D1546275

Also by Bea Carlton
in Large Print:

Deadly Gypsy Blue
In the Foxes' Lair
In the House of the Enemy
Moonshell
Voices from the Mist

Bea Carlton
Floyd Pierce
Ruth Burton

Thorndike Press • Waterville, Maine

Published in 2004 by arrangement with Bea Carlton.

Thorndike Press® Large Print Christian Fiction.

The tree indicium is a trademark of Thorndike Press.

The text of this Large Print edition is unabridged. Other aspects of the book may vary from the original edition.

Set in 16 pt. Plantin.

Printed in the United States on permanent paper.

Library of Congress Cataloging-in-Publication Data

Carlton, Bea.
    Where's Jessie? / by Bea Carlton, Floyd Pierce,
Ruth Burton.
        p.   cm.
    ISBN 0-7862-6103-X (lg. print : hc : alk. paper)
    1. Missing persons — Fiction.   2. Married women —
Fiction.   3. New Mexico — Fiction.   4. Large type books.
I. Pierce, Floyd.   II. Burton, Ruth.   III. Title.
PS3553.A736W47   2003
    813′.54—dc22   2003066289

Lovingly dedicated to our three families
who have been so encouraging and
supportive in writing this book.
God bless you!

As the Founder/CEO of NAVH, the only national health agency solely devoted to those who, although not totally blind, have an eye disease which could lead to serious visual impairment, I am pleased to recognize Thorndike Press* as one of the leading publishers in the large print field.

Founded in 1954 in San Francisco to prepare large print textbooks for partially seeing children, NAVH became the pioneer and standard setting agency in the preparation of large type.

Today, those publishers who meet our standards carry the prestigious "Seal of Approval" indicating high quality large print. We are delighted that Thorndike Press is one of the publishers whose titles meet these standards. We are also pleased to recognize the significant contribution Thorndike Press is making in this important and growing field.

Lorraine H. Marchi, L.H.D.
Founder/CEO
NAVH

* Thorndike Press encompasses the following imprints: Thorndike, Wheeler, Walker and Large Pr int Press.

Acknowledgments

I wish to thank those who have contributed much to the writing of this book:

The Deming Chamber of Commerce was extremely helpful in supplying materials and information on the Deming area, the setting for Where's Jessie? Tom Kelly, who was a volunteer there, also graciously gave permission to take pictures on his ranch and soak up atmosphere. Thank you Mr. And Mrs. Kelly!

Al Pierce, our co-author's son, put in many hours taking pictures of his wife Elaine, our book-cover model for Jessie. Many thanks Al and Elaine!

Alvin Levine supplied us with much needed expertise on drugs and their effects. Thanks so much Alvin Levine!

John Mallinak, editor at Messenger Publishing House, did his usual great job of designing the book cover. Thanks John!

Brian Ramos, print manager at Messenger Publishing House, has been so helpful, encouraging, and supportive, not only with this book but also through the printing of three others Messenger Publishing has printed for SonLife Publishing. Thanks much Brian!

My husband Mark always efficiently proofreads my books and this book was no exception. Thanks for your support and encouragement, as well as for your work Mark!

I want to express my appreciation for my co-author, Floyd Pierce, and his wife Rose (who is also my sister) for their untiring labor on this project: researching extensively, proofreading, writing and rewriting. Thanks a million, Floyd and Rose!

Ruth Chaote Burton, our other co-author, has been fun to work with and is a good friend. Besides writing fiction, she also is a cowboy poet. Thanks a lot for your work Ruth!

And I am grateful for the help of God on this project. Without Him, we could do nothing worthwhile! Thank you, Heavenly Father!

Bea Carlton

Prologue

Ann Helm, her sandy red hair glinting in the bright El Paso, Texas sunlight, stooped to place her two geraniums on the front floorboard of her Volkswagen bug. A friend who lived in her apartment complex handed her the last box which she shoved into the back seat.

"Just think, Linda," she exulted. "This will probably be the most rewarding photographic experience of my career! Something I have always wanted to do! Imagine getting paid to do a photographic story of life on a typical ranch. And at the ranch I grew up on!"

"I envy you," Linda said wistfully. "Just be sure you don't get lassoed by a handsome cowboy, forget about being a professional photographer, and never come back!"

"Not a chance," Ann declared with a chuckle. With a wave she climbed into her car and headed for the freeway out of El Paso, Texas.

But as Ann began her drive to the Helm

Ranch near Deming New Mexico, for her new photography assignment, she had no way of knowing her life would never be the same again. She also couldn't know that in the next few weeks she and those she loved would face many painful challenges: extreme trauma, danger and mental anguish — even despair.

She missed her brother Tobe, his wife Jessie — her special friend, their two lively youngsters, her Aunt Rachel and cousin Harold, and looked forward to being with them for the weeks it took to capture the story in pictures. This assignment was a rare treat. She loved her work but it took her to far-flung places, out of state and even out of the country, so her time at home was limited. Wherever there was a story to be photographed, she went.

She had just returned from photographing the Tarahumara Indian tribe in Copper Canyon, Mexico getting fabulous pictures of their craftsmen engaged in weaving, making pine needle baskets, ceremonial drums, masks, wood carvings and large pottery vessels (ollas). It had been a fascinating photography assignment and a delightful personal experience in getting acquainted with the Tarahumara people and their unique culture. Although Ann maintained a small apartment in El Paso, it was really just a place to sleep off exhaustion after a strenuous job. It was going to be glorious to be back in New Mexico for a while.

After she had signed a contract for the new assignment, it took her almost no time to pack. After all, she stayed in a mode of suspended animation with moving so much. She didn't even telephone her brother when she was coming, just packed her cameras, a few clothes, and two geraniums into her black Volkswagen bug and took off. On the way out of El Paso she stopped at a grocery store for some bread, butter, soup, crackers, milk, a few other items, and a bag of jelly beans.

Ann reveled in the feel of the late winter afternoon sun shining on the front seat of the VW bug. It was warm enough that she rolled down the window. The desert air circulating through the car felt good. It only took about an hour and a half to get home. Even when she turned off the pavement onto the rutted dirt road, no wind stirred up the dust as happened so often this time of year.

She had a (silent) part-ownership in Tobe's part of the ranch, inherited from their father when he died. The old original two-room cabin was hers to use whenever she chose to return — electricity always on and the refrigerator always running. So when she arrived, she quickly put away the food she had bought, unpacked her blue jeans and hung up her shirts in the living-room/bedroom closet.

She noticed the two books that were laying on the kitchen table and the clean coffee cup resting on a dish-towel on the drain-board. *Looks like Jessie's spending some time here,* she thought. That wasn't unusual, however, as Ann always made Jessie welcome to use her cabin whenever she liked — and Jessie enjoyed her time alone.

As soon as Ann had unpacked she drove over to Tobe's house. As she arrived at their front gate, she took in the attractive ranch house with pleasure. Both Tobe and Jessie worked hard and deserved to live in a modern, comfortable home.

Jessie came running out and threw her arms around Ann, exclaiming, "How glad I am to see you! I really need someone to talk to, and you're just the one I need." The welcome and warmth in her eyes and face sent a thrill of happiness into Ann's heart. But as Jessie led the way into the kitchen, Ann's observing eyes also detected stress and tiredness, and something else that she couldn't put her finger on, in Jessie's face. A quiver of unease swept through her. I hope Tobe and Jessie aren't having marital problems, she thought. For some time, Jessie had hinted that things weren't going well with them.

But Jessie didn't launch into her own affairs when she sat down to finish peeling some potatoes for supper.

Instead she excitedly began to quiz Ann about her new assignment.

"I'm so excited about this opportunity to do the photographs for a book about life and modern times on a working cattle ranch," Ann said earnestly. "I'm to take pictures of the Deming ranch country and can use my own family in the pictures. Isn't that fantastic! About half the book will be photos showing spring roundup and many of them will show the riders on horseback. I'll need the help of all the family, you and Tobe, Bethann, T.J., Aunt Rachel and Harold and any hands you have working right now on your two ranches. I hope you all won't mind being photographed," she finished a little anx-iously.

Jessie assured her everyone was excited about the assignment — except perhaps

Harold. "I imagine you will recall he never likes to be photographed." She giggled conspiratorially. "Just sneak some pictures of him when he isn't looking." Ann's heart warmed. Jessie had always been so supportive and interested in Ann's work.

They were interrupted when Tobe and T.J. drove into the yard.

They had spotted Ann's car, because T.J. barely had the front door open before he came tearing into the kitchen — bright blue eyes shining, light brown hair falling into his eyes as usual — yelling, "Auntie Ann, I'm so glad you came to see me. I have a new colt to show you. Did you have a horse of your own when you were my size? Can you come out to the corral now? Did you bring me some jelly beans?"

Jessie and Ann grinned at each other. T.J.'s mile-a-minute questions and exuberance were usual for the five year old.

After Ann tried to answer a few of his questions, Jessie told him to go wash his hands and face, then he could come back and have some cold orange juice. They soon heard him happily splashing around in the bathroom.

Ann heard Tobe entering the room and ran to hug him. She could never get over how large her big brother was and the strength of his muscular arms. How proud she was of him, tall — an inch or so above six feet, dark-blond hair, good looking in a rugged sort of way and darkly tanned from his outdoor work. Tobe hugged her back, then drew back to survey her with a grin on his face. "Hello, little sister. Are you here for a little R & R, or did they throw you out of your apartment because you couldn't pay your rent?"

This was familiar teasing so she just grinned back and said flippantly, "No, big brother, I came to borrow a few thousand dollars from my wealthy rancher brother — for a luxury three month's stay in Europe."

He replied in a laughing voice, "Wait till I get my checkbook out and see how many thousand I can spare." They all laughed and Tobe sat down at the kitchen table. Jessie poured Tobe a cup of coffee and he chatted with them for a few minutes, then headed out the door to the barn to do some evening chores.

I wish Tobe and Jessie really were wealthy, Ann mused as she watched him go out whistling. Since having the new house built things were pretty tight for them, she knew. Most ranchers didn't have a lot of money.

Nine year old Bethann's school bus dropped her off at about 5:00. As she came running up the steps, Ann observed how much she had grown since she saw her last — and how pretty she was — with long light brown hair like Jessie's hanging down her back in a neat braid.

She even had Jessie's delicate triangular face, although Jessie had a dimple which would spring up unexpectedly in her right cheek when she smiled, and Bethann didn't.

Coming in quietly, with a bashful smile she gave Ann a quick hug. *She is so shy,* Ann thought, *that I'm amazed to hear from Jessie a while back that she won a speech contest.* 'Bethann's my scholar,' Jessie had confided. 'Straight A student and serious about everything. A little too serious for her age, I'm afraid. But I'm glad she likes school as much as I did.'

After a wonderful ranch supper of chicken fried steak and mashed potatoes, Ann stayed to watch a video of "Charlotte's Web" with the kids, and share the bag of jelly beans she had brought, before going back to her cabin.

Saturday the kids were excited and ready to help. Both had ridden almost before they could talk and were excellent riders. They were up early and had their horses saddled and waiting. The cows and calves were being rounded up today and brought into the corrals on the far side of the ranch. Round-up time brought hard work but excitement for everyone.

As Ann rode beside T.J. she was thinking of a little episode she had witnessed in the kitchen that morning when she stopped in to find out the plans for the day. She heard Jessie brusquely and firmly say she wasn't going to ride out with them. There was no remark from Tobe but he had a scowl on his face as he hurried out, scarcely acknowledging Ann standing at the doorway. Unease again stirred in Ann's heart. Trouble surely brewed in the Helm ranch house.

By mid-morning, the branding fire was hot and the irons ready to use before Aunt Rachel and Harold came riding over to help rope and drag the calves to the branding crew.

For the next hour Ann climbed up and down the pole fences, sometimes leaning over precariously, always trying to get just the right angle for her camera shots. She wanted to capture the warm light of the early spring day as the riders moved among the milling, bawling cattle.

By noon she felt as hot and tired as the laboring crew, and it didn't help her feelings that Harold was acting especially disagreeable. He gave a glare or a wave of the hand every time he saw the camera pointed his way. When Bethann climbed up beside her on the top rail, Ann complained out loud. "How in the world am I supposed to take pictures, always making sure Harold is not in the background."

Jessie drove up about 1:00 with their lunch in the back of the pickup. The beans, sliced roast beef, biscuits and apple pie had been packed in the specially made wooden boxes Tobe had devised to keep bottles and pans of food from being turned over as they rattled over rough dirt road. Ann saw Harold tie up his horse and help to move the food boxes onto the tailgate.

"I can do this, you're needed to help in the corral," she heard Jessie say. But he simply smiled, gave her shoulders a quick hug, and ambled over to start a fire in the outdoor grill so she could brew some coffee. Harold was a gentleman, Ann had to concede.

Jessie stayed to help in the afternoon and to Ann's immense relief, she and Tobe seemed to work together companionably as if their early morning grouchy mood was forgotten. I'm probably just imagining there's trouble afoot in their marriage, Ann thought.

Late afternoon shadows stretched long before the work rolled to a halt. The tired crew headed for the house. Rachel waved away the invitation to stay for supper and said she still had some work to do at home and Harold had chores to do and horses to feed.

When the table was cleared and dishes done, T.J. and Bethann were urged into bed, which didn't take much coaxing that night. Tobe watched the early evening news on the TV, then yawned. "You girls can sit here and talk if you like but I've had a long day and I'm going to bed."

Jessie settled on the sofa and motioned for Ann to join her. This was the opportunity she seemed to be waiting for and Ann felt a foreboding rise in her heart when she saw the serious expression Jessie wore. She loved Jessie but sometimes felt in a very uncomfortable "middle" when her sister-in-law talked candidly about her marital problems.

After a few minutes of random talk about the day's activities, Jessie said gravely, "Ann, you're a partner with us on the ranch, so I want your opinion on a problem that's just come up. Tobe wants another registered bull. You know I would like to see us better our calf crop here by buying another registered bull but we just can't afford one right now.

"I showed Tobe the books for the last six months and he knows a loan payment for the cattle is due at the bank. I feel that he just wants to keep up with Harold. Harold just went to a sale and bought a yearling bull with a very impressive bloodline and an equally impressive price. Maybe they can afford it but we can't right now."

Ann knew an answer was expected but she was reluctant to comment. "Jessie, Tobe hasn't mentioned one word about this to me. But I could see that something was worrying him when I asked about renewing that leaky saddle house roof. He just growled 'no repairs can be made right now, let's just leave it at that.' "

"Tell me, has he actually spent money on a bull or are you still in the talking stage."

"So far we haven't ordered the bull but Tobe is pushing me to do so. We have been talking about the bull and I acknowledge another bull might improve our herd. But in reviewing our bills and money to pay them with, I just don't see how we can afford to buy a registered bull at this time. But Tobe won't agree that it will put us into a very hard bind right now, even when I show him the figures. Our talking just doesn't get us anywhere. We don't agree on anything anymore, it seems. But back to the bull. What do you think we should do?"

"Oh Jessie, you know I try to be a silent partner on this ranch. I wouldn't even suggest that I know the answer to that question. If Tobe brings up the subject I'll question his reason, but that's the best I can do. You know that Harold and Tobe have always been competitive. Maybe everyone in this county finds Harold charming but there have been times when I want to wring his neck."

"Okay Ann," Jessie said with a wry smile, "you're right not to take sides in our argument. I didn't expect you to give me an answer but it is nice to be able to talk to my best friend.

"Perhaps I'm wrong. Maybe this registered bull issue isn't a competitive thing with Tobe. But even if it isn't, we still can't afford a new bull now. More and more, it seems to me that Tobe just isn't realistic when it comes to money. We need a lot of things, I know, but we can't have everything, when we want them. The money has to be available to buy them."

Her shoulders slumped and she said wearily, "Ann, there are times when I get so distressed I just want to walk away from all this. That's when I go over to your cabin. After I read and pray and listen to music for awhile I feel able to come back here and face our problems again." She squared her shoulders and smiled wanly, "Sorry to unload on you like this. Don't look so worried. You know Tobe and I love each other. We'll work through this with God's help."

Ann readily changed the subject. "Now, let's talk about those two books that I see you have been reading at my place. How did you like the mystery novel about the woman who found the diamonds in the New York City subway?"

They settled into a comfortable exchange of information and views on their favorite authors and new books they both wanted to read. It was almost midnight when they laughingly agreed that it was great to be together, but any more conversation would have to wait for another day.

Although tired, Ann spent a restless night, dreaming she was trying to walk a tight rope, and kept losing her balance. When she awoke, she wondered if she could do anything to help Tobe and Jessie. Where did her loyalties lie?

Ann sent 15 rolls of film to be developed but they were just a start. The publisher didn't pressure her for time; she set her own deadlines. That was the way she worked best, with personal deadlines.

Tuesday morning Tobe stopped by and asked if she wanted to ride with him a little later. He was breaking the colt that T.J. was excited about and needed to ride him every day. Ann loved to ride and welcomed the opportunity to spend some time with her big brother. Of course she took her camera, she might get some good pictures for the book.

They rode out of the corrals facing the mid-morning sun, then turned south. Before long they met several cows headed toward the tank for water. While she took some pictures, Tobe looked the cows over carefully and remarked, "I'll only be able to keep these cows a couple of more years before taking them to the sale." Ann knew old cows didn't produce yearly calves and had to be culled.

"I've got another nice bunch of heifers

that I'm going to keep. They'll be ready to calve next year. I've got to get a new bull. Harold and I went to a sale and I've found the one I want. It's kinda expensive but a good registered bull is." He frowned. "But Jessie objects and continues to be stubborn. She keeps the books, you know, and says she can't see a way clear for us to buy him. But I know we can swing it some way. You know how important this is to me — and to the ranch. What do you think?"

Ann's heart sank, here she was being put in the middle of their argument again. What could she say?

"Tobe, I trust Jessie's judgment. She is a good bookkeeper. Is there any way that you could wait another year, or find a bull that's not so expensive?" Without waiting for an answer she continued. "Harold bought a bull at that sale, didn't he?"

Tobe gave her a long searching look with anger and disappointment showing in his eyes. Ann felt a faint flush rise in her cheeks. Her brother pulled down his hat another inch on his forehead, looked off at the hills and roughly spit out his words. "I thought you might be on my side, Ann. I realize now that Jessie must have talked to you about this. That is pretty much the same thing that she said. What does it matter that Harold bought a new bull? That does not change the fact that we need one here with our herd."

As they rode along in silence Ann reprimanded herself for not using more tact. But why did she have to be involved in this decision anyway? Just as she had done with Jessie, she changed the subject and by the time they rode back to the home corral the question of buying a new bull seemed to be forgotten.

As Ann pulled off her boots that evening she realized that the soles were wearing pretty thin, and she mentally began to make a list of things to do on her next trip to Deming. First stop needed to be a visit to the boot department at the western-wear store.

Next morning she stopped by to talk to Jessie and see if she would like to spend a day in town. Jessie's day was planned but she gratefully gave Ann a list of groceries to pick up for her. Tobe needed some grain and told her to take his pickup.

Boot shopping was not very successful; they were either the fancy style that would be great for a dance but not very practical for riding, or just not comfortable. Ann hoped the old ones would hold out for a while longer. Lunch at the Cactus Café was good. Her favorite high school science teacher and two former girlfriends were there. They laughed at her stories of big cities and world travels, and reminisced with her about school days.

After a while Dan Alredd, the sheriff's deputy, strolled in, pulled a chair over and sat down with them without being invited, then insisted on being introduced to Ann. He was rather good-looking, about thirty years old with sandy hair, trim mustache, gray-green eyes and a muscular athletic build.

"So you're Tobe Helm's sister?" he said smoothly. "Heck, I didn't think you would be so pretty. Tell Tobe I'll come out to the ranch to talk to him soon and I sure hope you'll be there," he ended with a wink and an intimate grin.

She gave him a direct, unsmiling look but inwardly she cringed. *If you want to impress me that you are a ladies' man, this is not the way to do it,* she thought.

Next stop was at the church; Pastor Frederick didn't seem to mind being interrupted for a long visit. He was very interested in her travels and reminded her that he prayed for her safety even when he wasn't quite sure where she was. She solemnly thanked him for the "all purpose prayers" and said there were times when she had felt their comfort.

After getting some grain for the horses and a new joke from Hank at the feed store, the grocery shopping took longer than she had planned. The sun was coloring the few clouds on the horizon when she started for home. As she maneuvered the twists and turns of the ranch road she wondered why Alredd's remark had irritated her so. Of course she had been flirted with many times before, but she had a nagging thought that somewhere she had heard that he was married. Flirtatious married men always sickened her. She tried to recall his wife's name but failed.

A quick trip into the house took care of Jessie's supplies. She parked the pickup outside the barn door so Tobe could unload the grain. Her own few packages went into her VW. The wind had turned cold so she was glad to hurry home.

After the red geraniums were brought in off the porch, supper consisted of a warmed up bowl of soup. The long hot shower felt good and she put on an old pink quilted robe she found in the closet. It was good to be home. Curled up in the big chair with her feet under her, she opened a new book she had picked up at the library. The branches of the old lilac bush tapped gently against the window pane.

Chapter 1

Jessie stood at the window of the Helm ranch house and stared out into the dismal, gray sky. "That's just the way I feel," she said aloud, "as lifeless and drab as the weather. I'm only thirty years old, married to my high-school sweetheart, have two of the brightest and cutest kids imaginable and we have our own ranch and home. I should be the happiest woman alive! How come I feel as old as Methuselah and utterly miserable?"

She choked and blinked back the tears angrily. I know the answer to that, she thought after a moment. It's because of the eternal bickering that Tobe and I do almost all the time anymore. If only he were more reasonable! I love him but he's the most stubborn, mule-headed man in the world!

Turning her back to the window, she gazed about her kitchen wearily. The lunch dishes still had to be done and she hadn't made beds or — much of anything yet. "I'm glad Tobe will be gone the rest of the day," she said to the room at large. "Because when he comes home there won't be just a few sarcastic remarks and arguing. There will be an atomic explosion — when Tobe hears what I have done!"

Straightening up, she squared her shoulders and spoke defiantly, "Well, I'm not sorry for what I did! If Tobe doesn't like it, he can just-just leave!"

As soon as the last word was out, she felt a tear roll down her cheek. No — she wouldn't want that! However, with their constant disagreements lately, it would almost be a relief if he did.

The shrilling of the telephone broke in upon her brooding, bitter thoughts. It was Ann, her sister-in-law. Ann was Tobe's younger sister, single, bubbly and fun to be with. The kids loved her and so did Jessie. It was Saturday and the kids were out of school, so right after lunch Ann had taken Bethann — Jessie and Tobe's nine year old, and T.J. — their five year old to town with her for shopping and a movie. The kids were thrilled because THE PRINCE OF EGYPT was showing and they were on pins and needles to see it.

"Hi," Ann's springy voice spoke in her ear, "Is it okay if I keep the kids in Deming overnight? We've been shopping — and eating ice-cream — and haven't gotten to the movie yet. Those clouds look bad and the prediction is snow before night. And I'm not wild about driving in the snow after dark. We can stay with your mother's sister. She always loves to have any of us, you know, and I'd enjoy a visit with Carolyn myself."

"Sure," Jessie said instantly. "The kids will love to stay with Aunt Carolyn, and the weather does look bad. Just be sure Bethann wears her retainer to bed. I'm sure she skipped last night. I know a retainer isn't 'cool', but neither is $5000 in orthodontist bills."

"I'll be a mean old woman and make her leave them in," Ann said with a laugh.

"And do be careful if it snows, the roads even in town could get slippery."

Ann promised she would and hung up. Jessie wasn't really worried, Ann was a good and careful driver, especially when she had the children along. She sank down in a chair by the table. Well, she thought, at least the children will be out of the way when Tobe explodes. Tobe was so irritable lately that she was afraid it was affecting the children, especially Bethann. *Beth is so sensitive,* she thought, *and sometimes I'm not sure she even likes her father. If only Tobe*

31

would show her more attention it might help. He always has time for T.J. — but perhaps that's because he's a boy and carries his name.

She had let Ann know that the way wasn't really smooth-going in their marriage of late but she hadn't said a great deal. After-all Ann was Tobe's sister and she wouldn't want to say too much about Tobe to his sister.

Jessie had talked to the pastor about their problems but she had the feeling he thought she should give in to Tobe on everything. That would be a good testimony to him, he had said. But Jessie didn't buy that. Wasn't a marriage suppose to be a fifty-fifty proposition? She would like to see Tobe go to church and take his rightful place in their home as the spiritual leader, but was giving-in to him going to help? She doubted it would. Tobe just wasn't into going to church or serving God.

She felt a little guilty about her thoughts but she couldn't help how she felt, could she? She had prayed about their marital problems but so far she hadn't seen any results. *Perhaps if I didn't get so upset and angry and say hateful things back to him, it would help,* she thought. *But he makes me so angry!*

Jessie ran water in the sink and began the dishes. As she washed and rinsed the dishes and placed them in the drying rack, her mind raced. She dreaded for Tobe to come home. *I'm set for a rocky road when Tobe learns what I did. But I'm right,* she thought defiantly, *and he will just have to live with my decision!*

But isn't there something I can do to mellow the atmosphere, she pondered uneasily. "Bread! Of course! Tobe loves buttered homemade yeast rolls and crunchy-crusted loaves! And it's been ages since I made any," she said aloud.

Jessie loved a plan. She felt better already. Maybe there was hope for the evening yet — if she worked it right! Beginning to hum, she finished the dishes and got out the pans and ingredients.

When Tobe stomped into the house, the wind had turned bitingly cold, and although it was only 4:30 in the afternoon, darkness was creeping in outside. But the house was a warm and welcoming place. The wood stove glowed with a crackling fire and the yeasty smell of fresh-baked bread filled the kitchen.

"Feels good in here," Tobe said as he shrugged out of his coat and hung it on a peg near the door. "And smells good, too." He grinned as he crossed over and gave her a quick kiss.

I thought yeast bread would do the trick, Jessie thought. "The kids are in town with Ann," she said cheerfully. "They're going to see THE KING OF EGYPT and were really excited. Ann's taking them to Aunt Carolyn for the night since the weather reports says snow could be moving in this evening."

"It sure could," Tobe said as he rinsed his hands at the sink and dropped tiredly into a chair at the table. "It's sleeting a little already and spitting a few flakes now and then."

He inhaled deeply. "Say how about a bun or two of that bread with some butter. Don't think I can wait 'til supper."

She slid a plate with several brown, crusty rolls and the old-fashioned pale-green butter dish she had inherited from her grandmother, filled with chilled home-made butter in front of him. Sitting across the table from him she watched him devour the food hungrily. *This is the way it ought to be,* she thought. *Peaceful and happy.*

"This talk of snow reminds me of the time you and I and Harold took that ski trip to Telluride. Do you remember?"

She jumped up and went to the cork board she called her Memory Board and selecting a picture, brought it back and laid it down on the table. In the snapshot, she, Tobe and Harold, dressed in bright ski garb, laughed into the camera.

A scowl darkened Tobe's face. "Sure I remember," he said, punching the picture of himself with a cast on his leg, with a stiff forefinger. "Harold won the competition and I broke my leg!"

"It was your idea to race, remember?" Jessie said. "Harold didn't want to race you, but you insisted, even though you knew he was much the better skier."

"If I hadn't hit that icy spot and missed the turn, I would have won," Tobe muttered.

"Tobe," she said with spirit, "why do you always, and forever, feel you must compete with Harold. Even in high school and on through college you always seemed to feel you must show yourself to be the better man. And you're still doing it."

Tobe looked up quickly, "What do you mean?"

"Harold bought a new, thoroughbred bull and now you've ordered one!"

A slight redness suffused Tobe's face and

he said gruffly, "I'm not competing! I need a new bull."

Jessie took a deep breath and spoke patiently, "Remember, Tobe, that we discussed this. I did the figuring and we decided together that we couldn't afford a new bull right now."

"Well, I changed my mind!"

"You mean Harold got one and then you had to have one, too!"

Tobe hit the table with a balled fist and Jessie flinched. "I'm the manager of this ranch and I know what is needed to run this ranch effectively!"

Ignoring his glare, Jessie tried to speak quietly but firmly, although her heart was banging against her rib-cage, and her stomach was quaking. "But I'm your business partner and I'm in charge of finances. Have you forgotten you agreed that since I have the degree in business management, I should handle the finances?"

Tobe jumped to his feet, rocking the table and rattling the dishes, "How could I possibly forget with you throwing it in my face every ten minutes!" He took a deep breath and said grimly, "Well, this is one time that I made the decision. We needed a new bull and I ordered one. It's done with, so I'll hear no more about it!"

Jessie took a deep quavering breath and said softly but steadily, "I canceled the order for the new bull."

For a moment Tobe seemed too stunned to speak and then his question was a roar, "You did what?"

"We had agreed together that we couldn't afford a new bull," Jessie said doggedly, "so when the rancher called to give us a delivery date, I simply told him the truth, that we had decided not to buy a bull at this time."

Tobe's face went almost purple with suppressed fury and then drained to a dead white. He stared at her for a moment like she was an alien from Mars — or like he hated her. "You've made me look like a complete fool," he said raggedly.

"No, I haven't," Jessie said, trying to maintain a calm tone, "I told him we were sorry, but we had done some figuring and decided it wasn't possible right now. I said we had planned to call but hadn't gotten to it yet."

Tobe's lips curled in disgust, "So the good Christian lies when it's to her convenience! You're just like your goodie, goodie mother, just a hypocrite!" He turned his back on her and started toward the living room.

"You leave my mother out of this," Jessie spat out, cut to the quick. "And if I did tell a little lie, I was doing it to protect your precious pride!"

Tobe turned back slowly, "After being married to you for ten years, bossing me and telling me how to run my ranch, I don't have any pride left!"

Tears were threatening and Jessie certainly didn't want Tobe to see her crying so she turned her back on him and ran to the door. Reaching up to a peg near Tobe's coat, she grabbed his old sweater and opened the back door.

"I don't have to listen to this," she yelled and darted out the door, slamming it behind her.

The wind almost took her breath away and for a moment she stood outside the door, to stare in bewilderment about her, as she shrugged into the heavy sweater and buttoned it up to her chin. Snowflakes were drifting down and the sky was nearly as black as night. Hesitantly she ran to the end of the gravel path and stopped. Turning back, she looked at the back door. She should go back in the house. Her heart quaked. This was a real storm and the wind, tearing at her like a wild animal, felt cold as an iceberg.

Surely Tobe will call me back, she thought hopefully, when he sees how bad the weather is out here. But the door remained stubbornly closed. "I won't go back," she said through quivering lips. She thought again what terrible things Tobe had said to her and a sob escaped before she could suppress it. How could Tobe be so cruel?

Turning around she started up the track toward the little cabin, Ann's domicile whenever she came to the ranch. Not over a quarter of a mile away from Tobe's house, and never locked because Ann knew the old cabin — the first one built on the ranch years ago — was where Jessie went when she wanted solitude. And that had been pretty often, of late!

The howling wind strong against her, she hurried on. "I have to reach the cabin before the snow gets worse," she said aloud, but the wind tore the words from her mouth. She wished now she had grabbed Tobe's coat, instead of his sweater. Even though it was heavy, she already felt chilled to the bone and getting colder by the minute.

Suddenly she stumbled on something, she couldn't see what, and fell sprawling. For a moment she was too stunned to move. She had fallen hard. There had been no time to brace herself; one minute she was upright and the next she was down on the icy, gravelly roadway. "Must be more careful," she muttered as she drew herself up to a sitting position.

"I'm so cold," she muttered through numbing lips. "My nose and ears are freezing!" Suddenly she recalled that Tobe almost always carried a large handkerchief in his pockets. Searching frantically in the right pocket of the sweater, she came up empty. Reaching a chilled hand into the other pocket, she sighed with relief when she pulled out a large blue handkerchief. As quickly as she could with hands that were almost paralyzed with cold, she shook the snow from her head, pulled her hair over her ears and tied the handkerchief securely over her nose and mouth. That helped!

In the short time she had been on the ground, the wind had plastered her back and shoulders with a white mantle. Shaking off all she could, she scrambled to her feet and started on. Surely the cabin was near now, though she couldn't see it yet. Struggling against the savage wind, head down to avoid the snow splattering in her face and eyes, her feet began to feel like weights. Where is that cabin? I have to be almost there. Jessie felt she had been floundering about for an eternity.

Putting her back to the storm, Jessie looked around. Fear's frigid fingers touched her as she stared around her with unbelieving eyes. A solid wall of white surrounded her and there wasn't a sign of the cabin — or anything but white snow. Sticking out an arm, she realized that she could barely see the end of her arm.

Terror beat in her throat. This couldn't be happening! A short while before she had been in her warm kitchen, not even aware that a storm of this magnitude was sweeping down upon the ranch. This was March! Springtime! What should she do? Jessie felt so tired, she was tempted to sit down with her back to the tearing wind and rest a bit but common sense told her that would never do. With a shudder, she recalled stories of people who had died right in their own yards in a storm like this.

She stood braced against the bone-chilling wind. Surely the storm wouldn't last long this time of the year. If only the snow would lighten up so she could see where she was. Bending over, she felt along the ground all around her, through the thin layer of snow. Only the rutted roadway was beneath her fingers. Had she missed the little path up to the cabin? There was no way to tell. One thing she knew, she must keep moving.

She placed her feet carefully now. If she fell and broke her leg or foot or even got a bad sprain, she could die out here before help came. Help? Even though he was angry, Tobe would come for her, if she called. She opened her mouth wide and screamed with all her strength. "Help, Tobe!"

But, as if the merciless, icy-cold white monster had gobbled them up, her words seemed to dissipate into the snow-filled air and with them her spirit. She yelled again a couple of times, but it took strength that she didn't have so she fell silent and again lifted leaden feet to trudge on.

Jessie fell again after a bit but fought her way to her feet once more and went on. Her feet were so cold she could scarcely feel them now and even with her hands in the deep pockets they ached with cold. Was she going to die? She mustn't think that! "God!" Why hadn't she thought of calling on him before? Because she didn't think he was greatly pleased with her behavior these days? But she was desperate.

"God! Please help me! Forgive me for how I've been acting lately and please don't let me die. Save me, dear Lord — please . . ." Suddenly her foot struck something different from the rutted roadway: metal, round — and slick from the snow. The cattle-guard! She had missed the cabin path and was at the road that crossed over a cattle-guard onto the road that ran between Rachel and Harold's ranch and their own!

Careful now, she thought. Ease back. She had stopped instantly with only one foot on the cattle-guard and she tried to move back onto the roadway but suddenly an extra hard gust of wind blew against her and she floundered around trying to keep her balance. Her foot slipped off the slippery metal rail and before she could back off, it went between the rails and she fell. Agonizing pain ripped through her ankle and she screamed above the fury of the storm. Did she black out for a moment? She wasn't sure, but now she was down on the frigid, snowy ground, drawing her foot from between the rails, sobbing with pain, fear and panic.

"Dear God, I need you now," she sobbed. Was her ankle broken? If it wasn't, it was badly sprained, she knew. The pain in her ankle was full-blown now, almost unbearable. She strove to think. First she must try to stand. Carefully, putting her weight on her good leg and bracing herself with a hand on the ground, she drew herself upright, swaying in the gusting, biting wind.

Jessie placed her other foot on the ground and tentatively tried to shift a little weight upon it. Instantly searing, excruciating pain shot through her ankle, clear up to her knee. The pain was so intense, it left her sick to her stomach. She started to sit back down on the ground but she lost her balance and tumbled into the deep ditch that ran beneath the cattle-guard. Savage pain engulfed her. Perhaps she blacked out from the agony for a moment, she wasn't sure.

After a few minutes, the pain subsided to a throbbing ache and she sat up and tried to get her wits together again. At least the wind wasn't as bad down in the ditch. She must calm down and think! Jessie knew she was in deep trouble now. The most perilous of her whole life!

The road was just beyond the cattle-guard. Perhaps someone would drive by and she could get help. But instantly, she knew this was a false hope. The road was used very infrequently except by people connected with the two Helm Ranches. And neither family used a great deal of outside help.

"And in a storm like this no one but a nut like Jessie Helm would be anywhere except in a cozy house next to a warm fire, drinking hot chocolate!" For a moment she visualized herself holding a cup filled with comforting hot cocoa. Heavenly! She had never been so cold in her life! "Dear God, help me!" She had never prayed a more desperate or sincere prayer.

Suddenly above the howling of the wind, a sound came to her ears. Craning her head, she tried to see over the edge of the trench but the bank was too high. The sound was becoming more pronounced. A vehicle? Was Tobe coming for her at long last?

She had to get out of the deep ditch and on to the road. Her hands were so chilled she could scarcely feel them now but setting her jaws resolutely against the pain, she started crawling up the steep, slippery side of the ditch. The sound of the vehicle was growing more distinct.

She had lost the handkerchief, she suddenly realized, and the snow was blowing in her ears and her nose was freezing. But there was no time to be concerned about that now. She must be up on the road when the vehicle got to her! She could be missed in this blowing snow! Her whole body was trembling but she forced herself to crawl, inching up the slippery bank.

"Crawl!" she commanded her protesting limbs. She was nearly to the top of the steep ditch now. She was going to make it! Clawing desperately for hand-holds, she felt sharp rocks ripping at her finger-tips but she clung there and tried to drag herself up over the lip. Then her fingers began to slip and she tried desperately to cling to the slippery edge of the steep bank. She turned loose one hand and grabbed for a better hold but the edge crumbled as her fingers scrabbled for a hold.

She screamed, "Jesus," once before she lost her tenuous grip on the edge and went rolling back down to the bottom. A blinding stab of pain lanced through her head as it collided violently with the sharp edge of a large boulder that was sticking up from the bottom of the ditch. She gasped once as her hurt foot landed on another part of the boulder. Her body spilled out upon the snowy ditch bottom, then darkness swooped down upon her like a giant bird of prey and swallowed her up.

Chapter 2

Tobe's ranting voice, loud and harsh, grated on Jessie's nerves and she squirmed and twisted trying to get away from the sound. Tobe must hate her! So angry! So angry! Then suddenly, he reached out a foot and struck her on the ankle and she fell. Severe pain raged through the damaged member and she struggled to escape his strong hands, reaching to hurt her some more. She rolled away from him, the pain intensified and suddenly she found herself sitting up in bed, sobbing with pain and fright. The dream vanished like smoke but the sound lingered still.

She stared about her with wide startled eyes. For a second she couldn't place the loud noise — not a voice as in her dream but a deafening, vibrating, whomping sound that grew louder until the house trembled with the pulsation. Then the sound moved away rapidly, soon lost to her ears. A helicopter — low. Why so low over the house? Searching for someone?

The house? Where am I? Horrified, she

realized she had never laid eyes on this room before. She shifted to sit up and searing pain struck her foot and ran up her leg. Had Tobe really kicked her? Surely not, he had never done anything like that before, never! Changing her position gingerly, she pushed the quilt away from her body and stared down at her foot. It was hurt!

Someone had wound an elastic bandage tightly around her ankle. Who? As she bent to examine the foot, a stabbing pain in her head brought a gasp from sore lips. She touched a hand to her head and found a bandage there also — covering a very large lump, she discovered as she gently probed. A twinge of pain brought her attention to her left hand, which also sported a bandage made of clean white cloth, taped together.

What has happened to me, she thought wildly. Fear pulsed in her throat and her heart hammered beneath her ribs. *Where am I?*

Suddenly a weariness so severe swept over her that she could barely sit up — or was it weakness? She lay back on the pillow — that smelled faintly of tobacco — and searched the room with her blurry eyes. The double bed she lay on appeared to be metal, peeling and painted a garish green. She was covered with worn, unbleached muslin sheets and a well-used, though clean, handmade pieced quilt of varied strips of cotton print. Two small windows, one on each side, boasted slightly tattered shades. Her bed sat out from one of the walls, with a small table holding a gooseneck lamp on her left. Across the room to her right, she saw a door, closed. She wondered vaguely if the smaller door not far from the foot of the bed was a closet.

From her position in the bed, she observed a kitchen cabinet, a sink, a small stove on which rested a coffee pot and tea-kettle, a refrigerator, chest of drawers and a metal foot-locker. Placed under a window were a small drop-leaf table and two chairs. A wardrobe filled a corner. An efficiency apartment. But how had she come to be here?

Closing her eyes, she tried to think but she found it difficult to concentrate. Had she been given a drug of some kind — perhaps to help her sleep? At least the warm quilt kept the cold from her body. Jessie shivered. Now it was coming back to her. She had been so cold . . . the snow . . . the storm . . . and she had fallen and hit her head . . . at the cattle-guard near the road.

It all flooded back now. The argument with Tobe, her dash out into the storm; she had missed the cabin and come out at the cattle-guard near the road. There had been a sound of a vehicle but she couldn't get up onto the road because her ankle was hurt. She struggled to recall . . . yes, she had fallen and her foot went between the rails of the cattle-guard.

"Someone must have found me, after all, since I'm not dead," she muttered aloud and grinned to herself. It hurt to laugh, her lips felt sore and chapped — probably from the icy snow-laden wind that she could recall vividly now. She shuddered. Looking down at her clothes, she saw that she still wore her own blue jeans and blue shirt, but they obviously had been washed. They should have been wet and muddy! *How long have I been here?* she wondered.

"Well," she said decisively, "I had better get up and go talk to whoever rescued me, and get on home. Tobe and the kids will be worried about me if my rescuer hasn't called."

She saw her athletic shoes sitting beside the bed — they had also been cleaned, she vaguely comprehended. Sliding out of the bed, she painfully hopped — in her stocking feet — to the door and turned the doorknob. "That's strange," she puzzled. "It's locked. Why would someone lock the door?" An uneasy chill prickled at the base of her head.

Turning around, steadying herself with a hand on the wall, she made her way to the other, smaller, door. It opened easily and she looked into a small darkened bathroom. The only light came from a slit of a window high above a mirror over the wash-basin. Flipping on a switch near the door, the light revealed a shower stall, a flush toilet and a small cabinet under the wash-basin. She limped over to investigate and discovered a few towels, wash-clothes, soap, new still-in-the-package tooth brush and toothpaste, and other odds and ends.

Returning to the main room, she hobbled to a window — being careful of her ankle that throbbed with a dull pain — rolled up the shade and looked out. Strong sunlight poured into the room, causing her to shade her eyes with a hand. The sun was a flaming ball not too much higher than a high canyon wall that loomed perhaps a hundred yards from the house. Was the sun coming up or going down? She couldn't decide.

A high, live ocotillo fence enclosed both

sides of the house, clear back to the canyon wall. The tightly-fitting natural fence, surrounded divided corrals, a small barn, shelters and mangers. Goats of varied sizes and colors moved about inside the enclosures. A goat ranch! She knew of no goat ranches near where she lived. That quiver of alarm quickened again. *Where am I?*

Hopping to the opposite window, she looked out into a small bare yard, also inside the ocotillo enclosure. Not far away stood an old Ford pick-up and a couple of lawn chairs made from willow branches — weathered to a soft gray, and beyond the tall fence she glimpsed a dirt road winding away toward low hills.

She had heard no voice but suddenly the sound of music blared, Mexican music, as if someone nearby turned on a radio or television. After a moment or so, the music went off and rapid Spanish was spoken, obviously an announcer. There must be another house or another room on this one, she decided, but they weren't visible from her windows. She couldn't be in Mexico, could she? Panic beat in her throat, threatening to overwhelm her but she quickly squashed it. There had to be a rational explanation for all of this!

Hopping over to the main door, she

again tried the doorknob. Still locked. She rattled the doorknob and then pounded on the door, yelling, "Let me out of here!" Mexican guitar music and a husky-voiced woman singing in Spanish drifted to her ears again but no other sound. It didn't seem to be coming from her quarters, but nearby.

After several minutes of banging on the door and yelling, she gave up. Exhaustion again overwhelmed her and she retreated back to her bed, climbed in and sank into a deep sleep almost instantly. Pain in her stomach awoke her. She needed food! She didn't recall ever being so hungry before.

Would the refrigerator contain food? At the thought her stomach twisted with ravenous hunger. Hopping to the refrigerator, she hastily pulled open the door. One shelf held a stack of plastic-wrapped tortillas, a chunk of some kind of white cheese and a covered dish of chopped green chilies. Below them were three eggs in a chipped yellow bowl and a glass fruit-jar of milk. Probably goat milk, she thought, but starving people can't be choosy.

Jessie gulped down a glass of milk first. Wasn't bad, she thought, though a little odd-tasting. Then quickly she located dishes, pots and pans in the cabinet. Even with her out-of-commission ankle, it didn't take long to make an omelet of eggs, cheese and green chilies, greasing the pan with some white-looking butter she found in a dish. Wrapping it up in a warmed tortilla, she devoured the lot. Never had anything tasted more delicious! Whoever said hunger was a good sauce surely knew what he was talking about!

Hobbling over to the window again she noticed the sun was lower, almost resting on the ridge. So it is evening-time, she mused. How long had she been in this place? Suddenly overwhelming weariness descended upon her and she could hardly keep her eyes open. She wondered foggily, did someone give me a sleeping pill — or something — and I'm still feeling the effects? Stacking the dishes in the tiny sink, she retired to the bed and slipped into slumber almost immediately.

A sound nearby snapped her from a sound sleep. A key rattled in the lock on her door. Sitting up quickly she felt a stabbing pain in her ankle but ignoring it, she stared at the door that was slowly opening. In the doorway stood an old Mexican woman, with a shawl wrapped around her head and shoulders. Gray hair straggled beneath the shawl and about the weathered, wrinkled face. Black eyes regarded her steadily.

Struggling to a more upright position, Jessie asked, "Where am I? What am I doing here?" The woman moved a step into the room, alert eyes quickly taking in the dishes in the sink, then back to Jessie. Without a word or expression of any kind on her aged, wrinkled face, she turned to go.

"No — don't go!" Jessie entreated. "You must tell me where I am."

Glancing back, the woman hesitated on the threshold, opened her lips to speak and then closing them resolutely, she stepped out the door and Jessie heard the key turning.

"No — No!" Jessie cried out. Springing from the bed, she almost fell to the floor from the wracking pain in her ankle but recovering her balance, she hopped frantically to the door and tried to open it. It was locked and she could hear slow footsteps moving away.

"Come back," she called frantically but no answer came. Utter quiet prevailed, even the earlier pulsing Mexican music somewhere in the vicinity had silenced. Jessie began to beat on the door and yelled and screamed for several minutes until exhausted, but no one came or answered.

Jessie hopped back to the bed and fell down across it, sobbing with anger, frustration — and terror. Yes, she admitted to herself as she tried to stop her violent torrent of tears, I am afraid. What kind of place is this? Am I a prisoner? If so, why?

"You must calm yourself," she remonstrated sternly. "Think this through. What do you know so far? Think! Think!"

Her mind was clearer now. Rolling over cautiously, she sat up, pushing the two pillows to support her back. With extreme effort, she pushed back the fear, that had rapidly accelerated into full-blown terror.

"Be calm, now," she admonished herself softly. "No one has harmed you yet. In fact, someone has wrapped your ankle, treated your wounded head and hand, washed your clothes, and provided you with a clean bed and food. So you are okay so far. You just need to find out why you are locked in. There may be a completely logical explanation.

Part of her mind argued, "Yeah, and what could that be, you're a prisoner?" But she refused to listen to that voice. "If I keep my head and don't let panic take over, I can better deal with whatever I must face," she told herself grimly.

What do I know? What do I last remember? Her argument with Tobe, of course, and running from the house into the storm. She recalled she had thought surely Tobe would call her back when he realized the fierceness of the storm. Why hadn't he, she thought bitterly. Was he so angry with her that he didn't care if she did die in the storm?

She realized suddenly that tears were running down her face. "Stop that, you are just feeling sorry for yourself!" she commanded. "Of course Tobe wouldn't want you to die!"

She thought back to her struggle through the storm. She fell down a couple of times or so, she remembered, missed the path to the cabin and reached the cattleguard. There she severely sprained her ankle, and heard a vehicle coming. After tumbling into the ditch, she crawled madly, terrified she couldn't climb out quick enough for the person in the car to see her. The numbing, gripping cold, she recalled vividly. Her hands had slipped right at the top of the ditch and she fell back down into the trench, and struck her head on something sharp. Flashing lights and violent pain exploded in her head then, and in her ankle too. Then darkness reached out and pulled her down.

What of the lights and sound of the car, or could it have been a pick-up? She couldn't remember. During such a gale, distinguishing one sound from another would have been difficult. Who's vehicle had it been? Where did it come from? Had she seen a faint glow above the bank? From the direction of her house, she thought, but she couldn't be sure. She had been disoriented with the raging wind and bitingly cold snow that had mostly blotted out both sight and sound.

Had Tobe come for her, after all? That had to be the most logical explanation but she couldn't be sure. And if Tobe had rescued her, her imprisonment in a strange house she had never seen before, was inexplicable. And who could that unfriendly old Mexican woman be who had just now locked her back into this room and refused to talk to her or answer questions?

The helicopter she had heard when she first woke up! Were they searching for someone? Perhaps for her? Of course, that could be it! Tobe would turn the earth upside down if she were lost! She knew that as a certainty! Or did she? When she informed him she had canceled his order for the registered bull, he looked at her like he detested her.

Perhaps I did a terrible thing, she thought guiltily. I should have talked with him, reasoned with him, instead of just taking the bull by the horns and canceling the order. Perhaps Pastor Frederick is right, maybe the man should have the last say on things. What she did would be hard on a man's pride.

Well, the question now was: would Tobe have come after her? Of course he would, she thought, but a little doubt remained when she recalled the anger on his face. But after he cooled off, he'd have come, she decided. And yet, no one had come for her right away. How long she struggled through that storm, she had no idea, it had seemed like an eternity.

But if Tobe had come after her, what was she doing here in this strange house?

Jessie studied the room with speculating eyes. I must get out of this place, she thought. What is going on anyway? Was she in Mexico? The pulsing Mexican music, goats — and she thought she heard the bray of a donkey somewhere in the distance, but couldn't be sure — it all sounded like Mexico. But what could she be doing in Mexico?

A sudden terrifying thought made her

catch her breath in a gasp. Could the vehicle she heard before she blacked-out have been driven by Mexican illegals and she had been taken to Mexico — for some vile purpose? After all the ranch was not far from the border and often the Border-Patrol came by searching for illegals. "And I am a prisoner," she said aloud, aghast at her own morbid thoughts.

"Of course not!" she scoffed at herself. "What would illegal immigrants have been doing driving around in a storm on our back roads? Perhaps they got lost in the storm just like you did," that persistent imp of pessimism seemed to taunt.

Jessie tried to push away the terrifying possibilities and again studied the room. Perhaps I could climb out a window. "That's a joke," she said aloud sarcastically. "With my sprained ankle, I doubt I could climb out a window, and if I could, I couldn't get far hopping like a frog with one leg! But if I did get out, where could I go? I don't even know where I am — or even if I'm in the United States."

She shuddered. The unknown outside was more scary than the inside. The ocotillo fence was tall and tightly woven and enclosed all the space she could see. But she hadn't been harmed yet and she didn't know what lay in wait for her out-side, even within the walls. Perhaps guard-dogs, although she hadn't heard or seen one in her short excursion to the windows. And she didn't know who lived within the fence. Fear ballooned like a baseball into her throat and threatened to choke her. Quickly she closed her eyes and tried to shut all thoughts from her mind.

After a while, she opened her eyes and realized she had drifted off to sleep again. Her eyes rested on the ancient wardrobe and felt a stirring of excitement. Perhaps there was something there that might give a hint of her surroundings. Slipping from the bed, she hobbled to the door of the closet and pulled the door open. Hanging on a rack were several shirts and pants on hangers, most of them she observed were well-worn. There was also a musty-smelling sheep-skin coat and a faded blue sweater. A scent of stale tobacco perme-ated everything and made her wrinkle her nose in distaste. Flipping through the line-up of garments, she concluded that the usual occupant of this room was a man, and with such a scanty supply of clothing, she surmised the person was not residing here on a regular basis. There was only a worn suit and a couple of work shirts and pants that were passably presentable.

Leaning against the wall of the wardrobe to rest her ankle, she removed several articles of clothing. Holding them up to the light from the window one by one, she saw they would fit a fairly tall man but of sturdy build. Replacing the garments, she lifted down a hat from a shelf above. With a chill, she recognized it was of Mexican origin, conspicuously so. On trips across the border she had seen hats such as this on sale and also on men's heads!

Of course, anyone could have bought the hat in Mexico, she reasoned — but this hat had seen much wear, was basically worn-out, in fact. This surely meant that the person who originally used this room did wear a Mexican hat. A Mexican laborer?

Standing as tall as she could, she slid her hand along the shelf and along with dust that made her sneeze, she swept off a coiled leather belt that fell to the floor with a clink. Stooping, she took up the belt and uncoiled it. It smelled strongly of cowhide leather, but the belt buckle is what drew her attention. Made of heavy silver, the buckle glittered with bright blue, genuine turquoise stones — and in the center of the belt nested the carved head of a goat with wicked horns.

Excitement beat in her throat. She had seen this belt somewhere before! But where? Closing her eyes, she tried to place the distinctive belt buckle in her recollection but no memory surfaced. Opening her eyes, she stared at the buckle for several minutes trying to pull a memory from her foggy mind but could not.

She coiled the belt up and slid it to the back of the shelf again. That belt probably held the answer to her whereabouts if it would only give up it's knowledge. For that reason, she didn't plan to keep it out where someone coming in might confiscate it.

Scattered on the floor of the wardrobe, were several pairs of worn-out and semi worn-out boots and high topped leather work shoes but nothing else. She spied something in the corner of the closet and leaned in and lifted it out. A cane! That she could use! However, her excitement faded when she tried to place a little weight on her wounded ankle. Sudden excruciating pain made her sick to her stomach and so lightheaded she almost fell. Dropping the cane, she leaned against the wardrobe until the savage pain subsided somewhat and the faintness receded, then she hopped to the bed and collapsed upon the bed.

"I'm not going anywhere for a while," she groaned. Why am I so very tired and weak? From my ordeal in the storm? She recalled hearing that pain caused weakness and she had plenty of pain when she tried to use her ankle! Stretching her ankle out carefully, resting it the way it pained the least, she closed her eyes. She didn't really plan to sleep but quickly slipped away into exhausted slumber.

The sound of a key being turned in the lock once again jarred her awake. She lay still but turned to face the door, apprehensive but alert. The wrinkled old lady stepped into the room. Carrying a tray, she crossed the room with quick nervous-like steps and placed it on the table. Behind her in the open doorway, stood an elderly Mexican man, swarthy of skin with snowy white hair, his wind and sun blackened face was slashed by a slightly yellowed handle-bar mustache. The elderly woman was already retreating to the door.

Jessie quickly sat up and swung her feet to the floor. "Please tell me where I am? Who are you and why am I here?"

The old woman was already edging out the door but the old man touched the woman's arm and she stopped. "Señora," he spoke in a heavily accented voice, not unkindly, "do not be afraid. No one wishes to hurt you."

"But why can't I go home?" Jessie tried to still the tumult in her breast and keep her voice calm and rational — while she really wanted to scream and yell and demand answers.

Shrugging his thin shoulders expressively, the elderly man, dressed in soiled Levi pants and worn gray shirt, spoke hesitantly, "Quien sabe, (which she knew meant 'Who knows')" and turned to move out the door with the woman.

"Please — I must get back to my children and my husband," Jessie said desperately. "They're going to be worried sick! Please let me go home to my husband and children!"

The old woman had been watching Jessie with keen, black eyes. Now she turned to the old man and spoke in rapid Spanish — words that were spoken so softly Jessie could only catch the word "niños" a couple of times, which she knew meant children. Obviously the answer from the elderly man seemed to puzzle her as she turned back to Jessie to study her face for a moment. Then she spoke again to the old man and he frowned and shook his head.

The old woman's voice raised now — and her staccato words were angry, it seemed as she spit out more words to the man. He only shook his head sternly.

She took a step back into the room and spoke gently, "Me —" she pointed to herself, "Juana Nuñez, y mi esposo," she jabbed a bony finger toward the man, "es Luis."

Jessie tried to stay calm. Now she was finally getting somewhere — she hoped. She held out her hand and spoke slowly, "I'm glad to meet you, Juana and Luis. My name is Jessie Helm."

Juana hesitated, glanced at her husband and then stepped across to take Jessie's hand in a quick clasp. Looking doubtful, Luis moved to the bedside and extended his hand also, but quickly withdrew it, not looking at Jessie.

Jessie quickly went on, "My husband is Tobe Helm and my two children are T.J. and Bethann. We live on a ranch out of Deming, New Mexico.

"I had an accident during a storm and fell and hit my head. Were you the ones who saved me?"

Juana turned to her husband and spoke a word or two and he spoke rapidly for a moment. He seemed to be arguing and then he put a hand on his wife's arm and began to urge her toward the door again. At first she resisted, spitting out Spanish words in a steady stream, and then she stopped to listen to his urgent angry words for a moment, shrugged and seemed to give in.

"Buenos noches, Señora Helm," she murmured and hurried from the room. The door closed with a decisive click.

"No! No! Please tell me why I'm here," Jessie cried as the door closed. A sob rose in her throat almost choking her when she heard the key turn in the lock. Then she lifted her head defiantly and brushed away the tears. This was no time to be a crybaby! She had to be strong and not fall to pieces. She must get out of this place and back to her family. She must! T.J. would be crying for her and Bethann was having enough problems right now, without losing her mother, too.

"I WILL GET OUT OF THIS PLACE!" she said aloud. "I will get back home where I belong! Even if Tobe is still angry with me, I'll make it right with him. And I'll try to be a better wife than I ever was, even if I have to give in to him a dozen times a day." How foolish her argument with Tobe seemed now! Her heart ached to see him — even if he was still mad.

A longing swelled up inside her so intense she felt she couldn't bear it. If she could only put her arms around her kids again, feel their warmth, and smell the scent of their clean bodies after a bath, and feel Tobe's strong arms about her, even feel the bristles of his face before a shave, it would be heaven! "Oh, God, take care of them and let us be back together again. Please God! Please!"

Suddenly she remembered the tray that Juana had brought and realized with surprise that she was again voraciously hungry. Hopping over to the table, she slid into a chair. The tray contained a large bowl of delicious smelling chili con carne, several warm tortillas, wrapped in a paper towel, a warm empanada (fried pie) and a cup of black coffee.

The chili, rich with well seasoned, garlic-scented chopped meat, and green, peeled hot peppers, brought tears to her eyes but she ate every drop, washed down with coffee and a glass of milk from the refrigerator. The dried-peach fried pie, no doubt fried in lard which was a no-no in Jessie's fat conscious household, tasted delicious. She consoled herself that a body had to eat.

After showering and brushing her teeth — she hoped the brush was new, as it appeared to be — she could scarcely keep her eyes open again and even though her watch said only eight o'clock, she dropped on the bed and fell asleep at once.

Chapter 3

Chet Upshaw stepped briskly out of his bright red Chevrolet Tahoe and entered the offices of the Las Cruces Herald. His high heel cowboy boots were shined to a high polish, and his light gray Stetson hat — cocked slightly to the right — only partly covered his slightly long sandy colored hair. He stopped at the reception desk where Paula Malory, the firm's general flunky and girl Friday reigned supreme.

"You better get up there," she said. "The Chief wants to see you ASAP."

Charles Creighton, owner and managing editor of the Herald, and Chet had an unusual relationship. Boss and employee they were but they also liked and respected each other. Creighton gave Chet almost free rein and it had paid off.

Jumping up the stairs two at a time Chet soon reached his editor's office. Just outside the door he whipped his Stetson off and stepped inside.

Creighton, seated at his desk, was talking to a woman of about fifty who was sitting in one of the two chairs that faced the desk. Chet recognized her right away.

"Mrs. Miller," he cried as he strode over, sticking out his hand.

"Chet Upshaw, it's good to see you," The woman's dark brown eyes were warm with welcome, "Charles and I were just talking about you. And Chet, we are old friends so please don't call me Mrs. Miller, call me Clara."

Looking down at her, Chet thought, despite the inevitable encroachment of time, she looks almost like she did the last time I saw her ten years ago.

"Ok, Clara it is then. Tell me about the family, Jessie and . . ."

Creighton interrupted at that point. "Where have you been, Chet? I expected you two hours ago." He didn't really expect an answer so he quickly continued, "Clara's a good friend of mine. Her daughter Jessica has disappeared."

"What?" Chet exclaimed, "Not Jessie! I used to date her. What happened?"

Creighton held up his hand in a placating gesture. "Hold your horses. Since you're from Deming, I'm sending you up there to look into the matter."

Chet looked over at Clara and started to speak but Creighton again held up his hand.

"Clara said she witnessed an argument between her daughter and son-in-law," Creighton continued. "She's afraid there's been violence. I called the Sheriff; he said they're working on the case but haven't gotten much so far. He didn't sound pleased that we wanted to get involved. You've had some success uncovering things when the police didn't have much luck. I want you to hear Clara's story."

While Creighton was talking, Chet again took Clara Miller by the hand. Her hand was cool and dry. Chet looked into her eyes with sympathy.

"I'll have Paula get you a reservation at the Holiday Inn in Deming," the editor continued. "There should be a good story in it for us. Call when you have something."

"Ok, Chief," Chet said, "I'll leave this afternoon." Turning to Clara, he said, "We have a conference room, let's go there while you fill me in. The chairs are much more comfortable and it's quieter."

"Yes, maybe a quieter place would be better."

Chet led her to the conference room. When they were seated, Clara said, "Chet Upshaw, I never dreamed I would see you again. You may not know it but I now live in Denver. I was offered a good job there when Denver National bought the Deming bank. It was a good opportunity to get Jessie into a bigger place. When Charles told me who he was sending, I was glad it would be you because you know Jessie and all of us. I know it has been a long time but many people and the town should be familiar to you. Where do you want to start?"

Chet thought for a moment. "Let's assume I know nothing," he said, "and you start from the beginning."

"Good," Clara said. "You probably know, in spite of all I could do, Jessie married Tobe Helm two years before she finished college. I never liked Tobe even when they were in high school. I didn't want her to marry one of those land-rich, money-poor ranchers."

"I always thought they were pretty well fixed," Chet said.

"Well, I guess they are if you count all the land and cattle but they never have enough cash. Jessie handles the books and does most of the money managing. Under Jessie's managing and Tobe's hard work the ranch has grown. I've got to hand it to him, though, he really knows livestock and range management. In spite of the lack of money they seemed to be happy until a little while ago. They have two children. Their daughter is nine and their son is five."

"Did you ever learn to like Tobe?"

"In a way I did. You see, in the beginning and for most of the last ten years Tobe Helm has been as good as any son-in-law. He has taken good care of Jessie and their two children and he has been pretty good to me, too." For just a moment she was silent, a haunted look on her face. Then she continued. "Sometime in the last several months I noticed a change in him."

"What kind of change," Chet wanted to know.

"He would hardly talk to me on the phone and according to Jessie he was not as attentive to her either. He was still very good with the children, especially T.J., but with me he was short and sort of surly. Sometimes he was downright rude. I could sense a deep anger in him and I felt that somehow he blamed me for something, I don't know what. I got this feeling while talking on the phone so I'm not exactly sure why I felt that way."

"What about Jessie? What did she say about all this?"

"Jessie too was more distant and seemingly troubled about something but she didn't confide in me. It was obvious something was going wrong with the marriage but I never dreamed it had gone that far. I wanted to know more so I decided to make a trip back to visit my sister Carolyn. She still lives in Deming, you know. I also expected to see Jessie and the children frequently."

"What kind of reception did you expect from Tobe."

"I guess I expected him to be what he always was, not overly nice but at least friendly. So when Jessie invited Carolyn and me out to lunch we were both glad to go. We were greeted warmly enough but soon I could tell there was trouble afoot. Jessie was preoccupied and Tobe was stomping in and out."

"Wasn't he normally in for part of the day."

"That's one of the things Tobe is noted for, he is a hard worker. Usually he is out doing something and not in and out of the house often. Finally we went in to lunch and Tobe was there also. He was obviously in a foul mood. After a while he got up and went into their bedroom and after helping us pick up the dishes, Jessie followed him."

Not good, Chet thought visualizing the scene.

"Carolyn and I went out to the porch to wait for Jessie. We heard loud voices coming from inside the house. We also heard a loud crashing noise amid the torrent of words."

"Didn't you go check it out?"

"Oh no, we could never interfere in a domestic argument. In fact, we really didn't know what to do. After a while Tobe came out, his face red with anger, his boots tromping loudly on the porch. He didn't speak to us, just went on out towards the barns. A little later Jessie came out. She was crying. I made an attempt to speak to her but she went right on by. She went out and leaned against the corral fence. I was flabbergasted and hurt but I went out to see if I could help."

"What did she say to you?"

"She told me that her marriage was in deep trouble and that she was at her wits end. She said she had talked to Pastor Frederick about it and wanted to talk to me but not at that time. She knew I was flying back to Denver the next morning so she told me she would call me. She did call after I got back to Denver but nothing was mentioned about the fight. I put it out of my mind figuring it was probably just a passing problem."

"Many times couples do work through their problems," Chet said. "Please go on."

"About a month later, along about two o'clock in the afternoon, Tobe called. He said Jessie had left in the middle of the night, running out into one of those cold March snowstorms with no coat. She had grabbed one of his old sweaters on her way out. She didn't return. He thought she had gone to the old cabin where Ann stays when she's home. Jessie had done that before so he said he didn't worry too much at first."

Chet sat up straighter in his chair, alert for more information. "Didn't he look for her."

"He said after about an hour he did. He searched for her that night until late. She wasn't in the cabin or anywhere in or around the house. He had called the sheriff and a search was being organized. I panicked and started making arrangements to fly back. I was able to get a flight out the very next day. Carolyn picked me up at the airport.

"On the flight I calmed somewhat and started to think it out. I knew I would not be of any use out at the ranch because I am not physically able to do much riding or walking. I decided to go to Carolyn's house in case Jessie called."

"Did that sound logical to you that Jessie would run out into a storm when she was angry?"

"Not really. I have grave doubts about his story. Jessie would not have gone out into that storm without a coat. She has lived in this country all her life. She knows how miserable one of those storms can be. I am positive something has happened to her. She would never leave her children this long and if she was able she would get in touch with me. The whole story seems more and more fishy to me."

Chet, thinking of Jessie the way he remembered her, nodded his head. He was inclined to agree with her.

"Chet, Tobe has a violent temper," Clara went on.

"Yeah, I well remember," Chet said.

"I believe Tobe hit her the day we were there or at least threw something." At Chet's skeptical lift of eyebrow, she hurried on. "She was more upset that day than I ever saw her — like she was at the end of her rope."

She paused and looked directly into Chet's eyes, "And now I think he has done something terrible to Jessie. I am desperate. The sheriff seems to have done a good job on the search but I feel he believes everything Tobe has told him. He just shrugs off my suspicions and refuses to investigate further, even though nothing has been heard from Jessie for two weeks. If Tobe has done something to Jessie — and I can think of no other explanation — I want him punished."

"Did no one else search for her?"

"Oh, yes, there was a massive search all around the ranch and surrounding area but finally nearly everyone gave up. Tobe and the family say they are still searching. But I don't believe she will be found.

"I hope you can find out something. Charles told me you were better than any police detective or private investigator. I will give you all the help I can."

She paused, "I told the sheriff I didn't feel he was doing enough and he got huffy so we are no longer on speaking terms but I am a good friend of two county commissioners. They should be able to keep him in line in case he gives us trouble."

They sat quietly for a while, each with their own thoughts. Chet was deeply troubled and convinced there was more to this than just Clara's suspicions. *I need to get up to Deming and talk to other people involved,* he thought. This was a strange situation. Could the Tobe Helm he remembered really have done away with his wife in a fit of anger?

"It's lunch time," Chet said, "Would you let me take you to lunch."

"Yes, I'd like that and I am hungry."

They left the building together. As they passed the reception desk Paula told Chet his reservation was made.

Chet drove to Joe's Sandwich Bar & Grill, on Loman Avenue. Joe was long gone. A former football player and bouncer named Wilton G. Bascomb now owned the Grill. No one knew where Wilton learned to cook but he surely knew his stuff.

Chet led Clara to a table in the rear, as far away from the noise as possible. Wilton's teen-age daughter was there to take their order.

"The food here isn't fancy, it just tastes good. I usually order the special," he said. Clara opted for Grilled Halibut and a tossed green salad topped with blue cheese dressing; neither ordered dessert.

The food was served quickly and they began to eat.

"You haven't said a thing about yourself," Clara said, "Please tell me about the last ten years."

Chet, who didn't like to talk about himself, made the narration as short as possible. "After Mom and Dad were killed in a car crash, shortly after my graduation, there was little money left. The grocery store went to satisfy debts but there was a small trust put away for my schooling. I was offered a place to stay in Las Cruces, so I enrolled at New Mexico State University."

"Who did you stay with down here," Clara said.

"Roberto (Bob) Vijil and his family. Bob worked in the store for a while and became good friends with my father. I took Journalism for my major and Law Enforcement for my minor. I managed to get a part time job at the Herald. At first it was clean-up but a little later I got the chance to write school news."

"I know you were on the football team in high school. Did you participate in any sports in college."

"Football was not my game so I tried out for wrestling and kick boxing. I managed to make both teams. It kept me in good physical condition and instilled in me a desire to stay that way. Anyway, after I graduated I was offered a permanent job on the Herald and I have been there ever since."

By this time they had finished eating so they left the restaurant.

In front of the newspaper office Chet said goodbye to Clara. "I'll do my best to find out what happened," he said, "Jessie meant a lot to me and she still does. I'll get in touch with you up in Deming. Are you staying with your sister?"

"Yes, I'll be there until my daughter is found. I would like to be involved as much as possible. Please let me help anyway I can."

It took Chet very little time to pack a bag and get under way for Deming. As he drove down Main to catch Avenida de Mesilla, he waved nonchalantly at several people he knew. When he reached the interstate he took the on-ramp and accelerated smoothly up to speed.

Driving west out of Las Cruces up I-10 to Deming there is very little to see — a large State Prison, a couple of tourist stops and desert in between — but he didn't mind the drive. Setting the cruise control at a steady seventy, Chet relaxed, one part of his brain driving the car, another part looking back into the past.

Jessie Miller, he mused. He couldn't think of her as Jessie Helm. She had been full of energy, a cheerleader, voted the most popular and the most fun. They had been pretty thick for a while and he still had a soft spot in his heart for her. He couldn't bear to think of her lying in some lonely place never to be seen again.

He overtook and passed a large semi pulling two trailers labeled SWIFT on the side.

Jessie and Tobe had begun to see each other early in their junior year. In fact, the way he remembered it, they were inseparable. Tobe hit Jessie? I just can't imagine it but I can't imagine her running out in that storm with no coat either. That does sound fishy.

As he drove past the Akela Flats exit, he turned his thoughts to Tobe. Tobias James Helm, how he hated to be called Tobias. He had insisted everyone call him Tobe. In this he had his way because if a person didn't, he got pounded.

Actually Tobe and he were never close friends. Probably partly because of Jessie. Tobe had a quick temper even then. Still I just can't imagine him killing anyone, but killers have no face. They could, like Ted Bundy, be very personable.

He guided the Tahoe off the exit into Deming.

Deming seemed rural and small-town flavored as usual, he thought as he drove into it. The Holiday Inn Motel, located at the east end of town not too far from the interstate, appeared deserted at this time of day. It was reputed to have a fair restaurant and good beds.

By 3:30 he was in his room and unpacked, with plenty of time to call Tobe Helm and get started. Tobe answered the phone himself.

"Tobe, this is Chet Upshaw. I am here representing the Las Cruces Herald. I would like to meet with you and talk. Would that be possible."

"Chet, it's good to hear from you after all this time but I'm tired of talking to reporters."

"How about we meet as friends then and just talk over old times."

"Sure, I'll meet you at the Down Town Bar on Gold Avenue at 7:30 this evening but leave your questions about my wife behind." With that he hung up.

Whew, Chet thought, that sounds almost as if he's hiding something. May be more to this than I thought.

With about three hours to kill Chet

84

decided to drive around town to look at any changes since he had left. Afterwards he could pick up a bite to eat. In the lobby he asked the desk clerk about interesting changes and perhaps a good place to eat other than the motel.

"You could drive out Gold Avenue to Florida Street and see our new mid-high school and there's a new housing project on North Country Club. As for eats, the Mexican food buffet at the Cactus Café is very good," she added.

Chet killed a couple of hours driving around, and arrived at the Cactus Café around six. Selecting a seat in the no smoking section, he proceeded to fill his plate at the buffet. He chose a beef enchilada, a couple of chicken taquitos, some Spanish rice and pinto beans. He put lettuce and tomato on the enchilada and salsa on top of that. Back at the table he found a large bowl of chips with red and green Salsa to dip them in. After demolishing all of this he was served two large sopapillas with honey. The desk clerk had steered him right — this was good food! He now felt ready to meet Tobe.

Chet had spotted the bar earlier so he parked his car a block away. After making sure his Stetson was cocked just right, he strode briskly down the sidewalk. He covered the ground swiftly, his high heel boots striking with a dull thud. In front of the Bar he checked his watch. It was 7:30 on the dot.

Stepping into the dim interior of the bar, his light blue eyes swept back and forth. Tobe Helm was not in sight but standing at the end of the bar, under a dim light, he recognized John Albright, Tobe's cousin. One boot rested on the stainless steel rail, and near his elbow on the polished surface of the bar, stood a shot glass full of a dark brown liquid. Chet remembered John was the bully-boy of Tobe Helm's high school crowd. Chet sauntered over.

"Hi, John, remember me? Seen Tobe around tonight?"

"Been waiting on you, Upshaw. Neither Tobe nor I have anything to say to you."

"Now, don't be that way, John, I'm just trying to do my job."

"Well, do it some place else then. You and your kind are driving us crazy. Tobe told me to tell you to keep your nosy snout out of our business." With that John raised his glass and downed the shot with one gulp, then turned and left the bar.

Nonplused, Chet could not understand Tobe's change of attitude. Hostility was one thing he had not expected.

Chapter 4

Back in the motel, Chet, who sometimes could think better when he had things written down, sat at the round table in his room to write down what he knew about the case. His notebook was in the top half of his large brief case. Starting on page one he listed facts in the order in which he had become aware of them:

1. His boss informed him of Jessie's disappearance.
2. Clara Miller witnessed a fight between Tobe and Jessie.
3. Clara suspected Tobe of hurting Jessie — or worse.
4. Tobe wouldn't meet with him and warned him off.
5. Conclusion: I don't know enough to make any assumptions.

After writing down these thoughts Chet spent some time in prayer seeking guidance from the Lord. He then went into meditation, both for relaxation and hoping his subconscious would dredge up some answers, with God's help. He awoke feeling refreshed but with no profound thoughts. What he needed to do next was get in touch with the sheriff. It was too late to contact him tonight so he called the desk to leave a wake up call for five a.m. He showered and went to bed, not feeling at all sleepy.

The next thing he knew the phone was ringing for his wake-up. He pulled on sweats and tennis shoes while he thought about last night's events. His jogging run took him down Motel Drive toward town, turned left on Platinum past the court-house, back down Poplar to Country Club and back to the motel. His muscles felt loose and warm and his breathing easy. He felt ready for the day. From experience he knew the solution to his problem with the Helms was to just keep pressing. He would ask questions of anyone he could think of; someone somewhere would know something. Going to his room, he showered, changed into casual soft gray slacks and a light blue pullover short sleeve shirt and went down to breakfast.

He ordered coffee and orange juice along with whole-wheat toast, sausage, a boiled egg and a bowl of fresh sliced fruit.

As he ate, he thought about the people he needed to contact and interview, praying silently for patience and guidance.

Back in his room, Chet called the sheriff's department and asked to speak to Sheriff Brady. He was put on hold. While he waited he tried to picture Brady as he remembered him from high school. Jim Brady was somewhat of a bully but a politician even then. One who could look mean as all get out in his eyes, but smiling all the time with his mouth.

"Hello," the voice was deeper but Chet thought he recognized it. "This is Sheriff Brady, who is calling, please."

"Yes, I am Chet Upshaw, I represent the Las Cruces Herald."

"Are you the same Chet Upshaw I knew in high school?"

"Yes, I'm the guy."

"Well look, Chet, our officers are doing all they can to solve this case. I'm not too sure I want an outside newspaper involved and muddying up the waters. Just what would you want from me and my department."

"Well, I'd like to talk about the investigation and look at your files on the case."

"Uh — uh, I don't think I should let you see our records or talk to any of my department. Not unless you have some official connection to the case."

Chet knew from past experience that it would not be wise to argue with him. Nor did he think it would be a good idea to threaten him with bad publicity so he said, "Ok sheriff, thank you for your time. If you change your mind I'm in the Holiday Inn, room one twenty one."

As soon as the phone was on the hook, Chet looked up the number for Clara's sister. When the phone was picked up he asked if Clara had gotten back yet. "Yes, she has. Just a moment."

"Clara, this is Chet, the sheriff has refused to see me. See if one of your commissioner friends can jar him loose. Tell him to make it sound like he hasn't heard from us, if he can."

"I know just how to present it to him. I'll call him right away."

Not more than thirty minutes passed before the phone rang.

"Chet, this is Sheriff Brady. I've decided to let you see what you can find out about the Helm case. But you are to let us in on anything new that you dig up. If you could drop by about eleven I think we can find some time."

Whew, Chet thought, that was fast work.

Clara's friend must be a very good friend indeed.

Leaving the motel Chet timed it so he would arrive at the Sheriff's office — located in the Park Plaza near the Courthouse — just before eleven. He parked his car across the street. As he got out he noticed the sheriff's car pulling away from the curb and wasn't surprised. An underling would give him as little as he could get by with as a token gesture, he imagined. He walked half a block and entered the sheriff's office. Inside the building looked like most law enforcement offices and smelled like one, too.

"Hi, I'm Chet Upshaw," he said as he stepped up to the counter, "I called earlier. Sheriff Brady told me I could see him at eleven."

The woman behind the counter was small, not more than a hundred and ten pounds, badge, gun, uniform and all. She gave him the scowl that many police officers reserved for reporters. "Oh yes, he had to make an emergency trip down south. He left word for Deputy Alredd to meet with you." She must have pushed a button with her foot because Chet could hear a bell ring somewhere in the rear.

A large man with very broad shoulders

stepped through the door. The first thing Chet noticed about him, other than his size, was the gun on his left hip with the butt facing forward. A very unorthodox way to wear a gun. He walked with a swagger that marked him as a lawman who had been around for awhile — or thought he was a big-shot.

The woman at the counter smiled — coquettishly, Chet thought — at the officer and said, "Deputy Alredd, this is Chet Upshaw the reporter Sheriff Brady said was coming in."

Alredd didn't offer to shake hands, he just motioned Chet to follow him. Behind the door was a wide hall with four offices branching from it. Alredd turned into the second office on the right. He sat behind a desk facing the door, after kicking a chair toward Chet. There was no window in the office. Chet felt claustrophobic. He wondered if this was where prisoners were interrogated. A person would be inclined to spill his guts to get out of this place!

For a moment the big deputy Alredd glared at Chet, his rather odd shade of yellow-brown eyes, derisive. "Ok, so you have a little pull," Alredd said, with a sneer. "But it won't buy you much here. Just what do you think you can accomplish that we haven't?"

Chet, determined not to antagonize the sheriff's department any more than necessary, ignored the sneer. "Well actually, I don't think I can do any better than you but I can put all my time on it. You have done all the real investigating. Now I can just poke around hoping something will turn up. If I do run into anything you will be the first to know."

"Ok, I have been ordered to give you all the help I can. What I won't do is disrupt my whole week. Maybe we should get to it. What do you want to know?"

"What about starting with the call about the missing woman and what happened after that."

"All right then." He reached into the right hand top drawer and pulled out a police folder. It was obvious to Chet he had gotten it ready before hand. "Let's see, we got the call at two thirty a.m. There was a deputy dispatched to the scene at that time. I arrived on the scene at eight the next morning. On the way out I picked up a tracker, Juan Alvenardo, who is the best in the state. Sheriff Brady handled all the first interviews. They are here in the file, you can read them later."

"That would be fine," Chet said, elated

he would get to read the file. He bet Sheriff Brady would never condone that.

"I organized the search," Alredd went on, "By four we had better than a hundred people but we couldn't really start until the tracker got through. The next morning the volunteers had swelled to over two hundred. For two weeks we covered the ground around the ranch like a blanket. We searched on foot the first day. The next day we mounted as many as we could on horses and spread our search further out. The National Guard loaned us two Helicopters. We used those to cover the rough ground over the mountains."

Chet wanted to interrupt to ask about the tracker but decided against it.

"It was impossible to keep every one in the field every day but we kept it up for two full weeks. She just wasn't to be found. We talked to everyone who might have seen or heard anything. No one gave us a clue. We found nothing, not a trace. There was nothing that suggested domestic violence but I have my doubts about that. To my way of thinking Tobe Helm is the only one who knows exactly what happened. Alvenardo didn't find a thing except a bloody handkerchief — with Tobe's initials on it. We thought we had something there but we couldn't do a thing with it. In other words we have zip. We haven't actually closed the case but it is on the back burner."

Alredd handed Chet the file. "You can use this office, I have to make another call. Just put the file back on my desk when you're through." He stood up and left the room.

Chet spent an hour looking through the file. He was especially interested in the forensic report on the bloody hand-kerchief. Through DNA testing the blood was determined to be Jessie's. No one could say how it got out by the cattle guard. However, Tobe stated that Jessie grabbed an old sweater of his off a hook by the door as she left the house and that the handkerchief was in the pocket. Not enough evidence to arrest Tobe.

Alredd left no doubt he suspected Tobe of harming his wife — perhaps even of murdering her. They had definitely been thorough but Clara was correct, they had concentrated mostly on the search. Alredd had also been right, they had zip.

On his way back to the motel Chet stopped at a Burger King for a quick whopper. He ate it in the car while he went over everything that he had read and everything that Alredd had told him. It looked mighty black for Jessie. It seemed almost certain that something had happened to her after leaving the house. It also seemed reasonable that whatever happened was close to the house.

A thought came unbidden to his churning brain. Wives had been known to just take off on the spur of the moment. Fed up with things, there were spouses who just cut loose and fled. Or maybe another man? Could that be possible? Didn't sound like the Jessie he had known — loyal to a fault and steady as a rock. But anything is possible if a person gets pushed beyond his or her limits and feels they can take no more. Maybe she had planned it ahead of time and someone had picked her up. He realized he was going to need some real breaks on this one. Finished with his sandwich he drove back to the motel.

Back in his room. He changed into a pair of old boxer shorts, his tennis shoes and a cut off sweatshirt. He assembled his weight set and prepared for his daily work out. Using the small set wouldn't give him his usual full work out but it would have to do. He started with slow body stretches to warm up, then began. As he went through his routine he thought again about the possibility of Jessie meeting someone. He decided not to pursue that angle until he had exhausted all other possibilities. That angle just didn't seem to fit. Finished with his workout he took a long hot shower, dressed in fresh clothing and, even though it was a little early, went into the dining room for dinner.

The Holiday Inn had a buffet. Today they featured barbecue ribs with all the trimmings. Chet went through the salad bar first. He heaped his plate with fresh vegetables and added a small amount of ranch dressing. He sat at a table with a window overlooking a small area planted with grass and other greenery. After consuming the salad he went back through the line. He chose a small helping of potato salad, pinto beans and barbecue ribs. The cook had done well today and everything tasted good.

The waitress cleared the table and brought coffee. He decided not to have dessert. While he was slowly sipping his coffee and enjoying the view a woman carrying a cup of coffee approached his table.

"May I join you?" she asked.

Chet stood up and faced the woman. She was an older woman dressed in tight jeans and a man's western shirt. She was wearing high heeled cowboy boots and a Stetson hat. Her silver hair was tied back with a ribbon and her face was wrinkled and seamed from the sun. She gave the impression of having boundless energy and inner strength galore. Chet guessed immediately that she was from one of the nearby ranches. He nodded his head yes and they sat down.

"I have been watching and waiting for you," she said, "My name is Rachel Young, formerly Rachel Helm. I am Tobe's aunt, his father's youngest sister. Tobe asked me to talk to you and ask if you can come out to the ranch. He wants to see you. He was coming himself but one of his bulls got into barbed wire this morning and he had to wait for the vet."

The minute she mentioned her name Chet made the connection. She was the wild one, the one who had followed the rodeo circuit. She had married a rodeo clown named Buster Young. The marriage went on the rocks shortly thereafter. She was left destitute. Tobe's father had brought her and the baby son back to the ranch and she had been there ever since. She was supposed to be as good as any man around the ranch and had earned her keep.

"I'll be glad to meet with him," Chet said, "I'll come out as soon as I can in the morning."

For politeness sake they chatted for a few more minutes, then Rachel left. Chet sipped his coffee reflecting on the strange circumstances. First Tobe sends Albright to warn me off, now he sends his aunt to invite me out. She wasn't mentioned in the sheriff's report; he wondered why. He vaguely recalled a Harold Young, though. I wonder if they are kin? Could that be Rachel's son. I really don't know much about that part of the family, should get Clara to fill me in.

The next morning Chet stepped out to start his run at six. He had slept heavily and was a bit logy. He did stretching warm-ups for ten minutes and then started to run. His route was in the opposite direction away from town and up along the interstate. He ran well to the side to avoid the big eighteen wheelers that constantly crowded the road.

In just a few minutes he was completely loose, his body working like a well-tuned engine. He timed himself thirty minutes out and thirty minutes back. When he reached the motel he showered quickly and went down to breakfast. Breakfast over he was soon on his way to see Tobe.

Chapter 5

A cock crowing awakened Jessie and she looked at her watch. Five-thirty. After sleeping the night through, she suddenly realized she felt good. Moving her ankle cautiously, the usual stab of pain was absent. Good, she thought, I can't do much about getting away from this place until my ankle is better, and it's making progress.

Closing her eyes, she thanked God with great sincerity for the progress on her leg and her feeling of returning health — even in spirit. "Protect T.J., Bethann and Tobe," she prayed, "and help them not to be too worried. Please help me to get back home safely and help us work out the problems Tobe and I seem to be having so much any more." Even as she prayed, their problems seemed very small compared to being held prisoner here — in Mexico? She still had no idea of her present whereabouts. But maybe today she would find out — and the reason for her incarceration — and how she got here.

When she put her weight on the ankle,

searing pain erupted clear to her knee, but she determined she wouldn't be discouraged. "Help me to win Juana or Luis's confidence and to get some answers," she petitioned earnestly. She frowned, even as she prayed. Why would that old couple be holding her imprisoned in this room? It didn't make sense. Someone else must be involved — but who? And why? Her heart lurched with sudden trepidation. She didn't want to pursue that line of reasoning too much. The answers could be too frightening to explore.

Shrugging away her questions, she realized how hungry she felt. I must have been here a long time, she thought. I can't seem to get enough to eat. That was another thing she needed to ask: how long had she been here, unconscious — and perhaps drugged? She mentally backed away from that word. Someone had probably just given her something to make her sleep and take away her pain. But certainly something had been given to her — she had felt just too drugged-up when she awoke and could hardly keep awake afterward.

After scrambling her remaining egg, she put it on a toasted tortilla with grated cheese and chopped green chili. Not bad! It's a good thing I'm a Mexican-food lover, she thought.

Looking around for something to pass the time, she looked through the drawers of the battered chest of drawers but found nothing of interest — just some worn-out men's underclothes, socks and a few wrinkled handkerchiefs. The bottom drawer held a colorful red Mexican blanket, and perhaps a dozen old western paperbacks.

Twice she circled the room, hopping along as she held to the wall, chairs and whatever came to hand. She could hear the baaing of goats and the not-to-far-off call of a quail and the far-off musical warbling of a meadow lark. Raising the shades on the windows as she hopped past, she looked out but saw no sign of humans. Once she heard the pick-up start but by the time she got to the window, it was leaving in a cloud of dust and she couldn't even see who was in it.

The morning passed slowly. In a desperate state from boredom and mounting tension, she pulled the paperbacks from the drawer and piled them on her bed. Lying down, she examined them. She wasn't fond of western stories but the isolation and idleness rasped sharply on her nerves.

Several of the much handled and battered books were by an author named Louis L'Amour, she noticed. She vaguely recalled Tobe mentioning reading his books, which remained a mystery to Jessie. Why would anyone want to read about ranching and cowboys when the real thing unfolded daily all around him?

Oh, well, I have to do something or go bonkers, she thought wryly. Placing both pillows under her head, she opened one called Sackett's Land and began to read. Much later, she was shocked to glance at her watch and find she had been reading for two hours, completely engrossed. Wouldn't Tobe tease her about that! She who had spoken so disparagingly of those who wasted their time reading westerns. But this is a story about real characters, she decided. Real heroes, too, and she could use a hero about now!

Suddenly she sat up. The key grated harshly in the lock on her door. Sliding her feet off the bed, she saw Juana push into the room, her arms filled with packages. Luis slipped into the room behind her and stood — as if on guard — against the door. Crossing the room, Juana dumped the packages on the bed and retreated to the door, her face carefully unsmiling and emotionless. The friendliness of last night was gone.

"What are these?" Jessie asked.

"Clothes, Señora — for you," Luis said.

"Thank you," Jessie said. She ripped open one bag and saw it contained a new pair of slacks. The sack had the name of a store — in Mexico. Bewildered, Jessie stammered, "B-but who bought me these?" When she received no answer, she tore open another bag and saw it held several articles of clothing — a soft silk blouse, a colorful skirt, and a number of delicate under garments.

Anger swept over her. What is going on here! "Where did these come from?" she demanded. "I can't accept these gifts until I know who bought them for me!"

For just a second, Jessie thought she saw a glint of emotion — approval perhaps, she wasn't sure — in the watchful dark eyes of the old woman and the hint of a smile on her lips and then her face slipped back into a mask of indifference.

"A friend give to you," Luis said as he started to move out the door, drawing Juana with him.

Jessie jumped from the side of the bed, ignoring the flash of pain in her ankle, and hopped as fast as she could toward the door but before she could get there the two had slipped quickly through, closed the door and locked it.

"Please come back," Jessie called. Then angrily, "You have no right to hold me here. This is kidnapping!" But her only answer came as retreating steps on a gravel path. In bleak despair, Jessie hopped back to the bed and flung herself upon it. Why were they keeping her here? Why? Why? Why?

She lay on her back with her eyes closed for a long while, trying to get calm again. Fear set in. What were they going to do to her? She had heard of white women being sold into other countries for vile purposes. Oh, no, God! I couldn't bear that to happen. She opened her eyes and sat up! "This is ridiculous," she scolded herself. "You are scaring yourself right out of your skull! You don't know that anything like that or anything evil is planned for you. Get a grip on yourself!"

After all, nothing bad had happened to her so far and except for confining her in this room, all her needs had been met. Someone had even bought her clothes. Curious, she now turned to examine the packages — there were several, all with names of stores in Mexico — so she was being held in Mexico! Fear started to take hold of her again and she quickly squelched it. Don't jump to conclusions until you have the facts, she cautioned herself.

She marveled as she looked over the garments. The sizes were right! How would anyone know what sizes she wore, she doubted even Tobe would know her exact sizes! Perhaps the little old lady — Juana — had helped to select them? Possibly. After all, the pick-up had gone somewhere quite a while before. That must be the answer. But who had paid for them? The materials were good and all of them must have cost quite a lot. A quiver of fear ran through her. This was getting more and more mysterious.

Besides the frilly silk blouse, brown slacks, a colorful skirt and two of each undergarment — delicate and lovely — she drew out a pair of Levi jeans, two pastel cotton shirts, a terry-cloth robe and two nightgowns, one rose silk and the other a soft white cotton, house slippers and a pair of sand-colored sandals. Also a hairbrush and comb, deodorant, shampoo and conditioner tumbled out. Since there was no tooth brush or toothpaste the same person had obviously already purchased those and left them here for her use.

Plus — and this set her stomach to quivering in near panic — a very large box of chocolates — pecan turtles. Her favorite of all candies! Who would know that except someone who knew her well? Weird, weird! A cold chill snaked down her back and prickled her arms and scalp. Who was this strange person who kept her here under lock and key but who bought her lovely and personal things?

She tried to think rationally — which was hard because her heart was pumping wildly and her mind seemed to be in a whirl of conflicting, bewildering emotions and fears. Terror tried to clutch at her but she fought it back. She must think rationally. Did this bounty come from the person who had picked her up on the road after she hit her head?

What was the last thing she remembered? Vaguely, in her memory she felt sure she had heard a vehicle, just before she passed out. What type of rig, she had no idea. And she had thought she saw a glow coming over the bank of the ditch. From the direction of the Helm ranchhouse? She had believed so, and that Tobe had come to get her. Perhaps she wanted to believe that? But now she was unsure of anything.

Tobe — would Tobe be having her kept here to frighten her — to teach her a lesson? Perhaps to join her later for sort of a surprise second honeymoon? No — Tobe wasn't into romantic things like second honeymoons, candy — and certainly not a bunch of expensive, delicate undies and gowns and clothes. Their budget was always tight, and besides it just wasn't Tobe's way.

A key being placed in the lock on the door caused her to slide to the edge of the bed, her heart pounding. Was that strange benefactor — if such, he or she was — about to show? But it was only Juana — with Luis at her back to guard the door, no doubt — bringing her food. Luis stood in the doorway as Juana brought the tray inside and placed it on the small table. Her face was inscrutable; not hostile, Jessie decided, but detached and remote.

"Thank you," Jessie said faintly. Suddenly she felt very tired and decided to not pursue the seemingly hopeless task of getting information from the pair.

Juana said nothing and proceeded to the door. Jessie suddenly had a thought and spoke it. In as meek a voice as she could produce, she asked, "Would it be possible for you to get me a crutch? I need to walk

— and exercise. Please."

The two regarded her solemnly for a moment. Even Luis stared at her. He usually wouldn't meet her eyes. Then without a word they went out the door and locked it. "Well, at least I tried," Jessie said aloud, thoroughly deflated, as she hopped over to see what the tray held.

The spicy odor of green chili stew caused her mouth to water. There were more tortillas and cold fried pies, hot pinto beans and coffee. As she dived into the food like a starving person, she thought, at least Juana is a good cook. The green chili stew, deliciously rich with pieces of tender pork and onions, and very hot with green peeled peppers delighted her palate. She drank the coffee, some milk and even water with the food but with all their help her eyes still watered and her nose sniffled, long before she finished.

She did up the dishes and went back to the adventures of Sackett's Land. And the afternoon passed much more quickly than she could have imagined.

Late in the afternoon, Juana and Luis came to her door with — wonder of wonders — a crutch! It was old and the pad had been replaced with a crude handmade one but she could have hugged them for joy. Now she could walk . . . and perhaps escape! Luis had her try it and then sawed off the bottom with a small saw he had brought with him to make it fit. Obviously it had been used by someone quite tall in some distant past.

Then, Luis told her sternly that she would be allowed to walk about outside, if she stayed inside the fence. Walking cautiously with her crutch, Jessie felt truly as if she had been let out of jail. Her ankle hurt when she swung it back and forth as she strolled around the inside of the compound but she bore it gladly.

Exercise, she needed, if she were to be strong enough to escape when the opportunity presented itself.

Eagerly surveying her surroundings, she saw there were two stucco-plastered adobe buildings — her own small house and a larger one sitting beside it that looked to be about four rooms. The space between, roofed over, formed a carport, although no car was visible. Large flat stones smoothly cemented together, created a clean uncovered porch. Bird-of-Paradise shrubs, laden with orange blossom, grew in beds in front of the buildings. Chickens industriously scratched in the flower beds and about the grounds.

Both Juana and Luis watched her closely as she circled the yard, going down to the goat corral and moving along the enclosure, and down the sides of the ocotillo fence on three sides. She noticed a heavy chain and padlock secured the front gate. What kind of place was this anyway?

Pausing, she looked through the bars of the corral at the goats that ambled around and lay about the pens. There were not a great many but they seemed very distinctive, a special breed, she thought — especially the large buck goat that tossed his wicked-looking horns as she limped up. I wouldn't want to try to escape through there, she mused.

After two turns about the yard, Luis motioned her to return to her room. She wasn't reluctant to do so as she was extremely tired. I've got to get my strength back, she thought, if I want to escape from here. Surprisingly, Juana followed her back into her room. Pulling out a chair from near the table, Juana gestured that Jessie was to sit there. Mystified, Jessie complied. The old lady went into the bathroom and returned shortly with bandages and proceeded to clean her head and hand injuries and re-bandaged them.

Then, to Jessie's amazement, she went to

the bed and taking up the brush and comb, she brushed and combed out Jessie's long honey-blond hair and re-braided it. When she had finished, Jessie touched her arm and spoke earnestly, "Thank you so much, Juana. That was so kind of you."

A slight smile curved the old woman's parchment-thin lips and she said in softly accented English, "You welcome."

Emboldened by the old woman's friend-liness, Jessie asked, as casually as she could muster, "Juana, what is the day of the month?" When Juana didn't answer, Jessie tried another tack, "Today — what is today." A slight frown appeared on the old woman's face. Did Juana understand? Jessie suspected she understood much more English than she could speak. Then, without a word, Juana went to the calendar on the wall and pointed out a date.

"Thursday, March 12?" Jessie asked.

Juana glanced — guiltily, it seemed to Jessie, toward the door and then said softly, "Si." As Jessie reflected on this important piece of information, Juana laid the brush and comb on the table and turned toward the door.

"Then I have been here five days," Jessie exclaimed in amazement! "I've only been awake for two days, so that means I was here three days — asleep!" She paused, then said softly, "Juana, did you or someone give me something to make me sleep for three days?"

Jessie felt the withdrawal of the old woman as she moved rapidly toward the door.

"Wait!" Jessie pleaded. "Did you and Luis, or someone else, find me and bring me here?"

Juana said nothing and didn't look at her as she opened the door.

"Please, tell me who brought me here," Jessie implored.

The old woman turned to look at her for a moment, dark eyes unfathomable, then she shook her head and said softly, "Maybe talk too much already. No can talk more." She left the room, locking the door behind her.

For a long moment Jessie stared at the closed door, conflicting emotions roiling through her breast: discouragement and fright wrestling with hope. "After all," she consoled herself, "you did learn how long you have been here and what day it is. And you did get a crutch, and got to walk around outside some and see the grounds where you're imprisoned. All these things will help you when your leg gets strong enough to make a break for freedom."

But you still don't have a clue as to where you are, that imp of pessimism whispered.

"But I will find out where I am . . . and I will escape!" Jessie declared defiantly. "I will!"

Chapter 6

The Helm ranches were located about fifteen miles southeast of Deming, on the east side of the Florida Mountains. In Spanish Florida (pronounced Floreeda) meant flowery. Chet often wondered what flight of fancy could have inspired the early Spaniards to name these rugged peaks that.

Chet tooled along in his Tahoe, enjoying the scenery, glad he was still on the pavement. He turned right on County Road 143 towards the Rockhound State Park, then left on 8023 and the gap between the Little Floridas and the Florida Mountains. The ranch houses were about four miles farther along.

The pavement soon ended and the road was now rocky and rough causing him to slow down and drive more carefully. He didn't mind, it gave him more time to view the countryside. Off to his right the sheer rock pinnacles of the Floridas stuck up into the clear blue sky like jagged pieces of glass. The iridescent like colors shifted magically from rocky peak to rocky peak and down into the shadowed fissures that tracked in between.

After passing through the gap he looked far out across the Lewis and Akela Flats. The flats were checker boarded with cotton and pepper farms. In the far distance he could see the Oregon Mountains, behind Las Cruces, sixty or seventy miles away.

Suddenly he realized he missed these mountains. Nostalgia swept over him and he was gripped with a feeling of loss. The intense feeling lasted only a fleeting moment but it was strong enough to bring moisture to the corners of his eyes.

The road turned south down the east side of the mountains. There were numerous washes leading into the hills. Each wash was covered with shrubs and grass making this good cattle range. The side of the mountain, in between the washes, was covered with scrub cedar and farther up, the slopes were dark with taller trees.

He turned off the main road onto a narrower, not as well maintained, road that ran roughly midway between the two ranch houses.

He'd been told the old ranch house, tucked up against the mountains with a view of the valley below and the craggy slopes of the mountain looming above, now belonged to Rachel and her son Harold.

The new house, farther to the south, was set up higher on the side of a wash. It too had a view of the Flats and the Portillo Mountains. According to Clara Miller, Tobe had the house built after he married Jessie.

The road split in a sort of "Y". He turned left to follow the road leading up to Tobe's house. Along the way and about a quarter of a mile from the house he passed a small two-room cabin. It was sitting on a low rise about a hundred yards from the road. There was a track leading up to the house. He was intrigued by the curtains hung in the windows and the neat front yard that was behind a short rail fence. It was obvious someone was taking good care of the little house.

Driving into Tobe's ranch-house yard, he parked next to a black 1997 Ford F-150, three quarter ton, four wheel drive pickup with a stock rack on the back. There was also two other vehicles parked near-by. One especially caught his eye, it was a black 1998 three quarter ton pickup but it was a Dodge, sporting one of the new

Cummings Diesel engines, coveted by most of the men around. This one had a crew cab and the inevitable stock rack. On both doors was a sign that said YOUNG and beside that was a picture of a brand, then under that was the word RANCH. The brand was a capital R+Y inside a circle. Of course Circle R+Y, he thought.

Glancing inside he noticed a gun rack with a thirty-thirty lever action rifle hanging in the rear window. On the back seat was what appeared to be a blanket heaped in a pile near one side.

He leaned closer to the window to admire the quilted interior. Glancing down he saw a crumpled piece of paper laying on the ground near the pointed toe of his boot. He picked it up and unfolded it. It was a brochure advertising a ranch liquidation sale in Canutillo, TX, on March 1. He crumpled it back up and tossed it into the front seat of his Tahoe. I'll throw it away later, he thought. He disliked litter anywhere.

His eyes took in the other vehicle, a Volkswagen Bug; it looked clean and well cared for. In the back seat was a camera tripod and a black canvas drawstring bag that was open. He could see what looked like other camera paraphernalia sticking out of the bag.

Strolling up the walk he felt somehow like he was coming home even though he had never been to this place. His feeling probably sprang from knowing this was Jessie's house, he thought.

He rang the bell and somewhere inside the house he could hear chimes. When Tobe opened the door Chet recognized him immediately, in spite of the drawn lines in his face and the worry in his eyes.

"Hello, Chet," Tobe said, "We've been expecting you. Please come in."

Leading Chet into the front room, Tobe gestured toward another man standing near a chair in front of the window. "This is my cousin Harold Young," he said, "Harold, meet Chet Upshaw."

Harold, who was older than Tobe, had a very lackluster grip for such a stocky muscular man. He was shorter than Chet by three or four inches and had streaks of gray in his otherwise coal black hair. "Hello, Chet," he murmured, in a surprisingly soft voice, "I have been looking forward to meeting you. I understand you are a crackerjack sleuth. We all hope you can find Jessie and bring her back to us."

"I'll do my best," Chet replied.

"Harold was just about to leave when you rang," Tobe said, "He has to get back to his own place. Harold, thanks for your offer to help gather but I can manage. If I can stay busy it will probably help take my mind off of Jessie."

Harold said his goodbyes and headed for the door; Tobe went with him to show him out. A few minutes later Chet heard the big diesel engine fire up. So the Dodge diesel belongs to Harold, he mused, bet that set him back plenty.

Tobe came back into the room. Just for a moment the picture of utter dejection. Then seeming to shake it off he brightened up. "I saw your Tahoe outside, Chet. It seems to fit you."

Chet, pleased Tobe had admired his wheels, said with a low chuckle, "Thanks, I like it."

"Before we get started," Tobe said, "Come into the kitchen and say hello to my little sister Ann." Not giving Chet a choice he headed that way.

Chet was a little apprehensive, remembering that the "Squirt" really hadn't liked him that much but he followed Tobe into the kitchen. Ann was standing at the freezer, taking out a package. When Tobe called out, she turned to face the two men.

This is no Squirt, Chet thought, as he gazed in amazement at the lovely young woman facing him.

"Look who I brought in, Ann," Tobe said, "Do you remember Chet Upshaw?"

"Sure," Ann said with a smile.

Chet, struck speechless by the poised, attractive young woman, with shoulder length sandy-red hair and beautiful deep blue eyes, grinned back. The loose fitting shirt, with the smiling face on it, didn't quite hide her slender body. He wondered why she had a camera hanging from her neck. He hoped he would get a chance to ask her. As she lifted her hand he noticed that she wore no wedding ring. *Great,* he thought.

Ann hadn't exactly been hiding in the kitchen; she could always find something to do there. She had started a large potato salad and was just starting to peel the boiled eggs when she heard the car drive up and stop in front of the house. Then she heard the voice and low laugh. Yes, that was Chet and his voice still had charisma!

When Clara had first informed them she had talked to Chet Upshaw and asked him to help in finding Jessie, Ann was not impressed. He must have changed a lot she had thought; he used to be pretty irresponsible. But it might be fun to see him again. He had been Tobe's classmate in High School and she remembered that he once had an irritating way of acting superior and a bad habit of calling her 'Squirt'. She in return had called him 'City Boy'. Tobe had been into football and Chet into wrestling, she recalled.

"I wonder if he will remember me?" she said softly to herself.

Ann was listening intently as she went to take some hamburger patties out of the freezer. She heard Harold leave and then she heard Tobe's and Chet's footsteps in the hall coming toward the kitchen. Her heart did a couple of flip-flops of apprehension and then they were at the door and her brother was asking if she remembered Chet from high school.

When he came through the kitchen door she saw that Chet was even taller and better looking than she remembered. There was a suntan that said he didn't spend all of his time behind a desk in Las Cruces as she had supposed. She immediately wished she had put a little more attention into what she was wearing. The sweatshirt with a smiley face on it and the two-sizes-too-large, bleached blue jeans that she bought at Wal-Mart, were comfortable but certainly not becoming. The tan leather camera case around her neck was well worn and battered but she would have felt naked without it. She put it on when she left the ranch house in the morning and took it off only when she came into the kitchen. Today she realized she had forgotten to do that.

She was conscious of the fact that she was still the same size 10 as she had been when she left Deming eleven years ago. But she felt that all of the outdoor assignments that she did had not been kind to her. She hoped that those very small crinkles at the corner of her eyes were not noticeable in the light from the kitchen window.

Of course there was no hiding the windblown, fine, sandy-red hair that needed some time spent at Sherry's Beauty Parlor. She had planned on making an appointment one day next week for a cut and perm. It was too late to worry about that now, so she reached up to brush the tousled straight hair back away from her face. For some ridiculous reason, she hoped Chet would notice that there was no wedding ring on her left hand.

"I wasn't sure you'd remember me," Chet said.

"Of course I do." She grinned mischievously. "You were Tobe's friend in high school who used to call me Squirt."

Chet had the grace to redden slightly, to her delight. "I understand Jessie's mother asked you to help find Jessie."

Chet's light blue eyes were serious as he held her gaze. "I hope I can help. I'm an investigative reporter now and have had some experience in this sort of thing. I'm here to interview Tobe and would like to talk to you, too, if I may."

"I'll tell you all I know but I'm sure you have been told that I didn't even know she was gone until Sunday morning when I brought the kids' home from Deming. I wish I had been here, maybe Jessie would have come over to talk to me and we wouldn't be looking for her now."

Chet was all business. "I won't interrupt your cooking. I have to be back to my motel soon. Could I call and make an appointment to see you tomorrow?"

"Any time, Chet," she said sincerely. She felt suddenly that this grown-up Chet was someone she would like to get to know better. And she also felt he would hear much that was not complimentary to Tobe and she wanted to urge him to keep an open mind about everything he heard.

Tobe didn't give them any time to talk over old times nor to get reacquainted. He guided Chet back into the living room, leaving Ann still in the kitchen.

Back in the living room Tobe cut right to the chase. "I'm not all that sold on your getting in on this, Chet," he said, "Even though you lived in Deming when we were kids, and were classmates in high school, you are still an outsider. I just can't see you being able to find out something that we, who knew Jessie well, can't dig out ourselves better. Also, we know the country and people around here and you don't. So what's your interest in this? A big dramatic story at our expense?"

"I'm not just after a big story, Tobe," Chet said patiently. "Don't forget that I was once a part of this town. I cared about Jessie, and you were my friend. Still are, I hope. I have been invited to look into this by Jessie's mother. We have both changed a lot and perhaps you no longer know me. But, I am good at this."

Tobe's expression didn't change much, with Chet's speech. He still looked worried and skeptical. "Yes, Clara said you had a good reputation but I just don't want our troubles aired for everyone to see."

"I promise if you cooperate with me, I will show everything to you before I send it in."

"OK, I guess that's the best I can hope for, so here goes. From my stand point there really isn't that much. Jessie and I were alone in the house. Ann had taken the kids and gone to a movie in town. We, Jessie and I, had a big fight and Jessie ran out of here angry and crying. She grabbed my old black sweater off the hook near the back door. I thought she would cool off and return after a while. I didn't realize the storm was as bad as it was and I was pretty mad myself."

"You mean you didn't go after her?"

"No, and I have kicked myself ever since but I just didn't know the storm was so bad. I didn't even look out for at least a half hour, although vaguely I realized the wind was really kicking up. When I did, I began to panic. The storm was the worst we have had in years. The snow was heavy and the wind was really whooping it up. There was already a couple of inches on the ground and the wind was whipping it around. Visibility was near zero. No one could stay out in that for long."

"What did you do then?"

"I quickly got into heavy clothing and started looking. The first thing I thought of was the little cabin where Ann is staying and where Jessie goes when she wants to be alone. I got into the pickup and drove down. The visibility was so bad I missed the turn but realized quickly what I had done and turned around and went back. I spotted the little track that led up to her house. It only took a few minutes to search the place and see that Jessie wasn't there. Then I drove slowly back to the house searching as best I could along the side of the road in case she fell."

"Did you call 911?"

"Not at this time, instead I called Aunt Rachel's, hoping to get Harold to help search. She told me she was there alone, that Harold had gone to a sale out of town. She said she would come right away. I tried to talk her out of it because I didn't want two people to look for. She would have none of it. I didn't wait for her. I grabbed a flashlight and went out again, on foot, this time. The wind had died down some by then and visibility was better. I started searching near the back door, then circled the house. I couldn't find any tracks and there was no sign of Jessie. I saw headlights coming up the road so I went out front to meet whoever it was. It was Aunt Rachel in her old pickup."

"Had she seen anything on her drive over?"

"No, but she started searching around the barns and other outbuildings. I went out past the corrals and made a circle around the fence. There were cattle in the pasture, all huddled up against the storm. They were seemingly undisturbed. Up to this point I was sure we would find her at any moment. Now I was not so sure. We kept searching, clear out to the cattle-guard, and up and down the road, just going in now and then for a cup of coffee so we could keep going. I had already put in a pretty hard day and I was dragging."

"Did you then call 911?"

"No, that would have brought out the state police. I didn't want that, so way after midnight I finally called the Sheriff's office. I know most of those boys and I know Jim Brady the Sheriff. I figured he would put Alredd on the case and I'd heard he was a good man. They sent out a woman, she is Hispanic and petite."

"Yeah, I think I've seen her."

"They say she is very good in this type of situation but I don't really know her. I was frantic with worry by this time and so was

129

Rachel, but we were also almost dead on our feet. Rachel and I sat down on the couch to drink some more coffee. I leaned back on the old couch in the kitchen and closed my eyes and that was the last I knew until the sheriff arrived at two. Aunt Rachel didn't wake me when the deputy came, just gave her the story and lay down to get some rest herself. The deputy promised to have some one out early and they did."

They sat for a moment in silence. Chet thought the story was full of holes. Why would Jessie stay out in that storm for even a minute? What could have happened to her even if she had? If she had fallen and hurt herself she would have been found. How far could she have gotten in a half hour — or even in an hour in a storm like that?

Finally Tobe said, "I want her found, that's the only reason you are here. As soon as the papers heard about it we got reporters by the gross. They have pestered us unmercifully. We even had one from Albuquerque. There was someone from your paper, if I recall correctly. There was lots of publicity and even a good many calls from people who thought they had seen her but they were all duds. So even

130

with all the hassle with the reporters, we didn't get any results. Jessie just seems to have dropped from the face of the earth!" His voice quivered and he turned his head away and swallowed hard.

"I'm sorry," Chet said softly. "I know this has been rough but don't give up. People don't just vanish. And I'll try to see what I can do."

"I just don't see what you can do. We've covered everything." He sighed deeply. "I've even been watching the buzzards lately, hoping against hope that what they've found isn't my wife," he said grimly.

"I'll tell you just like I told Alredd. I can put all my time on it. If, like you say, you don't know what happened to her, maybe someone else will."

A glint of anger showed in Tobe's face. "I should probably bust your teeth in for even thinking what I know you're thinking but I promised Ann and Clara that I would hold my temper. You will have cooperation from me and any one on the ranch. If you need a horse, we'll supply it and the gear."

"I'll borrow the horse if I need it but there has been a thorough search. I doubt if I would be able to see anything that the rest haven't. If you can't think of anything else, I guess I'll get out of your hair." He got up and started towards the door. Tobe just nodded his head. He didn't see Chet out.

When Chet came out of the house he noticed Ann standing by his car. She had changed her shirt and done something to her hair. She was lovelier than ever. For some reason Chet didn't fully understand the already bright day seemed a little brighter. "Hi," he said inanely, "what are you doing here?"

"I'm waiting for you, of course. I want you to listen to what you hear with an open mind. Many people think Tobe harmed Jessie — because of the argument. But he never would, never!

"I heard Tobe say you could have the run of the ranch. That will include Aunt Rachel's part also. You will be talking to Aunt Rachel and Harold. I'm telling you, and they will tell you that Tobe would never hurt Jessie. Tobe is worried sick. He's out before sun-up every day. He claims to be checking the pastures but I know he's looking for Jessie because he is leaving a lot of the work undone."

She seems so sincere, Chet thought. If she doesn't believe Tobe did something to Jessie, just how does she explain the disappearance?

Before he could say anything Tobe stepped out on the porch. Ann, seeing him, said quickly, "You said you wanted to talk to me. I have to pick T.J. up from kindergarten at twelve thirty tomorrow. I could meet you somewhere for lunch at eleven and discuss it."

"Sure," Chet said, already anticipating being with her, "How about the Holiday Inn, the food's not too bad."

"OK," Ann said, as she walked away towards the house.

Climbing into his car Chet watched her walk away. What am I thinking, he mused, she's way too short for me.

Chapter 7

Starting his car Chet drove to the corner where the two roads split. On impulse he turned into the road leading to the Young ranch. It's almost noon, he thought, this could be a good time to catch Rachel Young. He wanted to talk to her and to Harold. They should both be in for lunch. As he crossed the cattle guard he could see Harold's truck sitting next to an older pickup. They were probably both in. Chet pulled into the yard and parked next to the older pickup. He spotted Rachel working out in the tool shed, which was off to one side. She saw him at about the same time and came over.

"Hello," she said, "Harold said you were over at Tobe's. Harold is around here somewhere. Come on in, we're just about to have lunch and you can join us."

Chet, understanding that Rachel would brook no argument, readily accepted. They walked together into the house. Just as they entered the kitchen Harold came in the back door. Rachel had put a pot of

134

chili beans in the crock-pot to simmer all morning so all that was needed was to heat the flour tortillas. In only a few minutes they were sitting down to eat.

Rachel proved to be a good conversationalist, keeping Chet entertained throughout the meal. Harold, too, was a smiling and pleasant host, adding to his mother's stories with a telling comment here and there. Harold ate quickly, soon excusing himself, leaving Chet and Rachel alone at the table.

After Harold left Chet began to quiz Rachel about the Helm situation, especially the day Jessie disappeared. "Jessie's mother seemed to think things weren't going well between Tobe and Jessie. Did you notice anything like that, Rachel?"

"Yes, I noticed the two seemed snippy with each other but I never thought much about it. After all, things have been pretty tight with them financially since they built the new house. Money problems can make everyone tense."

"Tobe said you were home when Jessie disappeared but Harold was away."

"I was home alone the night Jessie disappeared. Harold called to tell me he wouldn't be home that night. He was tired after the sale and would stay at a motel in

Las Cruces but didn't say which one."

Rachel lifted a cup to her lips and then put it down and looked Chet in the eyes. "Chet, I know you will hear a lot of negative comments about Tobe, and I know those kids had their problems, but believe me when I say Tobe loved Jessie and would never harm her, I can say that with no reservations."

"Do you think Jessie got tired of the fighting and perhaps the lack of money to meet the bills, and just shucked it all?" Chet asked bluntly.

Anger flashed into Rachel's eyes and she lashed back, "No, I do not! That girl never shirked her duties in her whole life. She would never — and I mean never! — have left her children for someone else to care for, even for a night, unless she knew they were in good hands."

"Sorry, I didn't mean that's what I thought," Chet swiftly back-pedaled. "Just wanted to see what you thought."

"I know Tobe and I know Jessie, so don't let people fill your mind with stupid, absurd notions," Rachel snapped.

Chet assured her he wouldn't. "I ask questions and listen to answers and watch for reactions, but I always take everything with a grain of salt until I know the truth."

Then he changed the subject and after a few minutes more of random talking the anger left Rachel's face and she seemed to settle down.

Finally, over fresh cups of coffee, Rachel said bluntly, "OK, Chet, you've asked me questions and I've done my best to answer truthfully. Now, what do you think so far?"

Chet was a little taken back by the brusque question said in a rather aggressive voice. He didn't answer for a moment thinking of just what he wanted to say. He certainly didn't want to mention that he was beginning to suspect Tobe of killing his wife and hiding the body, in spite of Rachel and Ann's declarations to the contrary, so he took the middle road. "Right now I really haven't seen or heard enough to make any kind of analytic conjecture," he said.

"Well," Rachel said, "I can see you are not going to say what you really think but if you think Tobe has done anything to Jessie you should think again. At first I entertained some thoughts along those lines myself but after watching him these past two weeks I can see he is not guilty. No one could keep up that kind of front for this long."

Not much was said after that so Chet

soon excused himself. "I can see myself out," he said.

Rachel said, "OK," and started cleaning the table.

When Chet came out he heard a commotion out back so he went around the side of the house to see what it was. Harold was working a young horse in a small corral beside the barn. Chet went out to watch.

He hoped Harold would pause long enough to talk awhile.

Harold, circling in the middle of the corral, had a halter on the horse with a long rope attached. He held the rope in his left hand and a long-handled, very flexible whip in his right. He used the whip to flick the air behind the horse's rump, never touching the animal. The horse, well aware of the whip, picked up her pace a fraction each time the whip flicked behind her tail.

Each time Harold's arm went backward and forward, Chet could hear a little jingle, mingled with the crack of the whip. Puzzled at first, he finally figured out it was the ring of keys clipped to Harold's belt. In this manner Harold worked the horse around and around the corral. Finally he grounded his whip and allowed the horse to stop. Coiling the rope, he unfastened it from the mare's halter allowing the horse to stand and rest. He walked over to the fence where Chet was standing.

"Looks like she's working pretty good," Chet said.

"Yep, she's coming along right smart," Harold replied.

"I'm trying to get a line on where everyone was on the day Jessie disappeared," Chet said. "Could you take a few minutes to tell me about yourself?"

"Sure, be glad to, but actually I wasn't anywhere around. I left early and went to a liquidation sale down in Canutillo. I didn't buy anything but I waited on the livestock, they came up last. It ran pretty late so I got a room at the Days Inn in Las Cruces. I left there early the next morning and was home by eight o'clock. That's when I heard about Jessie so I joined the search. I really don't know any more. One thing I do know for sure is that Tobe could not be guilty of any real violence. Now, if you will excuse me. I'll get back to work." He snapped his rope back on the horse's halter, picked up the whip and started the horse around the corral again.

Chet watched for a few more minutes and then left. At the corner where the road joined the main ranch road there was a little turn atop a small rise. Chet stopped his car and sat gazing out over the flats to the far distant mountains. His mind was churning, turning over the things he had heard today. Up until now he had begun to believe that Tobe had probably killed his wife but Rachel, Harold and Ann all believed strongly that Tobe was telling the truth. He would have put that down to family loyalty but Harold's attitude gave him pause. He had not expected that. In the past I have always looked at all the angles, he thought, but up to now I have been set on only one solution. I'll look at some other possibilities, he resolved, but what?

With that decision made he turned his car into the road towards Deming.

About a mile down the road he glimpsed the roof of a house on the right. It was almost hidden by the brush. He almost passed it up but decided to see if anyone lived there. A short drive, down a hill, ended in front of a small house, surrounded by brush on three sides. There was a barn and corral in back and an old pickup, with a four-horse trailer hooked on behind, parked parallel to the fence in front.

There was room enough for him to pull

in beside the pickup. He walked through an opening in the fence and down a path that led to the front door. He was about to knock on the door when a tall thin man walked around the side of the house. Chet recognized him, it was Rudy Penrose. Rudy was well known especially by all the high school kids. A cowboy poet and yarn spinner deluxe, he liked entertaining and was at every poet competition held. He entertained at least two high school assemblies a year and seemed to enjoy them as much as the kids. Holding no regular job, he just worked when he felt like it and was such a good worker he never had any trouble finding work.

He was dressed today in the same type of outfit he always wore. A long sleeved western shirt was topped by a checkered bandanna knotted around his long thin neck. Tight fitting Levi's tucked into stovepipe, low-heeled cowboy boots, adorned his long thin legs. "Hello young feller," he said, "What brings you to my door."

"Rudy, do you remember me? I'm Chet Upshaw, you were at my mom and dad's funeral."

"Why, Chet, I would never have knowed you. You've grown." Ever blunt, he went on, "What do you want?"

"I was asked by Clara Miller to look into Jessie Helm's disappearance. I have been asking around trying to find out if anyone could shed any light on the subject."

"Yeah, ain't it strange. I might not be able to help you any. My old mare was about to drop her colt. She's fifteen and she was struggling. I was up all night out in the barn trying to help her through it. The colt was born about six a.m. Mighty purty little feller too. I didn't hear the news until late afternoon, I went over to help search as soon as I heard."

"Did you hear or see anything at all."

" 'Fraid not. That storm was fierce and I had my hands full."

Chet was disappointed; Rudy Penrose was not in the sheriff's files. He thanked Rudy and turned to leave.

"Wait," Rudy called, "I just remembered somethin'. My barn is fairly close to the road and there was an unusual amount of traffic on the road that night. I heard what I took to be Ann's little bug go by early toward town. A diesel truck went by about eight o'clock p.m. I thought it was Harold headed to Tobe's house but I guess not because I heard it come back by a while later, going in the opposite direction.

Another truck went by a little while later, but I couldn't hear it plain, the wind was screeching so bad and a while later either that one or another vehicle came back the Helm ranch direction. As I said I really didn't pay much attention but I couldn't help wondering who would be out driving on a night like that. I doubt if that's any help but I can't think of anything else."

Chet thanked him again and got on the road back to Deming. So there were two trucks down this road about the time Jessie disappeared. He wondered if either of these people had seen anything? He wondered if they could have had anything to do with Jessie? Could one of them have grabbed her? How about that second truck, could that have been Tobe getting rid of the evidence? Deputy Alredd drove a diesel truck — and of course Harold did. Could Alredd have had a reason to be out here on that night? I wonder if he might have strong feelings for Jessie or a grudge against Tobe?

When he reached the motel, Chet went straight to his room to work out with weights. As he went through the familiar routine he thought about the problem. He was not one bit closer to figuring out what happened to Jessie.

Jessie told her mother she had talked her troubles over with Pastor Frederick. Maybe she had told him something that would be useful. Chet wanted to see the pastor anyway. He decided he would call to see if they could get together this evening. He knew the Pastor would normally not talk about anything mentioned in confidence but this was different, maybe he would make an exception. Finished with his workout, Chet took a quick shower then dialed Pastor Frederick's home. The phone was picked up on the third ring.

"Hello," the voice sounded older but Chet recognized it.

"Pastor, this is Chet Upshaw, how are you doing."

"Why, Chet, it's good to hear from you. It's been a long time."

"Yes, it has. I'm in Deming on an assignment. I'd like to visit with you. Would you consider having dinner with me tonight? Could you meet me at the Holiday Inn at seven thirty?"

"That sounds like a good idea. I'll just hold all my questions and answers until then."

"Great, I'll see you at seven thirty."

"OK, Chet, and may the lord be with you."

As he hung up the phone Chet had warm thoughts of the man who, next to his parents, was most instrumental in his own conversion. He recalled walking down the aisle to kneel at the altar at the age of ten, with Pastor Frederick's hand on his shoulder and the pastor's voice lifted in prayer. When he rose from the altar, his heart full of joy, he was a changed person. All it took was a simple supplication, "Jesus, please save me, I'm a sinner."

Chet used his credit card to make a telephone call to his boss in Las Cruces. Paula answered. "Hello, Chet, Creighton isn't in. He told me to take notes."

"Sorry, Paula, tell him I have nothing to report. I'll call again tomorrow."

"OK, goodbye then. We'll keep the home fires burning."

While Chet waited for the pastor he got out his notebook and began going over his list. Mentally crossing out number five, he continued the list:

5. The Sheriff's Department suspected Tobe but had no proof.
6. A bloody handkerchief, with Jessie's blood on it, didn't prove Jessie had gone that far. (The handkerchief could have blown there during the storm).

7. Ann, Rachel and Harold all thought Tobe to be incapable of hurting Jessie. (This could be due to family loyalty).
8. Tobe sounded convincing (?).
9. There was an unusual amount of traffic on the road for a bad night like that. Rudy had heard three different vehicles. At least one of them was a diesel. There could have been more.
10. Nothing makes sense.

He was aware the list wouldn't solve any mystery. None of his lists ever had but they somehow focused his thinking.

Glancing at his watch, he noticed it was time to go.

Pastor Frederick came through the lobby door just as Chet arrived. Dapper as ever, he quick-stepped toward Chet for a hearty handshake. As they shook the pastor's dark brown eyes gave Chet the once over. Chet, too, was eyeing the shorter man. He didn't seem to have changed much. A few more lines around the mouth and eyes. His grip was firm and his curly black hair showed very little gray. All in all, time had dealt kindly with him.

"Hello, Chet," the pastor said, "It's been too long."

"Yes, it has been a while," Chet replied,

"But you are looking well."

"I do feel good and my energy level is high." The two men entered the restaurant still talking.

A young, pretty hostess met them at the entrance and escorted them to a table near the windows. Both ordered coffee and looked at the menu, deciding what to order. By the time coffee came, Chet had decided on a small grilled steak and baked potato, the Pastor would try the sautéed chicken breast and rice.

"Chet, I heard from the Helms you are investigating Jessie's disappearance. I won't be able to tell you anything that I have been told in confidence. I can't. I would only if I was sure it was a matter of life or death." Chet studied the minister for a moment, "I understand, sir, but this could be a matter of life or death. Could you answer this, do you think Tobe capable of harming Jessie?"

For a moment the pastor looked down at his hands on the table and seemed to ponder his question. Then he said slowly, "I suppose anyone is capable of harming someone else if driven to the limits of their endurance. However, even with his quick temper, I can't see Tobe harming his wife. He loves her, I have no doubt."

"It seems to be common knowledge that Jessie and Tobe were having marital problems," Chet said. "Perhaps canceling the bull he ordered was the limit of his endurance."

"Perhaps," the pastor said, "but that would have to be proven, beyond a shadow of a doubt, before I would believe it."

Chet was relieved enormously. Pastor Frederick was a wise man, Chet recalled, and his words meant a great deal to him. "Do you have any idea where Jessie has gone?"

When the pastor didn't answer for a moment, Chet asked pointedly, "Do you think Jessie just walked away from it all?"

The words were scarcely out of his mouth when the pastor was shaking his head. "And leave her children behind? No way! Those kids are her life."

"What do you think happened to her?"

Stark grief misted the minister's eyes, "I have trouble keeping my mind from the horrible things that could have happened to her."

"Such as?" Chet pressed.

"Illegals from Mexico could have grabbed her and taken her back there to sell. Someone from our own neighborhood could have attacked and killed her and taken her body far away before it was dumped — in a desolate, uninhabited place where she wouldn't be found, perhaps."

"But you don't think there is the faintest possibility that she left on her own?"

The minister frowned, "If she had, why didn't she take her car? Or contact anyone to find out how the children were faring. You must remember that Jessie loves Tobe. And I can't imagine her wanting to hurt him by leaving without a word. No, she didn't leave under her own power. Because of the blood on the handkerchief they found, I feel that she was possibly hurt and someone took advantage of that and abducted her. Perhaps took her to Mexico since it isn't far from Deming."

"There is nothing concrete you can add — anything, even an unimportant thing, that you recall that might help us find her. Had she been threatened by anyone, was someone jealous of her, or holding a grudge? Perhaps infatuated with her? She is an attractive woman."

"I'm sorry, Chet, I have already racked my brain but there is nothing she ever told me that could be a clue to her disappearance."

That settled, Chet led the conversation

into talk of old times and on into future plans. A pleasant hour was spent eating the good food and talking. Nothing else was said about the Helms.

Finally Pastor Frederick, expressing regrets, said he had to leave. They parted company in the lobby and Chet went back to his room. He was soon in bed and fast asleep.

Chapter 8

(Friday-Sunday)

Jessie awoke the next morning to the lusty crowing of the big red rooster. This morning she felt exhilarated. Yesterday she had been able to exercise with her new crutch, she was growing stronger and perhaps today would hold even better success.

There wasn't much left to eat in the refrigerator and she again felt ravenously hungry so she made do with some goat milk and the remaining fried pie. Still hungry, she crumbled the last of the white cheese, added the chopped chilies on a tortilla and toasted them on top of the stove in an iron skillet. She had been reluctant to use the things the unknown person bought for her — although she did use the white cotton nightgown since she had no nightwear. But this morning the chocolate turtles kept calling to her and she finally gave in, broke the seal and ate one. Heavenly!

After a shower, she went back to her western novel. The middle of the morning, she heard some sounds of activity outdoors so limped to the window, using her crutch. Luis meandered about the goat enclosure, taking care of the animals. She noticed he kept the male goat at a distance with what appeared to be a cattle prod. So the buck wasn't to be trusted, as Jessie had suspected. As Luis moved around, never turning his back on the animal, the creature followed, tossing his head and even rearing up on his hind legs occasionally as if to show who was the king of the corral.

As Jessie surveyed the action in the goat-pens, Juana came out with a basket of wet clothes and began to pin the garments on a line in the back yard. If the two noticed her watching they ignored it. Finishing her work, Juana returned to the house and a few minutes later Jessie was surprised to hear the familiar turning of the key in the lock. Standing at the door, the old woman beckoned. Using her crutch, Jessie limped to the door, and took the basket Juana had brought. After thanking the woman, she glanced down to see that it contained a number of food items.

Juana spoke a few words in Spanish but Jessie shook her head. Her limited knowledge didn't cover the words. Juana looked perplexed for a moment, then frowning as if in deep concentration, she spoke a few heavily accented English words. Shaking her head she pointed at Jessie and said, "No bring food to you — party mañana — me make mucho food, take mucho time cook food — big party — Sabe?"

"Si," Jessie said, "I understand." She touched herself and asked, "Me — help you?" and indicated Juana with a hand on her arm.

Juana's thin lips curved into a faint, shy smile, "Me see," she said. She gently pushed the door closed and locked it.

Jessie put away the food in the refrigerator — a half dozen eggs, several cans of low-fat soups, sliced low-fat ham, a loaf of bakery bread — 100 percent whole wheat bread that she always used, she noted with a slight quiver in her stomach. The quiver became a pronounced trembling when she saw the other items: a few oranges and apples, small jars of decaffeinated coffee, no-fat coffee creamer, lower-fat mayonnaise and kosher-style dill pickles, all low fat foods or foods she especially favored, and would have purchased herself. How did anyone, outside of friends or family, know just what she liked? Had that strange unknown person who bought the clothes have also bought these, or could she just be paranoid?

Bewildered and distraught, Jessie turned toward the window and saw Juana trudging down to the corral. "She's going to ask Luis if I'm to be allowed to help," Jessie mused aloud. "She seems to be afraid of that husband of hers — or is she afraid of someone else? The person who is having me held prisoner here?"

After a few minutes of conversation, Jessie observed Juana returning and soon heard her at the door unlocking it. Without preamble, she said, "Si," motioning Jessie out into the yard. "You come — you help." She led Jessie through the car-port and into the back door of the other house.

The cleanliness of the kitchen, and the bright pottery, straw-bottomed chairs with Mexican designs, roomy cupboards and scrubbed linoleum floors pleased Jessie. Utensils and pans were already laid out on the plastic-covered table and counter for the food preparation.

All that day, and the morning and part of the afternoon of the next day — with a quick break for meals — Juana kept Jessie busy. Dutifully she chopped onions, fresh tomatoes, and peeled green chilies, shredded lettuce, and grated cheese. They prepared an enormous amount of spicy tamales, burritos and frijoles (pinto beans)

— seasoned with little chunks of lean salt pork. Juana informed her a fat goat-kid would be barbecued late the next afternoon. Luis had attended to the butchering before lunch and it hung cooling in the shed. Although neither Jessie nor Juana could speak each other's language, both knew some words, so using those and gestures and motions, they corresponded quite well, Jessie felt. She learned, while working the next day, that Juana's son, Julio, was coming tonight — Saturday — and bringing his friends. After the food preparations were completed on Saturday afternoon, Juana escorted Jessie back to her quarters. Juana stressed that no one at the party must know Jessie slept here. The guests would be using alcohol, Juana told her by motions and a mixture of Spanish and English words, and it might be dangerous for her if she didn't keep her shades drawn and all lights off.

Jessie didn't object, but she wondered if that was the real reason she wasn't to show herself. Perhaps the couple didn't want their son knowing they kept a prisoner here. Maybe I should try to attract the attention of some of the guests and see what happens, she wondered. But Jessie didn't ponder long on what to do, she was exhausted, even though the old lady had insisted on her sitting down as much as possible, and taking breaks periodically to drink something and have a sample of tamales — or other snacks.

She read a bit while she rested, but was too tired to concentrate so before it was even dark, she brushed her teeth and went to bed — fully clothed, since she didn't know what to expect from tonight's party or its guests. Her watch said only 7:00 p.m.

Hours later, Jessie awoke with heart pounding wildly and her mouth dry as cotton. Why she hadn't awakened before, was a living wonder! *I certainly must have been exhausted,* she thought. A party was going full blast with guitar music, singing, and loud rowdy laughter. Grabbing her crutch, Jessie crept to the window and lifted the shade slightly. In the next yard on the paved court-yard, she saw two men and one woman — all brightly garbed in Mexican fiesta-type apparel, playing guitars and singing.

Electric lights, strung up about the yard, brilliantly illuminated the whole yard. Several couples were swinging about the courtyard, laughing and dancing exuberantly. Several others — more men than women, she saw — were strolling about, or sitting in chairs scattered around, talking. Everyone seemed to have a glass, can or bottle of something. And from the boisterous manner they were all behaving, Jessie was sure it wasn't non-alcoholic.

A long table had been set up for the food on the side closest to the car-port. As she observed surreptitiously, Jessie saw people beginning to take foam plates and plastic-ware from the end of the table, and load them up. From where she stood, Jessie could smell the food, especially the barbecue, and it made her mouth water.

The refrigerator held plenty of food — food Juana had sent — tamales, burritos and spicy hot sauce. She debated whether she should move around, though, recalling Juana's warning. And now she believed her. She would be an alien out there, and they all looked half drunk or more. Especially a big, dark fellow, tall and broad and mean-looking. Everyone seemed to show him deference, she noticed, obviously he was a "big wheel" at the party. Could that be Julio. Juana had said her son was big. I wouldn't want to meet him, even with others around, Jessie thought with a shudder. He looks like one mean hombre!

Softly, she crept back to her bed and lay

down. No doubt she wouldn't sleep, with all the noise, but she could rest. *I must still not be up to par,* she thought. Her muscles still ached from the exertion of the day. But some time later — how much, she didn't know — Jessie awoke to a sound at the back door of her little house. She had never seen the back door used, in fact, had forgotten about it. But someone was there now, fumbling around the door-knob! Even though the boisterous laughter and noise from outside revealed the party was still in full swing, she heard it plainly.

Terror set her heart to pounding. She sat up and reached for her crutch. Should she hide? But where? In this open, one-room building there was no place to hide except in the wardrobe or bathroom, or under the bed, and all could be searched in minutes. She slid to the side of the bed. If she screamed, would Luis make an attempt to protect her? He seemed very meek, old, and runty in build. What could he — or Juana — do even if they had the gumption.

The front of her room showed dimly from the bright lights out in the courtyard but darkness cloaked the back of the long room. Jessie felt her heart would burst from the tension as she sat stiffly on the bed-side. A key grated in the lock and the door swung open with a creak. Jessie held her breath as a form draped in black appeared in the doorway. "Jessie," a softly accented voice whispered.

For a moment Jessie's relief was so great she could only gape. Juana! Then she found her voice and whispered back, "Over here, on the bed."

Juana moved into the room and closed the door softly and Jessie could hear her locking it. Then she glided to the front door and also locked it with the bolt. Moving like a wraith, she tiptoed to Jessie's side.

"Is something wrong?" Jessie scarcely breathed the words. Juana sat down on the side of the bed beside Jessie and the black shawl slipped from her head. Her pale wrinkled face was dimly illuminated by the outside lights and Jessie gasped. Juana's left eye was almost closed and a dark bruise covered her left cheekbone!

"Juana," Jessie whispered in horror, "what happened?"

"Julio," the old woman mumbled.

"Your son . . . Julio . . . did this?" Jessie said, touching the bruised cheek with a gentle finger.

The old woman nodded, "Tequila! Tequila make Julio muy malo. (very bad)"

"I'm so sorry," Jessie murmured. She touched the woman's shoulder and the older woman flinched. "Your shoulder's hurt! Did he knock you down?" she asked.

Apparently Juana understood the gist of her words for she lowered her head as if in shame and nodded.

"Come into the bathroom and let me see," Jessie said, taking her gently by the hand. The old woman allowed herself to be led. The bathroom had only a small window which was on the side away from the other house. Pulling down the window shade which covered it, Jessie turned on the light.

In the light Juana's face looked even worse — the eye was completely swelled shut now so the man must have recently finished his brutal act. Unbuttoning her dress, Juana turned her shoulder to the light and Jessie saw an ugly bruise at the top of her arm. Juana winced when Jessie gently moved the arm to see if it was broken. Evidently it's just badly bruised, Jessie decided. Juana's whole side and ribs were also bruised but her ribs didn't appear to be broken.

"Did Julio hit you there," Jessie asked as she touched her shoulder lightly. Juana shook her head, "Julio hit face," she said.

"Me fall on cement. Hurts bad."

"Why did he hit you," asked Jessie.

"No more tamales and he angry with me. Hit me."

"I'll get some ice for your face," Jessie said gently. Turning out the light, she went to the refrigerator, removed an ice-tray quickly and closed the door. She didn't want that big bruiser seeing even a small light in here and pounding on the door.

After she made an ice-pack from ice-cubes and a towel, she found some Tylenol in the medicine cabinet. Jessie held a glass of water for her which she drank thirstily with the medicine. Jessie helped her to the bed, took off her shoes and made her as comfortable as she could with the ice-pack on her hurt eye and cheek.

"Donde es (where is) Luis?" Jessie asked.

"Mucho tequila," Juana answered.

"Passed out from too much tequila?" Jessie asked.

"Si," Juana said in a dejected voice.

"Just sleep here the rest of the night. Everyone seems too drunk to go looking for you," she whispered as she stretched out beside Juana on the double bed.

"Gracias," the old lady said in a weary voice. And in just minutes, Jessie could tell

Juana was sleeping the slumber of exhaustion. Anger rose in her heart like a storm — that big drunken lout had no right to expect his little frail mother to cook for a whole army of his intoxicated friends — and to knock her around was atrocious! *It makes my blood boil,* she thought. As she seethed with fury, the sounds of revelry and drunken mirth gradually faded and she slept.

The next morning the cock's crowing didn't wake Jessie up, vigorous pounding on the door did. Jessie raised her head groggily and then sat up. The knocking continued and an accented, querulous voice ordered, "Open door!"

"Es Luis," Juana's voice spoke from the other side of the bed. Jessie turned her head and saw the old lady struggle to rise and then fall back with a groan. The sun glowing through the blind fell on Juana's parchment-like face and Jessie couldn't restrain a gasp of dismay. All around the frail old lady's left eye was puffed and the eye was swelled shut. An ugly purple bruise extended to above her eye almost to the hairline and down over her cheek-bone and spread down her cheek toward her ear.

Luis' voice was angry as he again demanded the door be opened "pronto".

"Stay here," Jessie said, gently pushing Juana back onto the bed as she again attempted to rise. "I'll go." Jessie was still fully clothed except for her shoes. She padded to the door in her bare feet and drew back the bolt.

Luis, his hair sticking up every which way and his clothes looking as if they had been slept in — which they probably had — surged into the room and raked the interior with bloodshot eyes. Stalking over to the bed, he shook an unsteady finger at Juana and let loose a torrent of angry Spanish words. Jessie couldn't follow most of it but from the words she did understand, he seemed to be ordering the old woman to get up and get him some breakfast.

Fury sprang up in Jessie like an erupting volcano. Using her crutch, she moved swiftly to the other side of the bed where Juana was trying to get up. "Don't you lay a hand on her," she said fiercely to Luis, raising the crutch menacingly.

Luis stopped in the middle of his tirade, swung his eyes to Jessie and his mouth fell open, as if in shock. She was unaware of the picture she made — dark eyes flashing, proud head held high, her lithe body poised for battle. Luis seemed struck speechless.

"Look at Juana!" Jessie said angrily, motioning toward his wife. "Look what that big brute of a son of yours did to his mother! He hit her and knocked her down! You need to get her to a doctor — not be yelling at her to get your breakfast!"

Luis suddenly regained his power of speech. "No — no doctor. She be hokay — always is. We poor people," he ended in a whining tone, shaking his head. "No can afford doctors!"

"Then take my watch! Sell it and get a doctor for her," Jessie said, her voice laced with contempt, peeling it off her arm as she spoke.

"No — not you watch, so bonito (pretty)," Juana said weakly from the bed. "Me soon be fine."

But Luis was already reaching for the watch. Jessie didn't miss the greedy gleam in his eyes as he said soothingly to his wife, "Señora ees so kind to geeve her watch, I get medicine for Juana — from pharmacy."

As she held the watch in her hand, reluctant to release it into Luis' avaricious hand, a pang suddenly shot through Jessie's heart. Abruptly she knew that the money from her precious watch — her special gift from Tobe — would never buy medicine for poor suffering Juana. It would go for more alcohol to feed the demon of drink that was the master of weak Luis. She began to draw her hand back when a new thought struck her. Her watch was distinctive and had personal lettering inside. If Tobe was searching for her, he might (Dear God, let it happen) find it where ever Luis pawned or sold it.

Suddenly — was it inspiration from God? — Jessie had another thought. Closing her hand over the watch, she said firmly, "if I give you the watch to sell, you must do a little favor for me. My husband and children will be worried about me. They don't know if I'm dead or alive." She paused to let this sink in while holding Luis' attention with her eyes, then continued, "Just call my home phone number and tell whoever answers that Jessie Helm is alive."

But Luis was already shaking his head, "No-no, Señora, no can do that. El Jefe be muy angry."

Opening her hand partially so Luis could glimpse the sparkling jewels on the watch, she said softly, "You don't need to tell your boss, and you don't need to tell your name to whoever answers my home phone. Just say, 'Jessie Helm is alive' and hang up. No one will know who you are and there's no way your boss will know." Opening up her hand, she displayed the watch tantalizingly and coaxed, "You should get enough for this watch to buy yourself something, too — after you buy the medicine and make the call, of course."

Jessie could see Luis weakening; he couldn't seem to take his eyes from the sparkling, diamond-encircled watch. *Dear God, please help,* she entreated as she spoke again, pleading coming through her words, "I know my family is worried sick and your call would be such a help to them — and me. Please, Mr. Nuñez, it would only take a minute."

"Hokay, I weel do eet — for you, Señora," he said expansively.

"Gracias," Jessie said softly. "I thank you from the bottom of my heart," — and she meant it. *Dear Heavenly Father, go with my watch and use it to help me get back home,* she prayed fervently in her heart.

Handing the watch to Luis, Jessie felt as if her heart were being torn out of her body — parting with Tobe's special gift to her. "I'll write down the telephone number for you," she said as she quickly moved to the bedside table and took out pencil and a pad that she had noticed there earlier.

Handing Luis the phone number, she

added, "The Pharmacist will surely know something that will help Juana. Besides her face, her shoulder, ribs — and I suspect her hip — is badly bruised." As she watched him turn toward the door, she said worriedly, "I just hope she doesn't have a broken bone."

Juana reached up to pat Jessie on the arm, "I be fine," she said soothing.

Almost as an after-thought, Luis turned back to take away Juana's key, and lock the door. Within minutes, Jessie heard the pick-up leave the yard in a hurry. To the cantina, Jessie thought, to get tanked up on tequila again. With a heavy heart, Jessie wondered if she would ever see her watch again. Or Tobe — or the children? *Dear God, she pled silently, please help me. I miss them so much.*

Chapter 9

Eleven days later Jessie stood in front of the calendar and marked a slash across the number 26. Ever since she found out the time she had arrived at this place, she had scrupulously marked off each day of the month. She had been incarcerated nineteen days, almost three weeks — the longest nineteen days of her life!

Today was the lowest point of her whole captivity. Since giving her watch to Luis, she had lived daily with the hope that "today" would be the day Tobe would find her but it hadn't happened — and expectation was now fading. She had begun to doubt that Luis had even made a call to her family and obviously her watch had not been found by anyone who knew her.

Close to despair, she felt utterly forsaken — by Tobe, and all her family and friends. Even God seemed far away as if he didn't even know she was clear down here in Mexico. If she was in Mexico! The fact was, she didn't even know if she "was" in Mexico. Since finding out the date she arrived here, she had gleaned nothing new. Juana was still kind — but distant. She was afraid, was Jessie's assessment — but afraid of whom? Surely more than just of Luis, who seemed to be a pretty good guy, except when he drank too much and had a hang-over.

When Luis had returned eleven days ago, after she gave him her watch, he had brought some anti-biotic ointment and pain medication for his wife and, Jessie was sure, a goodly supply of alcohol. For days, afterward, he smelled like a brewery, Jessie noticed every time she came close to him. But he was even tempered, for the most part, and even jovial when he was the most intoxicated.

Jessie had cared for Juana, easing her bruises with the ointment. The first three days she had slept a lot — partly due to the pain-killers but also from exhaustion, Jessie felt. Jesse had cooked the meals — which seemed to please Luis. She even made yeast rolls and loaves which both of the elderly people seemed to enjoy immensely, with lots of the white butter that she had found was made from goat-milk.

When Juana could limp about the room, she insisted on moving back to her own house. But Jessie still did quite a bit of the work, cleaning the small houses, washing clothes on an old but serviceable automatic washing machine, and hanging out the clothes. She was allowed to roam about quite freely in the enclosure but was closely watched. There was no chance for her to leave anyway with the tight, almost impenetrable ocotillo fence and the heavy lock on the gate. She was always locked into her room at night.

Even with the work she took pleasure in doing because she had never liked to be idle, time hung heavy on her hands. She read all the western novels, even though some held little interest for her. The L'Amour books were action packed and the characters well-done, she thought. All of western books were heavy into fistfights and gun battles which she never cared for but the reading passed the time away.

She asked if Juana had a Bible but the woman only had one written in Spanish. Juana was interested in the fact that Jessie wanted one and said once, rather shyly, that she loved God. Sometimes, Juana was withdrawn and uncommunicative but at other times she chattered away. During those times Juana and Jessie had interesting conversations — in a mixture of

Spanish, English and sign language. Both were becoming more proficient in each other's languages.

But neither Luis or Juana would give Jessie any answers as to who their boss was — that she presumed had her imprisoned here — or why she was here. It was maddening at times, especially at night when she lay on her bed, so lonely for Tobe and the children that she often cried until her pillow was wet. And she prayed — but it seemed that God had deserted her.

One day in one of her talkative moods, Juana — in her limited English — conveyed to Jessie that when she was very young she had been married to a wonderful young man who loved her mucho and that she had born him three children — bonito little girls. With a catch in her voice, she told how they had all died, her handsome husband Alberto — her eyes lighted with an inner glow when she spoke of him — and their three children from a cholera epidemic in their village. Juana, herself, had almost died. Her three siblings, two sisters and a brother, and her mother had also perished.

Heartbroken, with no family left and still weak from her illness, she had jumped at the chance to follow a group who were attempting to illegally cross over into the US in hopes of a better future. Luis had been one of the two coyotes who led the group and he had allowed her to come, without money, if she would marry him. Shyly, Juana said, "Me muy pretty then." They had been married in a little catholic church on the border. So their only child, Julio, had been born in the United States, she said proudly.

But it wasn't often that Juana was in such a conversational mood and the days dragged on monotonously. Twice the son Julio had come rolling into the compound but Jessie had been bundled quickly into her room before he got to their house, and ordered to stay out of sight on both occasions. Jessie decided he couldn't be the mysterious person who had brought her here because the couple were careful that she not be seen. He hadn't stayed long either time. Besides him, no one else came.

Numerous times during her confinement, Jessie brought out the belt with the distinctive silver belt buckle with a long-horned goat engraving. But as hard as she tried, her memory refused to divulge the mystery person who had worn the belt in her presence. It must have only been a time or two, she reasoned, but a vague person would rise in her memory and then disappear before she could recognize him. So frustrating!

A few times while she was out in the yard, limping about with her crutch, Jessie had an eerie feeling that she was being watched. But when she looked carefully in every direction, she could see no one except for the old couple and she was used to their close observation of her. One day when she had again strongly felt the sensation, she lifted her eyes to the hills above the corral and thought she saw movement on the highest ridge and perhaps she saw a flash of light. Then there was nothing although she kept her gaze there for quite a while, and she wondered if she imagined it.

This morning as she marked the nineteenth day of her incarceration, Jessie felt such despair that it frightened her. She had tried to stay upbeat, praying and looking for each day to bring about her release but today the future stretched before her as bleak and barren as Death Valley that she had visited once.

After helping with the washing and hanging out the clothes, she stood for a moment staring up at the spot she thought she had once seen some movement — as she had done often since then. Suddenly something did move up there. It was far away, but for just a brief few seconds she was certain she saw the shape of a man. A man who held something in his hand that flashed in the sun. Then, as before, the ridge was bare of life or movement.

"I did see a figure," she said softly to herself, "of someone who doesn't wish to be seen." Was someone spying on this place — or on her? Her heart was pounding with excitement. Could that be someone searching for her? Because by this time she was certain an extensive search had been made for her. If only she knew where she was! It was so infuriatingly maddening!

She scarcely felt a twinge now from her ankle — although she hadn't revealed that fact to her captors, and still used the crutch where they could see her. The ankle was still weak, however, and she was careful about walking on uneven ground. She didn't want to hurt it again. Did they know that her ankle was strong enough now to walk away, if the opportunity came? She didn't know but if they did nothing had been said.

Juana was watering her little brood of chickens and Jessie walked over and watched her for a moment. Glancing around to see where Luis was, Jessie saw him leaning over the engine of his old pickup. "Juana," she said softly, "did Luis make that call to my family?"

Juana stood up from cleaning the water trough and glanced in her husband's direction. Her face betrayed anxiety as she spoke equally softly, "No," she admitted. "He afraid someone find out. Be in trouble."

"My husband and the children must be frantic," Jessie said despondently. "They must have looked everywhere for me."

Juana looked at her from gentle concerned eyes. Touching Jessie on the arm, she whispered, "You esposo care — para you? Mucho?"

"Yes, Juana, my husband loves me very much," Jessie said. "Mucho," she added with a sad smile.

Juana turned and walked away to the house.

Jessie helped cook a large noon meal — she helped prepare and ate most of her meals now at the Nuñez house. After lunch Luis got into his pick-up and drove away, after locking the gate, of course. Juana usually took a short nap after lunch unless Luis had work for her to do. So Jessie started to go out the door to her room but Juana called her back.

"Come," Juana said mysteriously as she beckoned Jessie to follow her. The old woman led the way into the small neat bed-room which Jessie had never been into before. The door had always been closed when she was in the house and she was never allowed to clean this room. Going to a bed-side night stand, she opened a drawer and took out an object that set Jessie's heart to hammering. A cellular phone!

Holding the phone in her frail old hand, she said simply, "Me call for you . . . you no tell Luis . . . no one?"

"N-No, of course I won't tell," Jessie stammered. "Do you want me to dial the number for you?" she asked when Juana held the phone out to her. Her heart was almost jumping from her body in exultation.

"Si," the old lady said. "But only me talk."

After the number was called and began to ring, Jessie handed her the telephone. The wild thought came that she could overpower the old woman and talk as fast as she could to whoever answered but she knew she couldn't do that and live with herself. This woman was going out on a very high limb for her and she could not

176

cut it off and let her fall.

Jessie could hear Ann's voice clearly on the phone, "Helm residence, Ann Helm speaking," and her knees went weak and tears filled her eyes. Juana spoke only five words in her heavily accented voice.

"Señora Jessie Helm es alive."

Juana pressed the button to shut off the phone.

Tears were running down Jessie's face as she reached out and hugged the startled little woman. "Thank you! Thank you! You are a dear and I love you!"

Chapter 10

The jarring sound of the telephone woke Chet. He looked at his watch; it was five thirty a.m.

"Hello," he mumbled.

"Chet," it was Clara Miller, "I got a call from someone saying there was evidence of Jessie in Tobe's pickup. The voice was indistinct but it sounded male. He didn't say what the evidence was. Chet, are you there?"

"Yes, I'm listening."

"Well, this man said he saw Tobe hiding something in the truck. He was sure it had to do with Jessie. I called my County Commissioner friend. He got in touch with the Sheriff. The Sheriff got the judge out of bed and obtained a warrant. We are going out to search the pickup. I want you to come. Will you?"

The words tumbled out of the receiver like water over a falls. Chet, barely awake, knew he didn't want to miss this, so his answer was a resounding, "Sure."

"It'll be a while before they are ready but

they won't wait on us. I would like to ride with you. Will you pick me up?"

"I'll be there ASAP," Chet said, "Just give me time to dress."

"OK, but hurry. I don't want to get there too late." The phone was disconnected with a click.

Excitement pounded in Chet's chest. Maybe — just maybe — they were getting somewhere at last! He wasted no time getting into his clothes. McDonald's was just opening when he stopped for a sausage biscuit and a cup of coffee to eat on the way. He arrived at Carolyn's house to pick up Clara at six ten. They were at the Sheriff's office by six thirty.

Deputy Alredd met Chet with a scowl and a, "What you doing here?" But when Chet said Clara had invited him, the deputy offered no further protest.

Alredd and another deputy got into Alredd's big diesel dodge wagon and started out. Chet and Clara fell right in behind him. Another car, containing a reporter and a cameraman, from the Deming News, trailed along behind. It was beginning to resemble a caravan.

Since it was early, there was very little traffic. Alredd hurried, driving fast along the paved roads. He slowed very little when he reached the dirt. They all arrived at the Helm ranch at seven a.m.

Activity at the ranch had already started. Tobe was out by the corrals with a saddle in his hands. He dropped the saddle over the corral fence and came to meet them. Chet noticed he looked haggard and red-eyed as if he hadn't slept much in a while.

"Morning, Alredd," Tobe said, "What brings you out so early."

"I have a search warrant to search your pickup." Alredd said. "Is it locked."

"No, it's not locked but you'll play the devil searching it." Tobe's voice was a growl.

"You're wrong, Tobe, I will search it and if I find what I suspect, I'll take you in," Alredd said insolently.

"Listen, you dirty skunk, you have been trying to pin something on me from the beginning. I'll never let you search my pickup." His face was livid with rage.

Alredd, his hand on his gun, looked ready to kill. The air was electric with tension. Chet held his breath.

Suddenly Ann was there. Placing a restraining hand on her brother's arm, she said calmly, "You don't have anything to hide, Tobe, so why not let him do his search."

Without waiting for Tobe's answer she turned to Alredd, "What's this all about, Dan."

Alredd slowly relaxed the grip on his gun, never taking his eyes off of Tobe. "We got a tip there was evidence in Tobe's truck. Evidence we overlooked." His tone of voice was truculent and held just a touch of triumph.

"Ok, go ahead and look, there's nothing to hide."

Alredd began the search. He was professional and he was thorough. His search that took about fifteen minutes, produced nothing. Looking somewhat deflated, he motioned to his sidekick to do his own search. The sidekick had the same results, absolutely nothing.

Clara went over to Alredd who was standing to one side with a sheepish look on his face. "There's a hidden compartment in back of the seat, under the carpet," she said. "Jessie showed it to me. It's where Tobe carries valuables when he goes out of town. Velcro secures the carpet. It's only necessary to pull."

Alredd, looking skeptical, went back to the truck. Chet ambled over to watch. Raising the seat back, Alredd pulled on the carpet. Sure enough it came loose,

181

revealing a hidden cover that was removed by sticking two fingers through two holes and pulling up. Underneath the cover was a trench-like cavity. It was lined with felt. Stretched out along the bottom of the cavity was what appeared to be a piece of black cloth.

"Yes, and what is this?" Alredd said. He stationed his sidekick by the door of the pickup to hold all at bay. He went to his truck for a set of tongs and a plastic bag. Giving the plastic bag to the other deputy, he used the tongs to pick up the black object. When he swung the piece out far enough to put it into the bag, all could see it was a black sweater. There were clumps of dried mud stuck to the sweater and another stain that to Chet's knowing eye looked a lot like dried blood.

Chet turned to look at Tobe. Tobe's expression was one of consternation, surprise or what? Chet couldn't read it.

Tobe made a lunge forward. Alredd catching the move out of the corner of his eye, turned to meet him. Tobe was not jumping for Alredd, however, he was going for the sweater that had disappeared into the plastic bag. "That's my sweater," he gasped. "The one Jessie was wearing when she disappeared."

Alredd successfully fended him off, then shoved him backward. The backward shove gave him just enough room to draw his pistol and shove it into Tobe's midsection. "You better hold it right there," he yelled.

At the sound of those words and the sight of the gun, there was deathly silence.

Tobe's face was white as a sheet. Chet didn't blame him for the gun was cocked. "How-how did that get in my truck?" he stammered.

"As if you didn't know," Alredd said sarcastically. "Cuff him, Tom." Alredd's voice was grim. "Tobe, I'm arresting you for the murder of Jessie Helm. You have the right to remain silent. Anything you say can and will be used against you. You have the right to an attorney. I'll advise you even further and that's to keep your mouth shut." The other deputy went around behind Tobe and hand-cuffed his hands behind his back. With Tobe now secured, Alredd put his gun away.

At that moment one hundred thirty pounds of screaming clawing woman rushed by Chet. It was Clara Miller. She hit Tobe head on, her hands and arms swinging hard to hurt. Tobe, unable to fend her off, was slammed back against his pickup where he squirmed back and forth trying to avoid the onslaught. "You murdered my daughter," Clara screamed. "You gave her no chance."

Ann and Chet both moved to restrain her. Ann grabbed her right arm and Chet her left. Together they managed to haul her off Tobe. She subsided meekly, tears streaming down her face.

T.J., his face contorted, grabbed Alredd by the leg screaming, "Don't take my daddy, don't take my daddy."

Ann let go of Clara and retrieved T.J. Alredd loaded a scratched and bewildered appearing Tobe into his van.

Chet glanced at Bethann, her face was ashen but she was looking at her dad with what could be fear and loathing.

This is tough on Ann and tough for Tobe's children, Chet thought, first Jessie and now Tobe.

Alredd's truck left, leaving everyone standing around in shocked horror and silence. Suddenly Chet was aware of flash bulbs going off. He walked over to the news reporter. "Please knock off the camera. These people are devastated. They probably will feel more like making a statement after a while."

The reporter, who was younger than

Chet, started to protest. He opened his mouth, then looking closely at Chet's glacial blue eyes decided to close it. He and his photographer packed up their equipment and went back to Deming. Clara looking shocked but satisfied, went with them after Chet asked them to take her.

She's probably thinking Tobe got his just deserts, Chet thought. He, himself, felt deep sadness and empathy for Tobe — guilty or not. Was Tobe really a killer or had he been framed? If Tobe wasn't an accomplished actor, he looked as confused as his children and Ann, literally reeling and stunned.

Chet walked over to Ann. He had the absurd urge to put his arm around her in comfort. He restrained himself, realizing she might not want that. "Ann, this is none of my doing."

"I didn't think it was, but thanks for telling me," Ann said, "I will need to stay with the kids. Aunt Rachel and Harold will take care of getting Tobe out of jail."

"Okay. Since you can't meet me for lunch, would it be a bad time to have our talk here?"

"That would be fine," Ann said. "It would be good to have someone to talk to anyway. I'll get the kids some breakfast and then get them settled down first. I'll put on a video for them to watch and give them some cookies to eat. Then we can talk in the kitchen. OK."

"Sounds good," Chet agreed. "I'll just wander around a bit outside and you can call me when things are under control."

Chet thought glumly, *Wow, that rumpled, dirty and perhaps bloody sweater has really upset the apple cart. Poor Tobe, guilty, guilty, guilty!* Or so it appeared.

Chapter 11

Ann clenched her fists and tried to control her anger as she looked at Clara. Clara didn't like Tobe and had cast suspicion on him several times before. She tried to tell herself that after all this was the children's grandmother; a woman whose daughter had been missing for almost three weeks and she must be out of her mind with worry. But that certainly didn't excuse what she had just done, she thought angrily.

It was strange that Jessie had told her about that compartment. Had Clara fabricated the story about an anonymous caller? Had such a call been made at all? Was Clara trying to frame Tobe for murder because she felt he was guilty of doing away with Jessie. Maybe Clara had placed the sweater in the hiding place — but where could she have found the incriminating sweater? Surely Clara didn't murder her own daughter! It was all so confusing, even weird!

Ann felt her blood boil at the way Clara had attacked Tobe so savagely when he was in handcuffs and couldn't ward her off. She felt like pounding Clara the same way — even if she is older and Jessie's mother!

Calm yourself, she told herself. The children — and Tobe — need you to be strong, and falling apart and acting as bad as Clara wouldn't help a bit!

A sudden conviction came to her, more like a fleeting impression but it slipped away before she could get a handle on it. Something was crying out in her memory to be heard. I should know how that sweater got into Tobe's truck, she thought, but her churning mind refused to settle down enough for her to think rationally.

Tobe — in jail for the murder of his wife. Preposterous and terrifying. He could not have done something like that!

Or could he? The thought dropped into her befuddled and tormented mind and she almost gasped aloud. Of course not! But — that treacherous thought intruded again, it could have happened. Tobe was furiously angry with Jessie — and humiliated — and he had a violent temper that he had never been able to master.

For the first time, Ann, her heart pounding with fear and dread considered that Tobe could have done something to

Jessie. Not purposely, of course, but in a fit of rage and then in horror at what he had done, had hidden her body so successfully that no trace could be found!

Absolutely not! Ann felt for a moment that she had shouted it out but when she looked around she saw no one was looking her way so she must have only thought it. Chet was talking to Clara and then moved away to make arrangements with the reporter and photographers to take Clara with them into town. At least she wouldn't have to face Clara right now!

She was suddenly aware that T.J. was pulling at her hand, his face pale, and asking her questions which she couldn't hear at first because of the thoughts churning about in her head. Bethann was standing quietly, with big tears streaming down her face. She had to get her emotions under control. The children needed her.

Hoping to keep her emotions from her voice she said, "Kids, let's go into the house and get you some breakfast. "Her arms slipped around Bethann's and T.J.'s shoulders and she started walking them toward the door. She stopped suddenly, knelt down before them and began to speak as quietly as she could — words that

189

she needed to hear as badly as the kids.

"You both know — and I know — that your father is innocent of harming your mother. We all saw the shocked expression on his face when Alredd pulled that sweater out of that secret compartment." She instantly regretted mentioning the sweater although she knew that it could not be ignored. But when she looked down at Bethann's tear stained face she saw a tiny smile appear.

Then with the satisfied look that children get when they are able to impart some information that adults don't know, she said, "Oh, Auntie Ann, that really isn't a secret compartment, all of our family knew about it. It is just a good hiding place. Last year we kept Mama's birthday present there until it was time to give it to her. And Uncle Harold kept Aunt Rachel's Christmas present there. He said she isn't much of a housekeeper but every year about three days before Christmas she goes on a cleaning spree. When I asked what a spree was, he said it was another name for a Christmas present hunt."

The reporters and Clara were pulling out and Chet came toward her, his face plainly showing his concern for them. He asked permission to stay and talk and she welcomed the suggestion. She didn't want to be alone with only the children and their questions.

She talked with the children for a while and tried as best she could to soothe their fears. After she fed them and installed them in front of the TV with a video and some popcorn, she called to Chet who was waiting on the porch.

"We can talk now," she said, and seated him at the table with a cup of hot coffee and a plate of cookies. Pouring herself a cup, she sank into a chair and sighed. "I don't think I'm cut out to be a substitute mother. It's just too emotionally exhausting."

Chet's eyes were warm and kindled a flush in her cheeks, "You're doing a very good job in my opinion," he said softly.

A little flustered by the compassion and intensity in his voice and eyes, she quickly took a sip of coffee, cleared her throat and tried to speak like the poised photographer she was supposed to be.

"Chet, I'll tell you where I was and what I saw happen on the weekend that Jessie disappeared. But first make no mistake, I believe in Tobe's innocence. I have watched Tobe search every bit of this ranch, looking for her. I know he has not harmed her in any way. I think Jessie is still alive and if there is any earthly way for Tobe to find her, he will do it."

Did she believe that? Yes, she did, she told herself defiantly. Tobe would never — never — harm Jessie. He loved her too much to do that!

She continued in as steady a voice as she could muster, "You know what I mean when I say I felt the storm coming down from the mountains. Watching the clouds and seeing the signs is just a part of country living."

"Right," Chet agreed as he munched on a cookie.

"I went over to return two cookie pans that I had borrowed from Jessie and I realized there was also a storm brewing in the kitchen. Tobe and Jessie were sitting quietly at the table when I came through the kitchen door. But there was tension between them, and they weren't hiding it very well. Right then I decided to take the kids with me into Deming. We would get a burger at McDonalds and go to a movie. Lucky for me "The Prince of Egypt" was playing at the movie house.

"T.J. and Bethann were quietly playing a game at the oak table. I hated to talk about my plans in front of them just in case Tobe decided he didn't want them to go. But he seemed relieved."

Ann sipped her coffee and continued, "It was beginning to snow when the movie was over and I didn't want to leave town. The Volks is not the best for handling a snowy dirt road. So when I said, 'Kids, what would you think if we stayed in town tonight? We could call your folks and tell them we will be home in the morning.' Bethann was the first to agree that she would like to stay. T.J. seldom disagrees with his big sister and this time was no exception."

"That's an exceptional boy who agrees with a big sister," Chet said with a chuckle.

With a nod, Ann went on, "I called and talked to Jessie, telling her we planned on staying in Deming, if it was all right with her. I said we would be home about 9:00 in the morning. I thought the sun would probably be shining bright the next day. That's sometimes the way with our spring storms.

"While I made my call the kids were telling Carolyn about the beautiful Bible story. They went through all the motions of placing the basket with the baby Moses in it on the river, then dramatically started in parting the Red Sea. It looked as if T.J.

was going to be Moses and Bethann would be all the trusting people."

"Carolyn seems to be a good aunt to have," Chet said, starting on another cookie.

"Yes, she's a jewel," Ann said earnestly. "Anyway, Carolyn had beds ready for us in just a few minutes. The next morning she insisted on fixing a big breakfast. 'You won't get cold cereal at my house,' she declared. We were a little late leaving but I figured we could be home by 9:30.

"When Deputy Alredd passed us on his way back to town he gave a friendly wave. Sheriff Brady was close behind and the kids waved to him. They were both in their Official County Sheriff's department cars. And I wondered what they would be doing on official business out there on Sunday morning."

Ann paused here remembering how irritated she had felt when she saw Alredd; she was glad she had not been home if he was there to pay a visit to Tobe. However, she didn't think it necessary to tell this to Chet. She went on with her story.

"When we drove up I saw Aunt Rachel in the corral saddling two horses and her pick-up was parked out in front of the barn.

"Tobe was sitting in his usual place at the table as Bethann and T.J. rushed in all ready to tell him all about their evening out. I meant to only say a short goodbye and go home to my cabin.

"I came in just in time to hear him say, 'You kids go in and get some clean clothes and pajamas. I think it would be a good idea if you stayed over at Ann's cabin. Go on now, I want to talk to your aunt.' They were disappointed they couldn't tell their story, but they disappeared down the hallway to their rooms.

"I said, 'what happened Tobe, where is Jessie?'

"I don't remember his exact words but he told me that Jessie left the night before and he thought she had gone over to my cabin. When he got worried and went to look for her, she wasn't there.

"He said they had a really bad argument the night before she left, one of the worst. When he couldn't find her, he had called the Sheriff's department and they were going to start a search for her. He and Aunt Rachel had searched a lot of the night for her and were getting ready to go again on horseback.

"T.J. came back into the room in time to hear his last words and said, 'We saw the sheriff and deputy, Daddy; who are you going to look for?'

"Tobe put his arms around him, held him close for a moment, then I saw him look over his shoulder as Bethann came into the room. 'They're searching for your mother, T.J., she's lost. She went out last night and hasn't come home yet but I think she is going to be here real soon.'

"Oh, Chet, it just about broke my heart. I saw Bethann's eyes widen but she didn't say a word, maybe she was waiting for Tobe to finish talking. He didn't have anything else to say, just sat there looking kinda lost and bewildered. Bethann walked over and took T.J.'s hand, just like a little mother. 'Come on now, we better do what Daddy says, he needs to go look for Mama.' "

"I know it was hard for all of you," Chet said, his blue eyes warm with sympathy.

"The next two days were the longest I have ever endured in my life. The kids soon tired of watching the helicopter but they never tired of asking questions. It was horribly frustrating. I had no answers. I just tried to reassure them that their mother would come home.

"Alredd brought his search warrant and started going through my cabin, the kids wanted to help and I had to tell them they couldn't get in the deputies' way. That just prompted them to ask me more unanswerable questions.

"By Tuesday Tobe decided the kids should come home and asked me if I would come, too. When the kids got home from school T.J. raced to the barn to say hello to the dog, the cats and the horses. He asked them all if they missed him and began to tell them about the movie he had seen. We could hear his conversations from the porch. He soon came in to report that none of the animals had seen Mama, but he would question them again later.

"Tobe was horrified and told me, 'He thinks this is a game. What can I say? How can I explain to him?' I tried to reassure him T.J. was just handling stress his own way. He was talking to his friends the animals.

"Ever since I have been here at Tobe's house, helping with the kids, the housework, and answering the phone while Tobe frantically rides and looks for Jessie."

"I know it's been hard for you and the children, Ann," Chet reiterated, then hesitated and said gently, "Tobe's been arrested, Ann. Do you still believe he is innocent?"

"Yes, I do!" Ann couldn't keep the anger from her voice.

Chet grinned boyishly and held up a hand as if to ward off a blow. "I'm a reporter, lady and it's my business to ask questions."

Ann couldn't help but grin back.

"How's your assignment going," Chet asked. "Or have you dropped it until this is all over?"

Glad that he had changed the subject, Ann jumped up to bring a package of photos from a nearby table. "No, I don't plan to cancel out on my assignment, just delayed it for a bit.

"I haven't taken any since Jessie disappeared but these arrived in the mail a while back and many of them are pretty good, I think."

She spread them out on the big dining room table. Her practiced eye had already picked out about half a dozen good shots that she felt would be seriously considered for the book. She took these up and spread them out for Chet to look at.

"Yes, these are really good," Chet said, "especially a couple of these of Jessie. She looks almost as I remember her — not even a lot older."

"Yes, these really look natural of Jessie,

don't they?" Looking at them, Ann's eyes misted and she said with a catch in her voice, "When I saw these I just longed to talk to her and ask, 'What happened to you, Jessie, where are you now?' Are you all right?"

There was one picture of Bethann, waving from horseback. She looked very much like her mother. Off to the side, in the background, Ann noticed Harold standing at the door of Tobe's pickup. "Look at this picture, Chet. If I cut Harold out of the picture I could enlarge it and have it framed as a gift for Bethann."

"Bethann would like that," Chet said. He paused as he studied the picture. "You know Ann, you're very good at this."

Ann was pleased that Chet seemed genuinely interested in her photography career.

Just then the phone rang. I hope that's not another reporter," Ann said, irritation edging her voice. She picked up the receiver.

"Hello?"

"Señor Helm?"

"No, this is Senorita Ann Helm."

"Señora Jessie is alive."

Ann was struck speechless. What was she hearing? Before she could say more she heard the click of the receiver and the steady dial tone. Ann slowly hung up the receiver. Stupefied shock held her speechless.

"What is it! What's happened," Chet said and when she didn't answer but stared at him wordlessly, he leaned over and took her hand. "What is it? Who was that? What's wrong?"

At last she found her voice but when the words came out, they were a whisper, "Jessie's alive!"

"Who was that? Tell me!"

"I-I don't know who it was." She stuttered. "A woman's voice — heavily accented, just asked if I was Señor Helm and then said, 'Señora Jessie is alive.' Then hung up before I could say another word!"

Chet touched Ann's arm. "Don't get your hopes too high," he said gently. "It could be a prank call. It happens often in this sort of case. Someone wanting to get in on the act and be important."

Quick anger lanced through Ann. "I won't believe that! The person sounded so sincere, like a Mexican woman who could barely speak English."

"I'm sorry," Chet said humbly. "I just didn't want you to get too excited in case it isn't true."

"You think Jessie's dead and that Tobe killed her, don't you?" Ann accused, trembling with anger.

Chet looked at her for a moment without speaking and then said softly. "I apologize. It was unfair to be so pessimistic." He grinned wryly, "That's the old cynical reporter mind talking. Forgive me?"

Ann sighed, "I'm the one who should apologize. And that's the quick Helm temper speaking. Forgive me and I'll forgive you."

"It's a deal," Chet said, sticking out his hand.

They shook hands solemnly and then laughed, the tension broken.

Chet was now all business again. "You said the woman was Mexican? Old or young?"

"Quite old, I would say, with a very heavy accent."

"It's a good chance this is a real lead," Chet said. "Basically the search has been around the ranch and in the Deming area, hasn't it? Not along the border or into Mexico?"

"That's right," Ann said. "I don't believe any searching was done across the border, and very little on this side. At first the assumption was that Jessie had gotten lost in the storm and strayed off into the hills — perhaps was badly hurt in a fall and couldn't get back under her own power."

"Let's go down to the border — to Columbus and cross the border into Mexico and visit Palomas. We'll take a really good picture of Jessie to show."

"Yes!" Ann said enthusiastically. "Maybe someone has seen her down there! One of these snapshots of Jessie would do fine."

"I imagine your aunt and Harold should have Tobe out of jail by tomorrow morning and he could watch the kids. Could you go in the morning?"

"If Tobe isn't home I can get Aunt Rachel or Jessie's Aunt Carolyn to watch them. Give me time to get the kids up and fed."

"Get those pictures ready and in the meantime, we should do some praying, don't you think?"

Ann studied him thoughtfully. "You're still serving the Lord, aren't you," she said softly. "I still remember when you accepted Christ. I did, too, about the same time, in Pastor Frederick's church."

"I'm not always the best Christian, I'm afraid," Chet said earnestly, "but I sure wouldn't want to try to live without God in my life."

"I've always felt the same way," Ann said. "But Tobe was always the rebel. He has never made any commitment to God and was always a little contemptuous of people who did, I think — even of Jessie. She's the one who took the kids to church and taught them about the Lord. Tobe's attitude grieves my heart."

"Maybe this tragedy will make him see his need of God," Chet said.

"I don't know," Ann said. "When I suggested praying about this at first, he just seemed mad at God for letting it happen."

"We'll just pray for him," Chet said. "I've always felt that without a definite call from God, no one would feel a need for Jesus. We'll just pray that he feels that personal urge to accept Christ."

"Thanks," Ann said gratefully. "It will be good to know you are praying for him too."

Chapter 12

Chet called Ann the next morning and they agreed to meet in Deming after lunch. She dressed very carefully. The old boots wouldn't take much of a shine anymore but they were comfortable and the heels would make her at least one inch taller. The cotton shirt was an expensive one that was a 'spur of the moment' purchase at a Fort Worth store two months ago. She had a pair of Wranglers that fit well and had performed a new cut on the unruly hair.

It was a beautiful spring day. The days had all been warm after the snow storm. As Chet and Ann drove along they talked about the mesquite trees that were blooming and the scattering of wild flower petals that were blowing on a light breeze. They completely avoided mentioning the real reason they were driving thirty miles to Columbus with pictures of Jessie in the folder on the seat between them.

When they approached the little dusty town that was on the US border, Ann's heart sank. How could there be anything here that would lead them to her dearest friend?

A stop at the post office, showing a picture, got them only a shake of the head and no acknowledgment that anyone looking like that had ever been there. They walked the streets, showing the photo and asking if anyone had seen Jessie, until late in the afternoon. Their last stop was at a gas station, with the same results, so they headed south across the border to the little town of Palomas.

Here again, they walked the streets, stopping to show the photo of Jessie to all they met, at stores, service stations and any other likely places or people. Finally, dog-tired and rather discouraged — although neither acknowledged it to the other — Chet suggested they eat.

Ann was looking forward to dinner at the Cantina called Casita Rosa. She had never been there before but had heard the food was good.

The place looked small, but was cool and dark as they stepped in out of the sunlight. Several men were at the bar and one quickly turned his head away as she glanced his way. She supposed there were sometimes people here who were hiding out from the police and didn't want to be recognized.

The bartender motioned them into a hallway that led to the dining room. Here the lights were a little brighter. There were several tables of American tourists. They were obviously having a good time and enjoying the food and atmosphere of Old Mexico. The decorations on the walls were especially entertaining. There were remnants of pink and blue streamers, perhaps left over from a baby shower. One wall had a smiling Santa with a sign over his head saying, "Toma Pepsi." White bells above the small bandstand meant there had been a wedding party here at some time in the past.

When their food arrived, it was steaming hot and delicious. Chet managed to engage the waiter in a long combination of English and Spanish conversation about the people that came here as regulars. He asked if the waiter had seen Deputy Alredd, or a woman called Jessie, or Harold Young, a cousin to his companion Senorita Ann. The waiter seemed reluctant to talk about any of the clientele. He did acknowledge that he had seen Harold within the past few days. Even with Chet's tactful questioning he would give no more information.

After paying their bill, Chet stopped for a few moments to talk to the bartender on their way out. Thinking, correctly that he was the owner, he complimented him on the excellent Chimichanga they had enjoyed. He happened to work Jessie's name into the conversation and showed the picture they had brought with them. Again there was no reply other than the fact that he saw many people each day; many of them were Americans.

When they came out of the cafe, the sun had set and many of the small shops were closed. After a leisurely stroll down the two inhabited blocks they stopped to peer in the dusty window of a small Mercantile. Earlier they had gone inside this store and spoken briefly with the proprietor and shown Jessie's picture — with no results, of course. They noticed now that the window display was crowded with shop-worn looking cans of Jalepeños, chili con carne, and other food items as well as pairs of men's, women's and children's shoes and a few clothes.

Ann glanced indifferently at a drab blouse and cheap-looking skirt hung on a paper-mache mannequin and started to turn away when a glitter caught her eye. A small dainty watch with what appeared to be real diamonds was resting on a piece of black velvet in the very front of the window. Ann leaned down to look more closely. Her heart began to pound.

"It can't be," she exclaimed, dropping down on one knee to examine the watch better.

"It can't be . . . what?" asked Chet.

"That's Jessie's watch! See how the diamonds circle around to make a heart on each side of the time-piece?"

"Are you sure?" Chet asked excitedly. He dropped down beside Ann and stared at the watch.

Ann felt light-headed with excitement and she had trouble getting her breath. "There's one way to find out! The watch has lettering underneath the time piece."

Chet jumped up and ran to the door of the store which had a slightly soiled closed sign displayed, and knocked on the door, then rattled the door-knob. When no one appeared, he strode next door to a leather shop which was also closed and knocked briskly on the door.

This time he heard slow steps inside and the door opened a little and a boy of about twelve peered out. In a very accented voice he stated the store was closed.

With a few Spanish words and a few

English, Chet made the boy understand they wished to find the owner of the mercantile next door.

"No-no," the boy was shaking his head. "No live here. Live out in country. Back mañana."

"Telephono?" Chet asked.

"No, no telephono. Come back mañana."

"Thanks," Chet said.

The boy continued to stand in the partially opened door, a sly grin on his face.

"I think he expects a tip," Ann said, suppressing a grin. "I might have some change," and started rummaging in her purse.

"I've got it covered," Chet said, pulling out a dollar.

The delighted grin which lit up the boy's face and his ecstatic "Gracias!" was worth the money.

The boy withdrew into the shop and Ann said resignedly, "We'll just have to wait until tomorrow. But I'm sure the watch is Jessie's."

Chet drew in a deep, satisfied breath. "At last we're getting somewhere. Tomorrow we'll buy the watch — and find out where it came from — if it's Jessie's."

Chapter 13

Chet, his spirits somewhat dampened by Tobe's arrest, started his Tahoe down Motel Drive. He was on his way to buy Jessie's watch. Something told him that today, in spite of recent events, he stood a good chance of learning something about the mystery of Jessie Helm.

He drove his Tahoe towards Columbus along one of the most dangerous stretches of highway in New Mexico. At first he didn't notice nature's spectacular display over the Florida Mountains, but it suddenly seemed to burst upon him, driving everything else from his mind for a few moments.

High clouds, moving in overnight, were bunched over the tops of the peaks. The sun coming up turned them light pink to dark purple and all shades in between. He stopped the car in a wide place alongside the blacktop and sat there spellbound by the sight. Each jagged peak was tipped with a rosy glow. The mountain itself was in shadow. Slowly, as the sun climbed, the shadows receded until only the steep sides were still black. The sky overhead lightened and brightened until the most predominant color was brilliant vermilion.

Chet watched until the glow left the peaks. Profoundly moved, Chet knew he had been blessed and breathed a prayer of reverent thanks. A once in a lifetime show. At peace now, he started the car and moved on towards Mexico. When he got even with the Tres Hermanas (Three Sisters) Peaks the sun was shining bravely through the high clouds. The Tres Hermanas were bathed in a light that softened even their rugged slopes.

He parked his car near the Pancho Villa State Park. Knowing he was too early for the stores to open, he decided to run the three miles to the town of Palomas and get some exercise at the same time.

As he ran along the road towards Mexico there was a steady stream of traffic coming to meet him. There were also a few people walking. All were going towards Columbus and other point's further north into the United States. These are probably day workers, he thought. Not much traffic going south, he mused, I must be too early.

Running across the border proved to be no problem; the Mexican official hardly even looked up. Most of the shops along the street were still locked up tight but a few shopkeepers were sweeping and getting ready for the day's business. He had no trouble finding the little shop where Ann had spotted the watch. Fortunately the door was open. An old woman was sweeping the sidewalk.

"Buenos dias, Señora. Is your shop open."

"No habla Ingles," she replied.

"She don't speak no English." A voice spoke up from slightly behind Chet.

Chet turned to see a young boy about nine or ten years old slouching against the wall. "Could you help me then? I am trying to buy one of the objects in her window."

"Sure, I help you, man, but not necessary. Shop owner speak English good. He just inside the door."

Feeling sheepish Chet walked inside. A man of about forty was sitting at a small table doing some paper work. "Are you the owner?" he asked.

The man eyed Chet up and down his running suit and canvas shoes. "I am the owner but we are not quite ready for business."

"I saw a watch you have displayed in

your window that I am interested in. Would you show it to me?"

"Si, I will show you the watch. It is very beautiful. Only get it recently," the man replied in an obsequious voice. Removing the watch from the window, he brought it to Chet. Holding it so it caught the light from the door, he added, "This is a verra fine piece, notice the handwork on the bracelet. It was made in the mountains of Sonora. There are no other pieces like it. It is one of a kind. I bought it from a local man who claims to know the maker." He handed the watch to Chet.

Chet examined the watch closely, turning it over to look at the back and looking closely at the diamonds on the band. The engraved letters t-j were there — it was Jessie's watch! Excitement flamed in his heart but he was careful to calm himself before he lifted his eyes to the storekeeper. "How much do you want," he said nonchalantly.

"As I said, this is a very fine piece, very rare," the owner paused, a calculating look in his eyes. Finally he said, "$1,200 Pesos."

Familiar with bargaining practices south of the border, Chet didn't bite on the first offer. He did a quick mental calculation coming up with $150.00. "Ok," he said,

"I'll give you $75.00."

"No — no, Señor, I couldn't possibly let it go for that. My sainted mother would never forgive me. Look at the stones, see, shaped into a heart. Perhaps for your sweetheart — yes? I could not take less than $140.00."

"Señor, you have me at a disadvantage, I'm not a rich man; I could pay you $100.00." The bargaining went on. Chet finally paid the man $125.00. The shop-keeper grumbling about Norte Americanos cheating poor Mexicans.

"Now, Señor," Chet said, "can you tell me a little more about the man who sold you this watch?" He laid a twenty-dollar bill on the counter.

The man eyed the money for a short while, then slipped it into his pocket. "I only know he is old man called Nunez. I see him around town more than once. I am told he comes from north of the border but his speech and accent are Sonoran. Other than that I know nothing."

Further questioning got Chet absolutely nowhere. So he decided the man probably didn't know more. He then went up and down the street asking anyone who would talk to him about the watch and the man who sold it. He received scowls and negative head shakes, and he received smiles with the same "No," head shakes.

After an hour of fumbling very poor Spanish and halting English he ended up in the Casita Rosa. He went directly into the dining room hoping for a little breakfast. Much to his surprise he spotted Harold sitting at a table off to one side. Harold glanced up at about the same time and waved Chet over.

"Hello, Chet, what on earth are you doing here."

"I came down to buy a watch Ann spotted in one of the shop windows. The watch belonged to Jessie."

"You don't say," Harold exclaimed. "How in the world did it get to Palomas?"

"That's what I'm trying to find out. It's the one Tobe gave her. She always wore it and she had it on when she disappeared."

"That's amazing. Let me see it."

Chet handed the watch over. Harold examined it closely.

"Yes, I do remember her having one like it. How do you know it's hers?"

"It has a tiny engraving on the underside."

Harold turned the watch over again, looking more closely at the underside. "I don't see it," he said.

"Look directly under the time-piece. It isn't noticeable at first but it's there."

"Sure, I see it now, it's tiny all right. Looks like a t-j."

"That's it. I suspect Tobe is out of jail by now so I need to get back and show it to him. I'll be getting back as soon as I have some breakfast."

"What! Tobe is in jail?" Harold's expression was one of surprise and outrage. "Why have they arrested him?" The last was in a very loud voice. Some of the other patrons in the restaurant were staring.

"There was . . . ," Chet began.

"Oh, never mind," Harold interrupted, "I need to get home now. They'll tell me everything I need to know." He put some money on the table and left the restaurant abruptly.

Chet was thunder struck. If I had been thinking I would have known he didn't know about Tobe, he thought. Well, I had better get breakfast and get on back myself. When the waitress stopped by he realized he wasn't really very hungry. He ordered toast and coffee and then only ate one piece of toast. He distractedly paid his bill and stepped through the front door of the restaurant.

"Meester." It was the same young boy he

had seen earlier. "I know about the watch."

"What about the watch?" Chet asked excitedly.

"Come thees way," the boy turned towards the rear of the building. "It's only a leetle way."

Chet followed him eagerly. At the rear of the restaurant was an unfinished cinder block building. The boy turned into the building. The main room of the building had no roof but along one side were three rooms that were covered. The boy disappeared into the center room.

Chet paused in the outer room, to look around, then followed the boy. The boy was nowhere in sight but in the center of the room was one big hombre. He was a good two inches taller than Chet and almost twice as broad. He motioned for Chet to come further into the room. Before advancing Chet looked carefully around the room. There were several jukeboxes, in various states of disrepair, stashed around the room. Chet couldn't see any one else and there seemed to be no menace in the big Mexican.

Wanting to know more he stepped boldly inside. Immediately he sensed another person behind him and quick alarm caused him to turn sideways where he could watch them both. The man in the doorway was shorter than Chet but he was built like a bull with bulging muscles in his arms and torso. From under hooded eyelids, black eyes glittered in a heavy, brutal-looking face. His whole bearing was filled with menace and he looked to be quick of movement. *I'm trapped and in trouble,* Chet thought.

"My name is Julio Nunez," the big man said. "I'm not Hispanic, nor Latin American. I am Mexican. And this, gesturing towards the first man, is Chudo, a muy malo hombre. Yes, a very bad man."

"What do you want with me?"

Ignoring him Nunez continued, "I was born in the U.S. but I am never the less Mexican. I have been told that you are very good. A kick-boxing champion in college and a wrestler also. I hear you keep in practice and work out regularly. We will be very careful with you."

Chet could see there was no use talking so he kept quiet awaiting developments.

"My father and mother work on a little ranch north of Columbus but I live mostly in Palomas. Here I am a big wheel; they call me El Poderoso and I have many followers."

Chet caught a slight movement behind one of the jukeboxes. Someone else was in the room. Three against one! *Dear God, help me now,* he prayed silently. He was given no chance to move for a better view, however, because at that moment the first man charged him.

Chet met the attack with a right toe kick to the jaw while Chudo was still coming in. This floored the man but Chet didn't see the results. He was already spinning towards Nunez, landing a foot in his solar plexus, swiftly followed by a toe in the groin. The big man folded over grasping his groin and gasping for breath. Chet landed a stiff left hook to the side of the man's neck and a hard right to the jaw. Nunez was knocked to his knees, where Chet was able to kick him in the head.

Chet felt a jarring blow in the middle of his back and was propelled sideways into one of the jukeboxes. Chudo was very quick but he was unskilled. Chet bounded back and planted another kick into Chudo's jaw, knocking him down again. Nunez waded forward, catching Chet with a hard blow in the chest which again knocked Chet back against the jukebox. From there he knocked Nunez to his knees with a kick to his head and a right hand in the windpipe. *I can take these guys,* he thought.

But a second later he heard a slight jingle behind him. He had forgotten the third man and was just turning to meet this new challenge when he felt a heavy blow behind his left ear. The blow sent sharp pain into his skull and sparks before his eyes. He fell to the floor on his right side. Then both of his first antagonists began to kick him repeatedly and he was powerless to stop them. *I've got to do something or they'll kill me,* he thought groggily. Blinding pain filled his head and now his sides. He tried to protect his upper body and head with his arms from the punishing blows but was only partially successful. He mumbled another petition for God's help — whether audibly or not, he didn't know.

Then Chet vaguely heard someone yell, "Bastante! Señors, No se matar! Don't kill him!"

Chet, only half conscious felt someone pulling on his arms, "Come on fellow. Let's get out of here before they come back."

Someone was trying to get him to his feet. He made every effort to stand up and with the other person's help he made it.

"That's it," he was encouraged, "come

on, you can do it."

Chet recognized that voice now, it was Harold, and he wondered what Harold was doing here now. Harold was supposed to be on his way home. They made their way out of the building. Chet had to lean heavily on Harold. Harold had parked his truck in the street where he loaded Chet into the front seat. As soon as he was in, Chet promptly passed out. The next thing he knew, Harold was pulling at him and shaking him.

"Come on Chet, baby," Harold was saying, "You've got to get on your feet."

With an effort Chet managed to slide out of the truck and into Harold's arms. Together they stumbled towards Chet's Tahoe. When they reached it Harold propped him against the fender. After several attempts Chet managed to stand alone. Harold fumbled in the zippered pocket of Chet's pants, fished out his car keys, opened the door and half-dragged, half-helped Chet inside the car. He heard the door close and then he was alone.

He must have passed out again and when he came to he stared bleary-eyed about him with one eye. His right eye was swelling shut and he ached all over. Wincing, he felt a big lump behind his left ear. He strove to pull his wits together enough to think. He moved and heard the car keys tumble to the floor. He stooped over to pick them up and everything went black again. He tried to breathe deeply — although felt like an elephant was sitting on his chest and pains like red-hot needles made him gasp. Then the blackness lifted and he could see the keys not far from his groping fingers. He picked up the keys and they made a slight jingling sound as he fumbled them into the ignition slot. That was the sound he had heard just before someone slugged him behind the ear.

Laying his head back against the head-rest, he closed his eyes to rest for just a moment. Thoughts went through his mind like lightening flashes. Harold helping him away from the scene of the fight. What had he been doing there and why didn't he stay to see that he got home safely? The young boy who led him to the cinder block building to be beaten up was hired, of course. And who was Julio Nunez? The son of the old man who sold the watch to the store keeper?

Julio's boastful voice seemed to be speaking in his ear again: "I am El Poderoso. I am powerful. I hear you are a kick-boxing champion." Now how would he know these things. Chet had never seen him before and he never mentioned, to anyone, that he was a champion. Someone knew a lot about him.

He dozed, his hand slipped off the steering wheel hitting the keys on the way down. Chet heard the jingle. It woke him with a start, ready to do battle again. Someone was behind him, he tried to turn, then came fully awake and found he was alone in his car.

Keys, that was the sound he had heard just before he was zapped. Another thought flashed through his head. He saw a whip going back and forth snapping behind a horse's tail. He heard the jingle as the hand holding the whip moved. Harold! Back at the ranch the day he had interviewed Harold and his mother!

Harold carried a set of keys snapped to his belt — but Harold had just saved him from being crippled or maybe even killed. "Bastante! Señors, Don't kill him." That had been Harold's voice. He was sure of it now! There was something else though. Was it the rustle of money?

Chet couldn't be sure. Why would Harold rescue him, then leave him before he was fully awake. He mentally shook himself. *I've got to get started,* he thought.

223

Tobe and Ann will be frantic to see the watch. He sat up straighter in the seat. All of his parts seemed to work. He started the car and put it into drive. He could only see out of one eye but it was enough. He had to concentrate hard and did some praying too and soon it got easier to drive.

Half way to Deming he suddenly had another thought. Harold had stated, "I wasn't here the night Jessie disappeared. I was in the Day's Inn in Las Cruces." He had meant to check that out but never had. Pulling over to the side of the road, Chet called his office, using his cell phone.

"Las Cruces Herald," it was Paula's voice.

"Paula, this is Chet, I need you to do some checking for me."

"Ok, go ahead," Paula said.

"Call the Day's Inn and see if they had a Harold Young registered for the night of Saturday, March 7, 1998. I'll get back with you later."

"Ok, I'll get on it right away. Anything else."

"Nothing I can think of right now, see you."

Chet got the car rolling again. Another voice came unbidden to his mind. "There was a lot of traffic on the road that night.

One of them was a diesel. It went up, then came back by in a little while." Harold drove a big black Dodge Diesel.

Blinding flashes of pain shot through his injured left eye. He could feel each and every sore spot on his body, indeed he felt sore all over. He wanted to go to the motel, wash off the grime, take a couple of Tylenol and go to bed.

I can't do that, he thought, *I have to warn Tobe and Ann. They'll never believe me though. My suspicions of Harold are all I have, there is no real proof. Maybe I'm just not thinking clearly but Harold was behind that jukebox. My gut feeling says it. He is probably getting desperate and he is dangerous.*

Chet didn't dare think too much about Jessie — if she was alive, or murdered and buried somewhere. It had been fifteen minutes so Chet pulled off the road again and dialed the paper.

"Las Cruces Herald."

"Paula, Chet. Any luck."

"None of the motels have a listing for Harold Young on that night." A slight pause, "Chet, Creighton wants you to call in tonight."

"Ok, Paula, thanks. You take care." Chet broke the connection.

Back on the road Chet began to hurry. In his mind Harold's involvement with Jessie's disappearance was now a certainty. Harold had hired a couple of toughs to lambaste him. Harold had lied about being in Las Cruces when Jessie disappeared.

I can see neither rhyme nor reason for Harold kidnapping or hurting Jessie but he is guilty of something, that's for sure. To have gotten desperate enough to sic those guys on me he must be cracking up. Ann could be next, and Tobe. I need to warn them. With those thoughts, he pressed a little harder on the gas pedal.

Chapter 14

Sometime during the following night — very late — Jessie was awakened by the sound of a vehicle roaring into the yard. Running to the window in her bare feet and twitching the curtain aside just enough to observe, she saw Julio standing beside his handsome red and silver pick-up, talking with Luis and Juana. He was motioning excitedly toward the little house Jessie was sleeping in but she couldn't hear anything that was said. Something's going down, Jessie thought fearfully, and I'm afraid it concerns me.

He only stayed a few minutes and after he left, Luis and Juana stood in the yard talking for a few minutes before they went back inside. She could hear Juana's voice raise a couple of times like she was arguing with Luis and once she saw Luis raise his hand as if to strike his wife. Juana turned abruptly then and went swiftly into the house, with Luis following more slowly.

Jessie had difficulty sleeping after that but finally slipped into a troubled, restless sleep where she dreamed she was being pursued by an unknown but frightening entity. She was awakened early the next morning, when the first pale rays of the sun was striking the windows, by someone at her door fumbling the key in the lock. Juana came breathlessly into the room and said excitedly, "Get up queek." Her eyes looked frightened but her chin was set determinedly. When Jessie stared, unable to comprehend, she grabbed Jessie's arm and tugged. "Now! Go! El Jefe coming for you today!"

Scrambling into her jeans and shirt, and throwing on an old levy jacket and jamming an old black hat on her head that Juana had loaned her for the cool mornings, Jessie tried to question Juana but the woman seemed too distraught to do more than urge her to get ready and leave "queek."

Hurried out of doors, Jessie immediately saw that the gate was wide open and the door to the old pick-up stood open, too. Juana almost hauled her to the vehicle and hurried her inside. Hardly able to comprehend what was happening, Jessie saw with rising excitement that the keys were in the ignition.

When Jessie was inside, the woman

pushed a small object into her hands and again implored her to hurry. Totally overwhelmed, Jessie saw that the object was the cell phone. Shoving it into her jacket pocket with a quick "thank you", Jessie asked, "Which way should I go? Am I in Mexico?"

"No — no! In US, just above border. No far to Columbus. Deming that way," Juana said, pointing.

"I'm that close to home?" Jessie asked in astonishment.

"Si, but you must go now!" Jessie saw that the woman was trembling, and stark fear showed in her face and eyes. "Must not let Jefe catch! He coming! He muy malo. Go now," she said and stepped back from the pick-up.

"What did you do with Luis?" Jessie asked as she turned the key, almost holding her breath because sometimes it was balky about starting, she recalled. But it started on the first spin.

"Put drug El Jefe bring for to make you sleep, in coffee," Juana said. Her voice rose another notch, "Go before he wake up!"

"God bless you, Juana," Jessie said gratefully as she slipped the vehicle into gear and rolled toward the gate. She was thankful Luis always pointed the pick-up toward the gate before parking. Leaving Juana huddled near the gate, she eased the vehicle out the gate as smoothly and quietly as possible but quickly picked up speed as she turned down the dirt track. She was amazed at the speed and capability of the old pick-up. Someone had certainly put in a more powerful engine than usual.

As she sped along as fast as the rutted dirt road would allow, she wondered what was in store for Juana. What would her husband do to her — and worse yet, what would El Jefe, as the Nuñez called him, do to her. She seemed in mortal terror this morning, Jessie thought, and swallowed a lump in her throat, as she realized what a sacrifice the old woman was making for her. "Dear God, don't let them hurt her, or worse," she besought fervently as she rattled along the dirt road.

As soon as she was around a couple of bends and out of sight of the house, Jessie pulled over to the side of the road. If that Jefe guy shows up I want Tobe to know where I am, she thought — not that I'm very sure myself. But to hear his voice would be enough to make me shout for joy.

Quickly Jessie snatched the cell phone from her jacket pocket and pulled out the aerial. Slowly and cautiously, with trembling fingers, she dialed her home-phone number. She must make no hasty mistakes. The battery could be low and time was short — El Jefe could be here any time — so she must not call a wrong number. Pressing the "send" button, she placed the phone to her ear, and listened with bated breath. Three rings and then she heard Tobe's voice strong in her ear. The voice that was the most beloved in the world to her — music to her ears!

For a few seconds, she could not speak, her emotions were so rampant and wild. Tobe again said, "Hello, Hello, whose speaking, please," before she could say a word.

Jessie's voice choked with intense emotion as she spoke, "Tobe! It's Jessie! I've escaped but . . ."

Tobe's voice interrupted — filled with delight and was nearly incoherent, "Jessie — honey — where are you?" To Jessie's horror his voice began to fade in and out. The battery must be going!

Almost hysterical, she shouted, "I-I don't know! Somewhere near the border, I think . . ."

Tobe broke in, "You're fading out . . . Jessie! . . ." the connection broke off abruptly.

For a moment Jessie held the instrument in her hand, panic-stricken. Then she quickly clicked off the "end" button. What should she do — try again? No, she quickly decided, she would try Rachel's number. Perhaps her phone might pick up better. It was worth a try.

She dialed the number and listened with rapidly beating heart as it began to ring. "Dear God, let me get through!" At the second ring, Rachel's voice answered.

"Aunt Rachel, this is Jessie. I'm somewhere . . ."

"Jessie," Rachel's voice broke in, excitement throbbing in every word, "we've been looking everywhere for you. Where are you?"

"Down near . . ."

"Jessie, I can hardly hear you. Wh . . ." Rachel's words were cut off and the phone again went dead.

Quickly pressing the end button, Jessie tried to think above her rampaging emotions. To hear Tobe and Rachel's voices was pure joy, but had she told them anything that would help them find her?

She waited several minutes, hoping the battery would regenerate a little but after two more unsuccessful tries, she threw the phone on the seat, started the pick-up again and pulled out on the roadway. No time to mope, she had to get as far away from the Nuñez house as possible.

The farther she got from the house the easier in her mind she became — until she began to dwell on what Juana had said: El Jefe was coming to get her! Who was The Chief and what was he planning to do with her? Her upper body began to feel tighter and more constricted until she felt like a cable was stretched tight around her chest, squeezing off her ability to breath. Her hands became slick on the wheel and her breath came in short gasps.

"Whoa there," she cautioned herself. "God is with you. The Bible says so. Trust in Him!" She forced herself to breath slowly and deeply, repeating over and over a part of verse 4 of Psalm 23, that had always been a favorite: "I will fear no evil for thou art with me." Gradually fear lost its grip on her and she was breathing normally again.

She had been so absorbed in conquering her terror that she had been driving unconsciously, following the winding road, oblivious to where it was leading. Suddenly almost without warning she saw that the narrow track suddenly dipped sharply downward and ran across a wash. The pick-up was running much too fast she realized instantly, and she put on the brake as hard as she dared.

Careening down the embankment the truck slammed into the sandy dry arroyo bottom. For a moment the truck rocked wildly as she tried to hold it on the harder part of the road. Then floundering and shuddering, the vehicle lost its traction on the main part of the track and plunged off into deep sand.

"Stupid-stupid-stupid," she lambasted herself, whamming the steering-wheel with her hands. "Why didn't you watch where you were going?" Needing to be as far from this place as possible, too, it was enough to make a person pound her head on the dash!

"Enough of that," she cautioned herself. With her heart beating wildly, she climbed out to look over her situation. She saw quickly that the main track had been built up with rock and gravel enough to make it passable but on either side sand had washed and drifted in until it was deep and unstable.

Without much hope, she climbed back into the rig and first tried to back onto the firmer roadway and then to drive onto it. But the more she tried the deeper the tires spun down until the truck was shortly almost down to the hubs in a sea of loose desert sand.

With a sob, she laid her head on the wheel and tried to think. If only she knew how far it was to a highway! Well, she certainly couldn't stay with the pick-up, that was for sure.

I'd better get moving, she thought. She grabbed an old pair of dark glasses from the dash and jumped out. Slamming the door, she set out resolutely. Slogging through the deep sand to the harder surfaced roadway, she crossed the wash, climbed out and started down the rutted road. She wished she had brought the crutch with her because her leg soon began to throb.

Walk, she told herself sternly. This road is hardly more than a trail, really, she thought, as she hurried almost at a trot. Thankfully the air was still cool but she would soon have to remove her light jacket. The sun felt hot on her shoulders and she was thankful for Juana's old black hat.

She hadn't hiked but a few minutes when she heard a noise on the road ahead. A vehicle? Yes — and it was coming fast! Panic gripped her for a moment and then she looked wildly around for a place to hide. Surely it was El Jefe! Or Julio — and she was as afraid of him as the one they called The Chief. To her right she glimpsed only short grass on the rocky, uneven ground that wouldn't hide a rabbit. A few yards off the road to her left she sighted a few mesquite bushes — not much but better than nothing!

Terror put wings to her feet as she ran toward the mesquite bushes off to the left of the roadway and threw herself down. Sand had drifted about the roots of the bushes and some short grass grew there. It wasn't good cover but the best available. She lay as flat as possible as she awaited the rapidly moving rig. She could hear the soft growl of the engine plainly now.

The gray branches of the mesquite bushes were still bare, and the grass, though greening, was short so they didn't impede her vision much. She could vaguely glimpse the truck now as it came spinning toward her meager hiding place. Little sharp stones that she hadn't even seen bit into her stomach, chest and face but she lay as still as the cactus that was pricking her elbow.

The hum of a powerful engine was bearing down upon her now and she could see its dust. Then it began to slow down and her heart almost stopped beating until she realized it was slowing for the coulee where she had left Luis' mired pick-up. Even if the driver didn't see her, he would see the stranded rig. But there was nothing for her to do but lie as still as possible and pray — and that she did!

Her face, resting on the earth, was facing toward the oncoming rig and she studied it with terrified eyes. It was slowing more now and she could hear the sound of the engine, and see it clearly. Suddenly her eyes grew wide with shock. She knew that truck! A black, trimmed with red, three-quarter ton Dodge, with a powerful diesel engine. It was almost as familiar to her as Tobe's! And she knew the good-looking driver — Tobe's cousin Harold! She had been found!

Chapter 15

When Chet sped into the ranch yard in a cloud of dust, there was activity everywhere. Rachel's truck was in the yard at an odd angle. Tobe was leading a saddled horse from the barn, T.J. right on his heels. Ann waved frantically from near the front door. Bethann was jumping up and down with glee. Rachel was just coming through the front door with a hamper in her hands.

Chet, took all this in at a glance. He couldn't understand what was going on but the scene conveyed excitement and happiness. He eased himself out of the Tahoe and started limping towards Ann. Everyone converged on him. They all came together in front of the porch, everyone trying to talk at once. Chet had eyes only for Ann. Her hand came up to gently touch his injured face. "Oh Chet," she said softly, "Who did this?"

Ignoring her question, Chet asked, "What's happening here?"

"Jessie called Tobe and Rachel. They could understand only a little of what she said but they both are sure it was Jessie."

Completely stunned by the news Chet was speechless. He stumbled forward, clutching at Ann. Ann's arm instinctively went around his waist to support him and Rachel grabbed his other arm, "Got to sit down," Chet mumbled.

Together they weaved over to the porch steps, where Chet sat down. "I'll get some ice for that eye," Rachel said and darted away. Tobe ran up and leaned over Chet, "What happened to you, man?"

Chet didn't answer. Taking the watch out of his pocket he handed it to Tobe. Tobe snatched it. "By the holy," he yelled, "That's it. That's Jessie's."

"Ok, so Jessie is alive and somewhere calling for help." Chet said, "Tobe, you tell me what happened."

"I received a call from Jessie. Her phone was breaking up and she couldn't seem to hear me at all. I couldn't get her to tell me where she is." It was obvious Tobe was near the breaking point.

"Just take it easy, Tobe," Chet said. "Jessie's alive. Just keep that thought uppermost in your head."

"Rachel got almost the same call. I was going to take a horse and start looking in the canyons."

"Bad idea! She must have been on someone's cell phone. Just listen to what I have to say, maybe it will ring a bell."

"Ok, just everyone be calm. Go ahead, Chet."

"I didn't have any trouble buying the watch. I'll give you details later. The shop owner told me an old man named Nunez sold him the watch. He is supposed to live in the U.S. but I couldn't confirm that."

"Oh, my, there's a man named Nunez living on Buster's ranch," Rachel said excitedly. She had just returned with an ice pack that she handed to Chet.

"Thanks," Chet said gratefully, holding the ice pack to his eye. "Who's Buster? Where's his ranch."

"That's it, that's it," Ann said excitedly. "That's where she is. She's on that old goat ranch of Buster's." T.J., catching the excitement, ran circles around the group.

Bethann for some inexplicable reason buried her face against Rachel and started to cry.

Suddenly, against all logic, it seemed possible. That's where Jessie was. Safe and sound — hopefully — at the goat ranch.

"That's only about forty five minutes from here," Tobe said, "I had better get started." He wheeled and started for his truck.

"You're not going without us," Ann yelled, "Come on, Chet."

She pulled Chet to his feet, put her arm around his waist and together they stumbled after Tobe. "Will you take care of the kids Aunt Rachel," she called over her shoulder. She didn't wait for an answer.

"Wait — wait," Chet said, "Let's get my cell phone, it's fully charged."

In the truck, with Tobe driving like a mad man, Chet dialed the number he had previously programmed into his cell phone. While he dialed, he stated, "I think Harold is the one who abducted Jessie." Both started shaking their heads. Then the phone was ringing. Before he could explain anything further to Ann and Tobe a woman's voice came on the line, "Luna County Sheriff's department."

"This is Chet Upshaw, let me speak to Deputy Alredd."

"Deputy Alredd is on the other line, can you hold?"

"Yeah, I'll hang on." While he waited Chet turned to Ann. "Who is Buster?" he asked.

"Buster Young is Harold's father and Aunt Rachel's ex," she said.

Now that's something that makes sense, Chet thought, as Alredd's voice rang in his ear.

"Alredd here, what's up?"

"Alredd, we have located Jessie Helm. She is being held prisoner on Buster Young's Goat Ranch. Know where that is?"

"Yeah, I've been by there."

"Well we're heading there now and we might run into a pretty rough crowd. Besides Jessie's kidnapping, I suspect there might even be drugs involved. Better come along for the ride."

"Now you just wait a minute. You can't just go barging in there. We'll need a search warrant. You wait for me."

"Sorry, there's no holding Tobe back. Better get moving." Chet pushed the end button, abruptly closing the conversation.

"What if he doesn't come." Ann said.

"Then we'll handle it by ourselves," Tobe chimed in. "Now, what did you mean you thought my cousin Harold kidnapped Jessie?" His voice was harsh with suppressed anger.

"Just don't get huffy until I've explained," Chet said irritably. He hurt all over and he was in no mood to be messed with.

"Go ahead," Ann said gently, as if she

sensed his mood.

Chet told them as briefly as possible about how he found the watch, had run into Harold, and was tricked into going into the building where he was beaten-up and slugged by three men. He explained how he was convinced that the one who slugged him from behind was Harold.

"That's pretty thin evidence," Tobe said testily. "After all, Harold is my cousin, so what possible motive could he have for kidnapping my wife!"

"I'm not wild about Harold," Ann said, "but I can't imagine Harold doing anything like that either."

I just don't feel like arguing with them, Chet thought wearily, they'll get the drift after we find Jessie.

After what seemed like an eternity to Chet — with each small bounce magnified by his battered body and throbbing head — Tobe finally turned off the highway onto a dirt road. Even though every bone ached, worse now on the rough road, Chet felt exhilaration begin to rise to fever pitch. Would Jessie be here, safe and sound?

The road was little more than a track leading toward the mountains. After a couple of miles they came to a large shallow wash. The bottom of the wash was

243

full of sand and the road angled across the wash. At the side of the wash Chet saw an older model truck stuck in the sand. The driver had spun the wheels until the truck was hopelessly buried.

"I'll take a look," Tobe said, as he slammed on the brakes.

Tobe's face was a grim mask when he ran back. "No one," he said.

He jammed his truck into four wheel drive. They had no trouble negotiating the wash and continuing on towards the goat ranch.

"That truck is souped to the gills," he said, "It's probably been used to run dope across the border. There's a cell phone in the floor on the passenger side. That could have been the one Jessie was using."

There was no more talk as the truck careened down the narrow track. About two miles further along Tobe again stopped. Chet could see a couple of small houses tucked in against a sheer rock wall, surrounded by an ocotillo fence. *That must be the ranch,* he thought.

"I wonder if we should be a little cautious," Tobe said.

Before anyone could answer, throwing caution to the winds, he shoved the truck in gear and roared off. The truck lurched

244

forward and at full speed blasted into the ranch yard.

A man stood beside a late model Chevrolet Pickup with a small two-wheel trailer hitched to the bumper. He was fairly tall, but dumpy looking. His long gray hair stuck out from under a floppy brown hat. His high heeled boots were slightly run over and had seen a lot of wear. He leaned back against the pickup with his arms folded across his chest. Seemingly unflappable, he calmly eyed their approach.

"That's Uncle Buster," Ann cried, "Let me out." She scrambled over Chet, being careful not to bump him too hard.

"Hola, Uncle Buster," she yelled, running toward him. "We're looking for Jessie. We had a phone call from her. Is she here?"

"Hold er down, Chiquita," Buster said, "You'll bust a gut." There was a big smile on his face. It was plain to see he liked Ann. Ann ran over and gave him a big hug.

While this tableau was going on, Tobe jumped out of the truck and walked quickly to Aunt Rachel's ex-husband.

Chet, stiff and sore from his beating, also eased himself out of the truck but much more slowly.

Ann by this time had flooded her uncle

with information while Tobe seemed to be trying to break into the one-way conversation.

"Wait a minute, will you just wait," Buster pleaded, "I haven't seen Jessie. Why would she be here?" He paused, "But someone has been staying in my cabin. I've only been here a couple of hours. I haven't seen Luis but Juana is here. Let's ask Juana about it."

"Juana, Juana venga aqui, por favor." At Buster's call an old woman came to the door of the cabin. Buster unleashed a flow of Spanish at her. It was too fast for Chet to follow any of it. She answered in kind, only a little slower.

"She says Jessie has been here for almost three weeks. She left this morning in the truck that is stuck in the wash." He turned back to the woman, speaking rapidly in Spanish again. "She says her husband went after her, but Harold beat him to her."

A gasp came from Ann, and Tobe's face went white as chalk.

Buster again conversed with the woman. "Harold has taken her to his ranch."

The old woman was pointing due west.

"That can't be," Tobe said. "His ranch isn't that way and besides we just came from Harold and Rachel's ranch, and she isn't there."

"Juana says it's another ranch that Harold owns, over west of here, on the other side of the mountains." Buster added, "This is news to me, too, it's the first I heard of Harold owning another ranch."

"But — but Harold wouldn't be able to buy a ranch, and — and how could he keep it secret, anyway?" Ann stammered.

Buster reached up and removed his floppy brown hat while he scratched his head with a puzzled look on his face. "Well, there is one possibility. For a little while I owned a small place over that way. I took Harold quail hunting there once when he was about sixteen. Wasn't much to the place — just an old shack and falling down barn, but Harold took a liking to it." He put his hat back on his head, shoving it well back on his head. "Since Harold liked it so much, I deeded it to him on his eighteenth birthday. Could that be the place Juana is talking about?"

He quizzed Juana closely, making her repeat herself again and again. Finally he was satisfied and nodded his head. "That's the place all right. She's been there but she says it's a very large ranch with a big grand hacienda now, with lots of cattle and growing crops." He shook his head in consternation. "I'll have Juana tell us what happened."

As the old woman talked in rapid-fire Spanish, there was silence in the group around her. She seemed to be enjoying the chance to tell her story. According to her, Harold had come upon Jessie after she stuck the truck in sand and sweet-talked her into going with him. Luis saw and heard it all — hidden behind a mesquite bush — and hadn't dared to challenge El Jefe. Juana also spat out the information that Harold's ranch was used in drug trafficking and that he had gotten her son involved — and that she was very angry about that.

"My son involved in drugs? It's unbelievable," Buster said in utter bewilderment. "How could he do such a thing? I never was much of a dad but Rachel is the best of mothers! This must somehow be my fault."

He shook his head as if overcome with shock. "Rachel got rid of me because I could never settle down — had to have excitement all the time. Being a rodeo clown fitted me to a T and satisfied my wanderlust. I was so busy running after my own enjoyment that I paid little attention to the kid when he was growing up and not a whole lot since he grew up — unless he sought me out — which he did quite a bit when he could catch me home."

"What's happened in the past can't be helped now, Uncle Buster," Ann said softly.

"I suppose not," Buster agreed with a sigh. He seemed to shake himself from his brooding and turned back to Juana, asking why she and Luis would keep the kidnapped girl here for Harold. She hung her head and wouldn't answer for a moment. But with Buster's gentle prodding, she admitted in halting English, "We no citizens. El Jefe threaten to turn us in to immigration officers if we say no help heem."

Every one was stunned. Even Chet had a hard time believing everything he had heard. It seemed incredible that Harold could be involved with drugs, threatened this old couple, and had abducted his cousin's wife. There big money in drugs and the people involved fought hard and dirty when they felt threatened, but why kidnap Jessie? Why? Why? It didn't make sense! But Jessie must be rescued, and now since Harold had fled with her, the task would be harder.

Buster was amazed to hear the old Mexican couple were not American citizens. "They've worked for me for years and I didn't know that," he said. "I'll certainly do the best I can to get them citizenship," he declared. Juana understood his English and grabbed his hand, kissing it — much to Buster's embarrassment.

"Ok, Buster give us directions," Tobe said, "We've got to get after him."

"All right, even though he's my boy, I can't protect him. You've got to get Jessie away from him. I hope he hasn't hurt her." Buster said, "Here's the way of it. Go to Columbus and turn west on State Highway 9 past Pancho Villa State Park, and on out past Hermanas. Watch out for those curves out that way, they are wicked. There will be about ten miles of Greasewood flats then some cultivated fields on both sides of the road.

He pondered for a moment and then continued, "Go on past Johnson and Sons Ranch, about a mile from the Grant County line there is a dirt road going back north toward the Cedar Hills. The road is county maintained so it should be in good shape. Almost exactly four miles you will come to a big wash, there is a road that turns left and runs along side the wash. When I was there last it was just a track, but you won't have any trouble. The property is at the end of that road. That's the best I can do. I'll wait here in case Harold should double back. Vaya con Dios."

Tobe, his face grim and set, spun on his heel and headed for his truck, Ann and Chet hard on his heels.

"Un momento! Por favor, un momento!" Juana called, in an urgent voice. All three stopped and looked at her. She rattled something off in Spanish and Buster translated, "She says to wait a moment, that she has something for you."

Juana ran back to the house and within two minutes she was back with a brown paper sack in her hand, which she thrust into Ann's hand. "You be hungry," she said, panting from her exertion, "Me just make. Hot."

"Thank you, Juana, that's so sweet of you." Ann said as she leaned over and hugged her. The old lady stepped back, beaming with pleasure.

All three climbed into the truck and Tobe roared off.

Chapter 16

Relief surged through Jessie like a tonic. As she scrambled to her feet her legs felt as weak as a new-born calf's. When she stood up, Harold's truck was almost even with her. Harold slammed on the brakes, jumped out of the vehicle and ran around the truck cab toward her with a big grin on his face.

"My, if you aren't a picture for sore eyes," Harold said, grabbing her in a big bear-hug. "We've been looking all over for you."

For a moment, Jessie let him hold her, sobbing against his chest in relief, and then realizing she was in another man's arms, even Tobe's cousin's, she pulled away self-consciously. "How did you find me," she asked.

"Your watch," Harold said. "I just found out today who sold it."

"Thank God," Jessie said, brushing away the tears that wouldn't seem to stop, with her sleeve. "Are Tobe and the children OK?"

"Just worried is all," Harold said gently.

"Ann's been caring for the kids, so they're in good hands."

"We'd better go," Jessie said anxiously, "Juana, the old lady who cared for me, said someone that she calls El Jefe is coming to get me today and she seemed terrified of him."

"Did this El Jefe kidnap you?"

"I'm not sure, but I guess so," Jessie said. "But I never talked to anyone except the old woman and her husband. Their son came a few times but I never talked to him. And I saw some people one night in their front yard at a wild party their son threw but I was kept under lock and key."

"This son wasn't the mysterious El Jefe?"

"I'm sure he wasn't. I don't think he was aware that I was here until perhaps last night. He came late last night, and early this morning his mother let me out and sent me away in her husband's pick-up. I would have been long gone but I got stuck in the sand in the wash and couldn't get out. I was walking when I heard you coming."

She laughed shakily, "I thought you were El Jefe so I hid until I saw who you were."

"Old Harold to the rescue," he chuckled and then sobered. "You haven't contacted Tobe or Ann at all?"

"Yes, I tried a while ago. Juana gave me the cell phone as I was leaving and I called Tobe."

"He'll be glad to know where you are," Harold said solicitously.

"I didn't get to tell him much — the phone battery quit on me. And I also tried Rachel's phone but I barely got to her and the phone quit for good."

"Well, don't worry about it, I'll get you home right soon. Come on and get in before your bad guy comes," Harold said with a wide grin.

Taking her by the arm, he led her toward the pickup.

"I can hardly wait to get home," Jessie said, pausing to brush the dust from her jeans and jacket. As she climbed into the truck, with his hand steadying her, she laughed softly. "It was so good to hear Tobe's voice that I could hardly speak at first — imagine me — speechless!"

Harold expertly maneuvered the truck around and headed back the way he had come. As soon as he was on the road again, he turned to her, "Your mother's here — staying with your aunt Carolyn."

Jessie's face lit up, "I should have known she would come when she heard I was missing."

Harold chuckled softly, "She's convinced Tobe murdered you and hid your body."

Aghast, Jessie exclaimed, "How could she think such a thing!"

"Your mother brought in the Las Cruces Herald's ace investigative reporter to help in the case."

When Jessie stared in amazement, Harold asked, "Do you remember Chet Upshaw, that you used to go to high school with? He's their big-shot reporter."

"Of course I remember him," said Jessie, incredulously. "I even dated him in high school. Does he think Tobe's guilty too?"

"I'm not sure — he keeps his own council. But he's really been on the job, interviewing and beating the bushes."

"Goodness! It looks like I've got things in an uproar!" Jessie said contritely. "I'm sorry this has been so hard on everyone and especially Tobe. What he must have been through."

"Yeah," Harold said. "The police thinks he did away with you too, even had him in jail over night."

Tears blinded Jessie's eyes and she wiped them away with her sleeve, "How unfair! He wouldn't have harmed me in a million years!"

They had reached Highway 11 that ran

between Deming and Columbus on the US-Mexican border. To Jessie's surprise, Harold turned south toward Columbus. Before she could say anything, he turned his wide smile on her and explained, "Chet's searching for you over in Columbus today, near the border. Ann may be there, too. We arranged to meet each other at about ten-thirty at a little store down there and compare notes. It's nearly that time so since we're this close, I'd better run down and make connection with him so he won't search all day and put in time for nothing."

Jessie's heart fell but she tried to not show her disappointment. Even if she wanted to dash home to Tobe and the kids, it made sense to take care of the other first. She'd caused enough trouble without taking up any more of people's time.

"I hope that's all right," Harold said anxiously.

"Yes — yes, of course. It shouldn't take long."

As he guided his truck toward Columbus, Harold filled her in briefly on the search, who had helped and other tidbits of interest about the family. Jessie mainly let him do the talking. It felt good to just be able to relax and know she was safe — and would soon see Tobe and the children. She listened with only half an ear as she meditated about how wonderful it would be to be at home with Tobe and the children again. In no time they were driving into Columbus and then turned west on State Highway 9.

They had passed the outskirts and were headed out into open country now and Jessie felt a prickle of unease. Where was Harold taking her? Surely there was no store out here. She opened her mouth to ask when Harold suddenly pulled off the road onto an open space under a small tree. Putting on the brake, he turned to her with a serious face. "Jessica, we need to talk — serious-like."

"Sure," Jessie said, mystified.

"You may be mad at me for what I'm about to say, but I want you to listen with an open mind. Okay?"

"I-I guess so," Jessie said uneasily.

Harold's deep blue eyes stared into hers with an intensity that unnerved her. "Jessica," (He had always called her Jessica when nearly everyone else called her the more informal Jessie.) "You said you don't know who abducted you. How much do you remember of that evening, from the time you left your own house?"

"Why?" Jessie asked. This was beginning to be irritating and she wanted to get home — not be interrogated.

"I have my reasons," Harold said gently, "please bear with me. I might be able to shed some light on who picked you up."

"Okay," Jessie said hesitantly, turning her eyes away from the intensity of Harold's gaze. "I remember being very angry at Tobe — we had had an argument — and running outside, heading for Ann's little cabin. I never dreamed there was such a storm brewing. The wind was blowing awful and it began to snow worse and worse. I recall getting colder and colder and wishing I had taken Tobe's heavy coat instead of the old sweater I grabbed as I went out the door.

"I fell down a couple of times or so, I think, and when I reached the cattle-guard I realized I had missed the cabin."

"So what did you do?"

"I was on the cattle-guard before I realized it and when I tried to go back, I guess my foot slipped or a wind gust hit me. Any way, I twisted my ankle and I couldn't walk. I fell down into the ditch. Then I thought I heard a vehicle coming so I crawled up the steep bank."

"Did you see who was coming or from

what direction?"

Jessie pondered for a moment, and then looked up into Harold's serious face again, "Everything was pretty foggy by that time — I was so cold and somewhat disoriented, I think — but I thought the vehicle was coming from the direction of our ranch house."

"You think it was Tobe coming?"

"I thought it might be — but obviously it wasn't or I wouldn't have been held captive for almost three weeks by strangers."

Harold touched Jessie lightly on the arm, "Perhaps it was Tobe. Have you given any thought to that possibility?"

"Why — why, that's preposterous, Harold, and you know it! Why didn't he take me home — or to the doctor, if it was him!"

Harold's eyes were glowing again with that intense fire, "Now keep an open mind here, Jessica. What if it was Tobe who found you and had you held captive all this time."

"But — but why would he do that?" Jessie's eyes were beginning to glint angrily.

"I wouldn't know what was in his mind, Jessica, but maybe he wanted to give you a good scare. Or — and I know this is far-fetched but just supposing, he had decided to do away with you at a later time when things settled down."

He held up a silencing hand when Jessie tried to protest again, "The police think it was Tobe who did something with you and so does your mother. I have always stood up for him but I see some evidence that is hard to explain."

"Such as?" Jessie asked weakly.

"The police found one of Tobe's handkerchiefs at the cattle guard — with your blood on it. And just recently they found his sweater — hidden in that secret compartment in Tobe's pick-up — and it had your blood on it. He admitted you wore it away that night, and you also say you wore it that night. That's why Tobe was put in jail overnight and is just now out on bail."

"But-but . . ."

Harold broke in relentlessly, "How did Tobe get that sweater if he wasn't the one who found you and secreted you away? You need to consider these things before you go back to Tobe, Jessica."

"I can explain the handkerchief," Jessie said defensively. "I was so cold and I remembered Tobe usually carried a big handkerchief in his pockets. I found it and tied it over my mouth, nose and ears. It was gone after a while, I guess the wind blew it off. I had fallen down and so I probably got blood on it. It was that simple."

"And the sweater the police found hidden in Tobe's pick-up?"

"I don't know," Jessie choked back a sob. "When I woke up in that cabin it was gone." She took a deep gulping breath, "But Tobe would never harm me — I know it!"

"It's common knowledge that you and Tobe have been fighting like two wild-cats lately," Harold said quietly. "Maybe Tobe got tired of the fighting and wanted out."

"But he wouldn't have resorted to kidnapping to accomplish that," Jessie scoffed — but even to her own ears it was a little weak. Her mind was racing, could there be any truth in this outlandish reasoning? Of course not! "Why not opt for the regular way: divorce? That's what normal people do."

"From what Tobe told the police — and the family — you had one of the biggest fights yet, over his ordering a registered bull and you canceling the order."

Jessie was recalling the anger and — hate perhaps? certainly intense dislike — in Tobe's face when she ran out. Then she recalled Tobe's voice a short while before on the cell-phone. It had rung with joy and love and he had called her honey. She said stiffly, "We love each other, Harold, and when I called a while ago, he sounded delighted and thrilled."

"Anything can be faked," Harold said. "However, who am I to try to convince you any more. I really care about you, Jessica, and I just don't want to see you abused and treated like dirt by that loser of a cousin of mine."

"Tobe is not a loser! And I'll thank you not to talk about him that way," Jessie said furiously.

Harold grinned that disarming smile, "Sorry, I just got carried away. It has pained me a long time to see the struggles you have to make ends meet and I don't think Tobe realizes how hard it has been for you."

Starting the truck, he pulled out on to the road and continued west away from Columbus.

"Harold," Jessie said, "Let's go back. Surely Chet wouldn't be down here. You're leaving the town behind. Please, let's go back!"

"I'm afraid I can't do that right now," Harold said smoothly. "There's something

I want to show you that will knock your eyeballs out."

Jessie was angry now, "Harold, I want to go home. Take me home — now."

"Can't do that," Harold said with a grin. He reached over and pressed down the switch that locked both doors. An icy chill ran down Jessie's back. Where was Harold taking her?

"Harold, this is ridiculous! I don't want to go sightseeing. I want to go home!"

"I just want you to see something before I take you home," Harold said calmly. "It won't take long."

When he glanced over at her, Jessie saw again the almost savage intensity that glittered there and fear struck deep in the pit of her stomach. This was not the easygoing Harold she knew — or thought she knew. Where was Harold taking her? *Dear God,* she breathed a prayer inside her heart, *please protect me.*

The miles rolled by and Jessie became more and more frightened. Harold seemed completely relaxed and even hummed now and then. What was going on? This whole affair was unreal — it couldn't be happening. Surely Harold wouldn't harm her! She had known him most of her life! Or had she? She had never seen this side of

Harold before. Didn't even know it existed! He seemed so self assured and — scary.

Casting about in her mind for something to get Harold to stop the car so she could get out — and get out, she must! — she noticed a small store ahead and said, "Is that the store where you were to meet Chet?"

"No, I've decided to go on out to my place instead of meeting him."

"Let's stop there anyway," Jessie, almost breathless from the fear that was banging away at her ribs. "I didn't have time to eat breakfast. We should be able to get some snacks and I'm starved."

"Open the glove compartment," Harold said with a complacent grin. "I always carry some snack crackers or cookies in there. They will hold you over until I can fix you a good breakfast, at my house."

Jessie suppressed a shudder. What was this all about? She didn't know Harold even had a house anywhere else! Opening the glove compartment door, she reached into the crowded interior. A couple of packets of peanut-butter filled crackers were there and as she drew them out, she bumped a small leather case which tumbled to the floor. When she stooped to retrieve the case, it fell open to reveal two photos. As her hand closed on the case, her eyes quickly took in the two pictures, in color. One was very obviously of a much younger Harold with a rather dumpy clown.

But it was the other photo that stilled her hand and set her heart to thudding harder. She felt suddenly sick to her stomach. It was a bust pose of a man — who wore a leather belt with a belt buckle which appeared to be made out of heavy silver. It was adorned with bright blue, turquoise stones — and in the center of the belt buckle was the carved head of a goat with wicked horns!

"Who-who is this?" Jessie spoke through trembling lips.

"My dad, Buster Young," Harold said readily. "He's a clown, you know, who performs at rodeos and other places. Dad trains goats to use in his acts and he's quite good."

"I met him once or so, I think," Jessie managed to speak through constricted lips. She had been staying at Buster Young's goat ranch! Of course, why had she not realized it before? Vaguely she now recalled hearing he owned one near the Mexican border. Was this amiable-looking clown her abductor? Her mind seemed to spin. But why would he kidnap her?

This was getting more and more weird!

"Harold," Jessie spoke firmly. "Take me home! I've had enough of this foolishness! Take me home now!"

A slight frown appeared on Harold's usually placid face. "I'm afraid I can't do that, Jessica. After I show you my surprise, I might consider it. We'll see."

"Did your father kidnap me?" Jessie asked, aware that her voice had risen.

"Of course not! What gave you that ridiculous idea?"

"I've been kept a prisoner at your father's goat ranch for almost three weeks!"

"Where did you get that idea?" Harold asked.

Jessie tapped the picture of Buster Young with a slightly unsteady forefinger. "That belt Buster is wearing is in the closet of the room I've been incarcerated in!"

Exasperated, Harold laughed. "My dad would never kidnap a woman! A goat maybe, but a girl, never!"

Jessie started to sputter a furious reply, when Harold turned off the main road onto a dirt road. "We'll soon be there,"

Harold said, "and you're going to love it."

"Love what?"

With his eyes on the narrow, graveled road, Harold spoke proudly, "My home, of course."

"But-but you live with Aunt Rachel," Jessie said. "I didn't know you had a house over this way."

"There are lots of things you — and nearly everyone else — don't know about me," Harold said enigmatically.

Jessie turned these things over in her mind. Yes, she decided there were a great many things she — and others — didn't know about Harold Young and she wasn't sure she was going to like what she found out!

Suddenly Harold rounded a small hill, drew the powerful truck to a smooth stop and pointed proudly. "There it is! My home sweet home."

Ahead of them, Jessie saw the top story of a white building, rising above a very tall wall. It appeared as large as a mansion and glowed like marble in the sunlight. The tops of trees and shrubs could also be seen here and there.

In spite of her anger of a moment ago, Jessie was struck speechless. "It looks immense. Surely this isn't your home," she said in bewilderment.

"It is immense," Harold said proudly. "And my ranch which stretches on back for miles, is also enormous. I'm breeding some of the best pedigreed cattle on the market today."

"B-but how could you afford a ranch like this?" Jessie stammered.

Harold put the truck in gear again and rolled toward the imposing structure before he answered. "There are ways," he said glibly. As he neared a large gate, he touched a button on his dash and it swung wide to admit them.

Jessie gaped at the vision of beauty and wealth that spread before them when they were inside the wall. A lawn of velvet green stretched on both sides, and beds of flowers, shrubs and trees, set in well-tended elegance met her eyes wherever she looked.

"Do you like it?" Harold asked, as the gate swung closed behind them and they parked on an immaculate paved driveway before triple garage doors.

"Of course I like it," Jessie said, still in awe. "Who wouldn't?"

"Wait until you see the room I had pre-pared for you," Harold said eagerly.

"For-for me? What do you mean, you

prepared a room for me?"

That penetrating, intense glow was back in Harold's eyes as he gazed at Jessie. "I really prepared all of this for you. I want you to be happy here."

Horror was beginning to clutch at Jessie. She spoke sharply, "What are you saying?"

For a moment Harold only stared at Jessie and she seemed powerless to look away from his hypnotic gaze, then he smiled as he spoke softly, "Surely it has always been obvious to you that I've never loved anyone else but you." His tone was slightly condemning. "I've never made it a secret that I like to be with you."

"Harold! You're my husband's cousin. I certainly never knew you had any more affection for me than for a cousin. I love Tobe! I've always loved Tobe. And he's my husband!"

"You think you love him but he can't even provide for you properly — and I can. You'll learn to love me, Jessica," Harold said confidently. He swept his arm out to encompass the house and grounds. "It will be so easy for you here. No work to do, no worries. Lovely clothes. Servants to see to your every whim."

Jessie was getting angry again. "Harold, where did you get the idea that a woman would leave her husband just for a beautiful home and fancy clothes. It's true things have not gone well with us financially at times, but when I married Tobe, I meant every word of my vows to him. I married him 'Until death do us part.' "

"That could be arranged, too, if you upset me," Harold said with a little crooked smile.

"Are you threatening to kill one or both of us, if I don't go along with this-this preposterous plan of yours?"

Harold chuckled and didn't answer. Jessie felt cold shock turning her blood to ice. Was Harold insane? She had always felt he was a little odd. But this was absurd!

"How were you able to-to kidnap me?"

"I didn't kidnap you," Harold said emphatically, "I saved your life!"

"But how did you happen to be there — when I ran out in the storm."

Harold's eyes softened and he said earnestly, "I finally had everything prepared for you. So I had been watching your house, trying to find a time when you were away from the house and alone, such as at Ann's cabin."

"So you saw me run out of the house and head for Ann's house?"

"Yes, so I went on ahead to her cabin. When the storm worsened I knew you had missed the house, so I went looking for you. And it was a good thing I did or you would have died — no thanks to your ever-loving husband!"

"I'm sure Tobe didn't realize how bad the storm was," Jessie said.

"He was only thinking of himself, you mean! Oh, well, that's over and done with. Come on, I'll fix you some breakfast before I show you the house," Harold said as he opened the pick-up door. "I let most of the servants go into town to a big fiesta of some sort but I enjoy cooking and it will be my pleasure to cook a meal for you. The first of many, I hope." He strode around the truck to open the door for her, a smile on his handsome face.

Terror turned Jessie's limbs numb as she tried to scramble out of the truck before Harold reached her and she almost fell. She felt his strong arm around her, steadying her and she drew back quickly.

Harold was looking down into her eyes with a strange possessive-like expression on his face that chilled her to the marrow of her bones. "Don't fight me in this, Jessica," he said softly, "because you're on my turf now."

Chapter 17

Jessie felt terror throbbing in every vein of her body. Clearly Harold was insane! Hysteria threatened to overwhelm her but she fought it down. If ever she needed a clear head it was now.

Trying to restrain a shudder at the touch of his hand, she allowed Harold to take her by the elbow and lead her toward a massive, carved door. It opened before they reached it and a grinning Julio held it wide for them. Julio spoke a few words in Spanish to Harold, with an insinuating smirk in Jessie's direction. Harold frowned and Julio's grin quickly was replaced with a solemn expression but the glint was still in his bold black eyes.

Harold spoke an obvious command in Spanish as they went into the house, and Julio quickly left them. In spite of her fear, Jessie was surprised that Harold spoke fluent Spanish — and that he was instantly obeyed by the formidable, hulking Julio. Harold clearly was El Jefe in this household. Terror again lanced through Jessie like the shaft of a spear and she trembled.

Harold still retained the hold on her arm and he quickly turned her to face him and said softly, "You don't need to be afraid of me, Jessica. I would never hurt you." The tenderness in his face filled her with a near panic. *Dear God, save me from this madman.* Or was he crazy? She didn't know, but either way, Jessie knew she was in deep peril.

"Come into the kitchen and I'll fix you a meal you'll not forget soon," Harold said, urging her through a small entry hall with pressure on her elbow. Jessie had no choice but to obey. After crossing a huge, elegantly furnished living room, he led her through a beautifully paneled dining room, with a gleaming oak table, sideboard and luxurious chairs, and into a large kitchen, filled with modern turquoise-colored appliances.

In spite of her terror, Jessie was awed by the opulence and splendor of Harold's mansion. Harold had always been a part of life with Tobe, but he had always seemed so insignificant and mild. No one would ever have suspected Harold had a dashing, romantic side or that he had the ability and acumen to acquire such wealth. In amazement, she mused, *I didn't think Harold* ever dated much — unless he did his courting in Mexico where she knew he frequently visited.

Harold's recent words rose to the surface of her mind, "I've always loved you, Jessica!" Her knees went weak. Appalled, Jessie struggled to understand. Had a fixation for his cousin's wife actually been with Harold all the many years Harold had known Jessie. Have I encouraged this weird obsession, she thought in horror.

She realized suddenly that she stood stock still in the middle of the room, and that Harold was speaking to her in an annoyed voice. "Jessica, I was asking you how you like your eggs!"

"Oh . . . oh . . . I guess I was just thinking of-of something else. No, I'm not very hungry after all. Let me just fix myself a sandwich, if you have the 'makings'."

"Sure, I have a well-stocked larder," Harold said, "but I was looking forward to fixing you a real meal. I really am an excellent cook."

"I don't doubt it," Jessie said — and she didn't, because anything seemed to be probable with this strange new Harold. "But a sandwich will be fine. And I don't wish to be a bother, I can fix it myself."

Harold's deep blue eyes held that

strange, almost hypnotic, intenseness as he answered softly, "You are never a bother to me, Jessica. I've waited for this such a long, long time!"

Jessie turned quickly away from his burning eyes, and said sharply, "That's nonsense, Harold. I'm Tobe's wife! Nothing will change that!"

Harold's strong hand was suddenly gripping her shoulder cruelly as he whirled her to face him. The look in Harold's eyes no longer held tenderness and his voice, was no longer soft. She tried not to cringe under the glare of those cold, marble-hard blue chips. Although his hand on her shoulder hurt viciously, she found herself totally unable to even squeak out a protest.

"I told you, Jessica, that you mustn't fight me in this. It never pays to fight El Jefe. I keep my claws curved-in for those I care about — which aren't many — but I can be pushed too far, and that I won't tolerate, even from you!"

Even in her fear-numbed mind, Jessie could now fathom why Julio, and probably anyone else, who ever saw this side of Harold's nature, didn't cross him.

After a long moment when terror held her silent and passive, eyes hypnotically locked with Harold's, she felt him suddenly release her shoulder.

"Now — I think we understand each other," Harold said gently. He turned from her, crossed the room to the refrigerator and opened the door. "Come choose what you want to eat." Glancing around, his face now lit with a big grin, he said graciously, "There's some delicious ham, different kinds of cheeses, turkey, and even some tuna in the cabinet if you want tuna salad."

On slightly trembling legs, Jessie moved a step toward Harold and said as calmly as she could, "Ham and cheese will be fine. And let me help."

"Sure, if you want to."

Amazed that she could actually eat after the former strange discourse, Jessie wolfed down the fat sandwich of boiled ham, cheese, lettuce and tomato on toasted rye, and chips, washed down with a tall glass of chilled milk. Harold, now the mild-mannered, but charming host again, also ate — with obvious relish — a turkey sandwich and Pepsi Cola.

Gathering up the few pieces of exquisite china and real silver they had used, Harold quickly stacked them in the sink while Jessie wiped off the kitchen table where they had eaten.

"Now," Harold said, pure joy radiating

from his eyes, "let me show you the lovely bedroom I have prepared especially for you."

Choking back the retort that came swiftly to her lips, Jessie followed him from the room with lagging steps. Terror beat like a hammer inside her brain, her hands felt slippery on the exquisitely carved stairway banister as she climbed, and her legs felt rubbery and weak. *Dear God, Help me!*

Crossing from the landing to a pristine white door, Harold stood back, and with eyes alight like an eager schoolboy, ushered her in ahead of him with a quaint bow. Jessie, who had always gloried in light and color, stood with her mouth agape as she stepped across the threshold.

No drapes covered the wide windows which lined the entire outside wall, light spilled in through wide, pale green, vertical venetian blinds. *He's even taken into consideration the allergies I suffer, and used no drapes, just like at my own home,* she thought, in amazement. *Even Tobe would not have been so considerate.* Then she was horrified at her thoughts. *How can I compare Tobe with Harold, at a time like this. Harold is a nut-case, even if he is a charming, thoughtful one, and I mustn't* forget it for a moment.

And I must be careful not to anger him! He scares me silly when he's upset.

A luxurious king-sized bed, covered with a silken quilted spread and heaped with colorful pillows, stood out from a wall. Glowing walnut furnishings, even to a dainty carved desk and chair, and large well-filled bookcase, occupied the spacious room. Through a door she could see a frilly dressing room, and glimpsed a bathroom with mint-green fixtures. Everyone knew she loved green in any shade.

"Look in here," Harold called as he opened a door. A pang of pleasure swept through her as she stepped inside the door. How she would like to own this for real! A small, cozy sitting room, complete with a Mexican fireplace spread out before her delighted eyes. She crossed to the huge window, also with wide vertical venetian blinds which had been drawn back and looked out upon a walled garden, with trees, shrubs and flowers in bloom.

"Beautiful, isn't it?" Harold murmured at her side. She moved away from him and then let out a gasp.

Two huge, powerfully muscled dogs moved into the peaceful scene below. As if they knew they were being watched, they both turned to look upward and Jessie's heart seemed to turn over. They were the ugliest dogs she had ever seen! They looked positively evil.

"Just my trained watch dogs," Harold said nonchalantly. "Don't try to go outside unless I'm with you, until you get acquainted with them. They'd rend you to pieces."

"They're so thin," Jessie said. "They look half-starved."

"Guard dogs need to be half-starved, makes them mean."

Jessie turned away. She loved animals and mistreatment always made her sick to her stomach.

"Do you like your suite?" Harold was again standing close and she moved away toward the living room.

"Yes, it is all very nice," she managed. It was more than nice, it was all gorgeous. She would have loved it if it really belonged to her — and Tobe.

"Good, I'm glad you like it, because I've tried to do everything just like you would want it!"

A chill ran down her back, and she said nothing.

"You do like it, don't you?"

"Yes, of course, who wouldn't?" Jessie's words were stilted.

"What's wrong then?" Harold asked, a small frown furrowing his brow.

"Harold," Jessie turned to face him, trying to choose her words with care, "I know you mean well. Everything is lovely — more than lovely, it's all exquisite. But you know that I can't stay here. Tobe is my husband and I must go back home to him."

Harold's brow furrowed more deeply and his mouth tightened, "I've warned you, Jessica, that you are not to fight me in this. I've dreamed and planned and worked too long to be thwarted."

Jessie held up a hand, "Harold, you are a good-looking guy. There are girls who would die to share this with you — but I . . ."

Anger flared in Harold's eyes and they became flinty hard and implacable. "I could have had dozens of girls in the past, Jessica. Girls run after men with money — and I'm wealthy." His tone softened into pleading, "But I only want you. I've never wanted anyone else. I can make you happy. I know I can. Just give me a chance."

Jessie's heart banged feverishly against her ribs, like an imprisoned bird beating against the walls of a cage. What could she say to make Harold understand? She stared at him in hopeless silence.

"Very well," Harold said calmly after a moment. "We'll talk more later. Perhaps some isolation would be good for you right now, anyway, and I can wait for you to see the sense of my reasoning. We have lots of time — the rest of our lives, in fact."

The rest of our lives? Jessie felt as if he had punched her in the stomach, and nausea threatened. This couldn't be happening — it was unreal!

He waved toward a closet door. "There's clothes in the closet — attractive clothes — so please change out of those grubby old jeans before I come back." It was an order and her stomach quavered uneasily. She must tread softly, not stir him to the violent anger he was capable of, but still not nurture his hope. *Dear God, I need you desperately. Please help me!*

Harold walked to the door but turned back with his hand on the doorknob. "I have to attend to some work in my office, anyway. There are books and magazines here in your room, and even a tiny refrigerator and cabinet in the sitting room, with food. Make yourself at home and I'll see you later, my love."

Unable to utter a word, Jessie watched him go. For long moments, she stood still, listening. Finally she stepped cautiously to the door. Although she had not heard retreating footsteps, surely he had gone. Gently she tried to turn the doorknob and then gripped it. Harold had locked her in! There had been no sound of a key turning.

In fact, she now noticed there was not a sound anywhere. It was as if she were sealed in a tomb. Was the room soundproof or was there no one else about? No, that wasn't true. Julio was here somewhere — but hadn't Harold said he had let most of the servants go for the day, to a fiesta or something? But if there were others, they must tiptoe about for she had heard no one. Of course, now that she thought about it, deep carpets covered all the floors she had seen, except the kitchen.

Sudden fatigue latched itself upon Jessie and she stumbled to a large couch and slumped down. Suspicion rose quickly. Had Harold some way drugged her again. Stretching out on the couch, she closed her eyes wearily. That was her last conscious thought until she heard a subdued sound that snapped her awake. Raising up quickly, she saw Harold standing a few feet from her, that hypnotic intense look in his blue eyes.

An almost sheepish grin twisted his lips.

"It's almost more than I can imagine," he said softly, "You're finally here with me."

Jessie stood to her feet and almost fell. Harold was instantly at her side, solicitously steadying her. She noticed the room was in deep shadows, lighted only by a small lamp. It was nighttime! "You drugged me again," she said angrily.

Harold chuckled, "Only a tiny sleeping powder in your milk. You need your rest."

"Is that how it's going to be?" Jessie said bitterly. "You plan to keep me drugged all the time, like you did the first three days of my incarceration at Juana's house?"

"Don't be angry," Harold said gently. "I only do what has to be done. And besides, I'm an expert when it comes to drugs. I know just the amount to use for the desired effect. When you accept my judgment about things, they will no longer be necessary."

"Yes," Jessie said sarcastically, "I imagine you are an expert with drugs! That's how you make your money, isn't it?"

Jessie warily watched as warring emotions seemed to spar with each other in Harold's face: anger, hurt, anxiety, his desire to please her? She was relieved when his smile returned. "Okay, I admit it. I do deal in drugs. I needed money to do all of this — for you." Eagerness brimmed in his voice, "But if you aren't pleased about that, I'll give it up. I can go back to ranching completely. Or — I wouldn't really have to work at all — and we could travel, see the world."

"You are forgetting something," Jessie said carefully. "I'm a married woman and also a mother. I could never live without my children."

"We'll get a quickie Mexican divorce and get custody of the children. Money can buy almost anything, you know."

Before she could think of an intelligent answer, Harold suddenly went taut and wary. Cocking his head, he seemed to be listening. Jessie could hear nothing but obviously Harold did. He made her think of a cougar, poised for attack.

Then Jessie heard it too, the purr of a vehicle, which quickly turned into a roar. The room wasn't soundproof after all! She heard the scream of tires as if someone were charging up to the house, and then the squeal of tires braking on gravel. The loud clamor of a vehicle's horn and the revving of an engine rasped loudly on her ears. It sounded like Tobe's pick-up horn and engine! Hope surged into her being. "Dear God, if that's Tobe, protect him and help him to get me out of here," she whispered in her heart.

"What the. . . ." Harold turned quickly and dashed from the room, slamming the door as he went out. Jessie sprinted toward the door but didn't reach it in time to catch it, and the door crashed to. Hopefully, she tried the door, but it was locked again. Angrily she kicked at the door but only succeeded in bruising her toes.

If that was Tobe outside, he was also in grave danger. Formidable Julio, and probably at least another thug or so, lurked somewhere on the grounds and they were surely armed — and those evil guard dogs! "Don't let anything happen to Tobe, Father," Jessie prayed fervently.

"Harold will be back," she said aloud. "And he'll drug me again and hide me somewhere!" She knew it! And then Tobe might never find her! "I've got to find the drugs if they're here." She tried to think intelligently, but her head was spinning with anxiety and her heart was raging almost out of control.

Although she listened intently, Jessie could hear nothing. Where had Harold gone? Would he come back right away? Would she be able to find the drugs before he came back. She had to try. This suite had been prepared especially for her and everything needed was here. If Harold planned to keep using drugs on her, logically they would be in her suite.

"Think!" she told herself, as her eyes flitted about the room. Moving quickly to the sitting room, she spied the small refrigerator and cabinet Harold had mentioned in a corner, and even a microwave. Looking into each, she quickly assessed their contents. The refrigerator held only milk, sodas, juices, cold cuts, cheese and lettuce. Only a few cans of meats, soups, and crackers lined the three short shelves of the pantry but nothing that looked like a drug.

She searched the medicine cabinet in the bathroom and the dresser drawers, which held such lovely lingerie that she couldn't resist briefly holding a silky garment to her cheek. Finally, after searching frantically for long moments, she stood in the middle of the bedroom and sighed. Maybe he didn't keep any drugs here. But, since he planned to incarcerate her here, it just seemed logical to assume the drugs would be kept here handy; everything else was.

She wandered about the room, touching items for several minutes trying to imagine where he would hide them — if, indeed they were hidden here. Sitting down at the desk, she slid open a drawer and was about to close it when she noticed the drawer was shallow. Excitement fluttered in her stomach. Pulling out the drawer, she set it on the desk top and peered in the drawer opening. A small box was tucked onto a little shelf at the back! With trembling hands, she drew it out. To her amazement, it wasn't even locked, and when she lifted the lid, she saw two bottles, and syringes in a plastic bag.

She scanned the labels. Both contained valium — quick to work and powerful! Even the dosage was inscribed on the bottles. I must hurry, she thought, before Harold catches me.

Chapter 18

Tobe wasted no time as they sped out of the goat ranch yard, headed for Harold's house to find Jessie. Before Ann put Juana's bag in the back seat she peeked in. "Burritos," she said. "It looks like about six of them and do they smell good! When we get back on smoother road, I plan to eat one of those. I'm starved."

"Sounds good. From the smell, I'd bet they're good," Chet said.

Tobe drove fast but kept the truck under control as he maneuvered over the dirt road.

Chet grabbed his cell phone to call the Sheriff's office; the same duty officer picked up the phone on the first ring. "This is Chet Upshaw, has Alredd left yet."

"Yes sir, he is on the way."

"Can you patch me in so that I can talk to him."

"Coming right up."

"Alredd here."

"This is Upshaw, Jessie has been moved, I repeat Jessie has been moved. Her abductor took her to his ranch on the other side of the Cedar Hills. He took her up a county maintained road just about a mile this side of the Grant county line."

"That sounds like Harold Young's old place."

"You got it. What's your location?"

"I just pulled into the court house. The Judge promised to have a search warrant ready, it shouldn't take long. Sheriff Brady will be just behind me. He's bringing a drug sniffing dog and his handler. I have two deputies with me, we should have plenty of fire power."

"How are you feeling, Chet," Ann asked when Chet pressed the end button. "Those guys really worked you over."

"You can say that again!" Chet said. "I think they would have killed me if Harold hadn't intervened and for the life of me I'll never understand why he did." He stretched gingerly. "I hurt all over but it's just a dull ache and I can move better now. I'm even getting a little sight back in my worst eye so the swelling must be going down. That ice-pack Rachel got me really helped."

They had arrived at the highway, and Tobe took the south end leading to Columbus and Highway 9. He drove as fast as he dared, slowing down some in Columbus as there seemed to be a celebration of some sort under way, and the traffic was thick. Ann and Chet each ate one of the burritos and told Tobe how good they were, but he was too revved up to eat, he said.

The rear end of the truck slid sideways as he turned onto highway 9, but Tobe caught it expertly and the engine roared anew as he straightened out in the new direction.

For awhile all three were quiet. Suddenly Ann's eyes widened and she sat forward with a jerk. "I've got it! I've got it!" she almost yelled.

Both men turned to stare at her in astonishment. Tobe swerved the truck and put his eyes quickly back on the road. "Don't yell like that. You want to make me wreck us!"

"What have you got?" Chet asked.

"I know when Harold put that sweater in Tobe's truck. I caught him in a picture, standing next to Tobe's pick-up with the door open. Everyone else was off working the cattle and I was taking a picture of Bethann. Harold was over by the barn, in the background and I didn't even know he was in the snapshot until I had them developed. I kept thinking that picture was trying to tell me something but I couldn't figure out what it was!"

"Yeah," Chet said excitedly. "I recall the picture. I'm not on the ball or I would have wondered why he was fooling around inside Tobe's pick-up."

"I can't believe Harold could be so rotten," Ann said, with vehemence. "Tobe, he defended you to the high heavens to everyone, and then planted the sweater to make you look guilty!"

Tobe only shook his head in unbelief.

"If only I had looked more closely at that snapshot, I could have blown it up and I believe we could have seen what he had in his hand," Ann lamented.

"No doubt it would have been in a sack, or wrapped," Chet said.

"But he would at least have had to answer some questions and we might have started looking at him as a suspect, maybe found Jessie sooner."

"We haven't found her yet," Tobe said grimly. He took a deep exasperated breath. "If Harold has harmed Jessie, I'll kill him with my bare hands!"

"Easy, Tobe," Chet said gently. "I know this is hard but we are all three going to need cool heads to do what has to be done.

So let's try not to think of "ifs", and do some thinking and planning about how we're going to handle this. Okay?"

Tobe took another couple of deep breaths and then said a bit unsteadily, "You're right, of course." Ann agreed and they all lapsed into silence and thought.

Highway 9 going west out of Columbus is a two lane black top with some snaky sharp curves. Tobe drove fast but with skill and some caution on the worst curves. They made good time and were soon at the turn off.

The county road, C001, Chet noted, was freshly graded and the going was fairly smooth. When they reached the large wash, they were surprised to find a good road leading off toward the mountains. The road was not as wide as the county would have made, but it was graveled and relatively smooth. Nothing could be seen of Harold's ranch house from there but they knew the road must lead there and Tobe didn't slow down much as he turned onto it.

Shortly after the turn Tobe abruptly stopped in the middle of the road. The sun was getting low, spreading a bloody glow over some hills about fifteen miles away. To Chet's utter astonishment Tobe said with utmost sincerity, "Why don't one of you say a prayer. We are going to need it."

"Absolutely," Chet agreed and at Ann's nod, he said reverently, "Heavenly Father, you see the mission we are on and we know you are always with us, but we ask right now for special blessings on the three of us and on Jessie. Protect her and us and direct us how to conduct this rescue effort. Please let there be as little violence as possible but if there has to be some, give us strength and courage to do whatever needs to be done to recover Jessie from her captors. In Jesus' dear name, we ask this. Amen."

Tobe and Ann voiced a quiet echo of his "amen." Tobe turned to face Ann and Chet and said with a catch in his voice, "While I was in jail I gave my life to the Lord Jesus." His voice quivered and he swallowed hard.

Chet and Ann both stared at him in stunned amazement as Tobe continued, "It's all my fault Jessie ran out in the storm. I've been a bear to get along with lately." He almost choked then steadied his voice, "I never hit Jessie like her mother thinks I did but I yelled at her and threw things and made her cry. I've been a complete jerk!"

His eyes still held the pain of remorse, but suddenly his lips quirked into a half-grin, "Do you guys remember Pastor Frederick reading that poem to us kids several times, about Jesus being the hound of heaven?" When both nodded, he chuckled softly. "The hound of heaven has been on my trail for months now and I've been the most miserable man alive and I took it out on Jessie. God had to get me in jail before I was willing to listen to His voice."

He turned back and started the truck. "I just wanted you both to know — and Jessie — that in case something happens to me in the next few hours — that everything's right between me and the Lord now."

Ann grabbed Tobe and hugged him hard and Chet congratulated him.

"Tobe, that is so marvelous!" Ann said. "Chet and I had agreed to pray together for you!"

Tobe grinned boyishly as he pulled out, "Thanks, I suspected you were. Now, let's go get Jessie."

"Yeah, we'd better get in there," Chet said quickly, "It will be dark soon and we need to look around while we can still see."

The road followed the wash as it curved slightly left and angled around the base of a hill. The taller hills behind it were bare of any trees. Chet wondered why they were named The Cedar Mountains, since there wasn't a Cedar in sight. In the valley off to the left Chet could see numerous cultivated fields, some of which were green; probably alfalfa.

When they rounded the hill to where they could see the other side Tobe pulled up. Before them was a mesquite flat. The mesquite trees had been thinned so that they created a park like effect. The ranch house was set higher on the hill and overlooking a small pond with some large cottonwood trees growing along it's banks. Someone had dammed the wash to form the pond but there must be a spring to supply enough water to keep it full, Chet decided.

The house looked enormous and rose two stories. There was a thick Adobe wall about ten feet high that circled the house. The wall had been plastered and white washed. The road disappeared into a wrought iron gate installed in the center of the wall. On the east corner of the wall, stood a guard tower. Behind the wall only part of the huge white house could be seen. Chet noticed the top of a rounded portico that he assumed to be the entrance.

"I can't see Harold's truck," Tobe said quietly, "It's probably in the yard behind the gate. I wonder who else is there. If the ranch is as big as Juana said it was there will need to be some Vaqueros on the place. Could be some of the drug people about also."

Using Tobe's field glasses, Chet examined the wall and the tower. There appeared to be no guards. "Tobe, we both grew up in this type of terrain. We know how to get around in it. Let's hide the truck behind that clump of mesquite and have a little look-see. Ann, you stay with the truck but keep your eyes open. We may need to get out of here in a hurry."

Ann didn't appear to be very happy to stay with the truck but agreed to go along with the plan. Tobe parked the truck and climbed out. Chet met him in front of the truck. "Why don't you go that way and I'll take this side. The brush should help shield us," he said, pointing. "Let's try to meet back here in thirty minutes."

Tobe nodded and trudged off in the indicated direction. Chet started off, crouching low and following a small coulee. He emerged behind a huge hackberry tree and using all available cover, worked his way to the back of the wall.

Thankfully, he saw that the wall across the back was unfinished. A gap of about fifteen feet had about three feet left to be finished in the center. The workers had left a scaffold in place, no doubt planning to work on it at some future time. Here was a way in. Chet could hear snuffling sounds coming from the other side of the wall.

He climbed the scaffold and looked cautiously over the wall into an impressive flower garden. A hedge of oleander stretched around three sides of the wall, its white and red blossoms bright against the thick adobe wall. Beds of brilliant-colored flowering plants were arranged artistically in the smoothly manicured lawn.

A path led around the mansion, going through a small gate on each side, disappearing toward the front of the building. Chet had been leaning over the wall when suddenly an enormous mongrel dog leaped up from the ground toward him, almost reaching the top of the wall. He jerked back in shock and almost fell off the scaffold. Another dog, a mite smaller but just as ferocious and determined to reach him, followed the first like a jumping jack, springing upward as far as his long legs could reach, then falling back. Neither dog barked. How very strange! Must be trained guard dogs — trained to kill, he thought with a shudder.

Other than the dogs, no living thing was in sight, and all was quiet. But how were they to get past the dogs? Chet sat back on the scaffold and thought for a moment. Then he grinned to himself. Reaching over to his right, he twisted a thin branch from an oleander bush that stuck above the wall, folded it's slender length until it would fit in one of the plastic bags he always carried in his pocket. Then he swiftly retraced his steps back towards the truck.

When he reached the truck, Tobe had already arrived. They met in front of the truck and Ann hurried to join them. "I didn't see anyone on that side," Tobe said.

"I didn't see anyone, either. If there are any guards they are keeping mighty low. Have you seen anything, Ann?" They had left her the binoculars.

"No, I didn't see anything moving. But it is getting late so we had better do something quick."

"Yeah, and we are probably on our own," Tobe muttered, "No telling how long it will take Alredd to get that search warrant."

"There are a couple of guard dogs," Chet said. "It looks like they have the run of the inner compound. They were completely silent so they are probably trained killers. We've got to get rid of them. I've got an idea, unless you two have a better one." He pulled the twig from the bag. "Oleander."

"Yes!" Ann said, quickly catching on to what he had in mind. "We can crush some and mix it with Juana's burritos to cover the taste. If the dogs will eat it, the oleander will put them out of commission for quite a while."

"Will that really work?" Tobe asked.

"I think so," Ann said. "It's worth a try, if they'll eat it."

"I think they'll eat it all right. They are as thin as rails," Chet said grimly.

"How long does it take?" Tobe asked.

"Should work immediately. I've read about it. We won't give them enough to kill them but they will be pretty sick and disoriented for a while," Chet said.

"Ok, hopefully that'll take care of the dogs," Tobe said. "There will probably be at least two or three guards — and if we guessed right Harold will be there, and Jessie. Any ideas of the best way to get Jessie out without her getting hurt — or one of us killed or hurt?"

"I have an idea," Ann said quickly.

"Harold is my cousin, so I don't think he will hurt me. So, if everyone agrees, you two could feed the bait to the dogs and when they are out of the way, slip inside the compound walls. You could give me a sign when you are in place beside the front door, and then I'll drive right up to the gate and honk the horn and blink the lights until someone comes out. Then you can try to disarm anyone who comes out the door."

"That sounds awfully dangerous," Chet said anxiously. "We could bring down an army on you — and us."

"I don't think so. You said it was very quiet around the place. And most Mexican people are not quiet — they love to chatter and play music and sing. Remember there was a big fiesta going on in Columbus and I'll bet most, if not all, of the hands have gone to that."

Tobe looked distressed, "Ann, I don't want to get you killed. They might come out shooting!"

Ann laughed, "I don't believe Harold would let them harm me. Unless you have a better plan?" Chet and Tobe accepted the plan reluctantly.

"I'll get the burritos then," and she went to the pickup truck.

"I'm not real happy about putting Ann at risk," Tobe said worriedly, but I don't think Harold will let anything happen to her, and I can't think of anything better."

"I'm not happy with it either," Chet said, "but we can't do anything from here and we will do our best to protect her."

In the fading light Tobe broke the remaining burritos into halves and fourths and handed them to Ann. Chet tore off a few leaves, crushed them and the small stems, and Ann pressed them into the halves and pulled the edges around them so the oleander was inside. She formed some smaller baits — using the quarters of burritos, and some larger.

"The bigger ones are for the big dog," she said. She wrapped the baits in the wax paper Juana had wrapped the burritos in, and handed them to the men. "Good luck," she said.

Tobe handed Chet a piece of the rope he had taken out of his pickup and coiled a piece about his own shoulder. "We might need this," he said. They set off, Chet in the lead. He followed the same route as before. They could barely find their way as the desert quickly darkened. By the time they reached the break in the wall, objects were barely discernible but Chet could clearly hear the snuffling sounds behind the wall and knew the vicious guard dogs were waiting.

Chapter 19

Chet and Tobe climbed the scaffold, peering cautiously over the wall. Sure enough the big dog leaped for them, scrabbling at the wall with his claws, trying to reach the top. The smaller brute sprang a second later. The huge one nearly reached the top. Unwrapping the bait balls, they leaned over and waited for the next leap. Chet had the bigger balls, Tobe, the smaller. The next time the dog leaped, mouth wide open, Chet tossed a ball directly into the gaping maw. The big dog had no choice but to swallow it. A second later Tobe tossed one of his balls into the smaller dog's wide-open mouth when she bounded upward. She gulped it down with one snap of her powerful jaws. Just for good measure they fed them all the balls, which they seemed to relish.

Now there was nothing to do but wait until the dogs went to sleep — hopefully. They sat down on the scaffold, listening carefully to the sounds from the other side. Shortly, no sounds could be heard. Chet looked over the wall but by now it was full dark and nothing could be seen. There was a lighted window in the house with no blind. Chet saw two men sitting at a table drinking. It was Julio and Chudo.

Chet let out a small gasp and pointed. "It's the two who stomped me," he whispered.

Tobe nodded and pointed down. Chet felt his heart hammering against his ribs as he poised on top of the wall. Fervently, he breathed a prayer that the dogs were asleep and not at the foot of the wall, silently waiting. They slipped over the wall and dropped to the ground together. Chet landed on something soft and quickly stepped aside. He knelt, groping. He felt a dog's rough hair and hot breath on his hand and jerked his hand back; a tingle of fear slithered down his back. Then he heard the even breathing of the animal and stood up with slightly quivering legs and moved after Tobe. He didn't wait to check on the other dog's whereabouts.

They felt their way around the house, heading for the front. Dim light spilled from the windows, helping them to avoid objects. The yard was mostly clear, indicating no children played there. When they reached the front Chet, discerned a small rock wall about three feet from the house. A concrete walk ran along the building to the entrance portico. A bushy shrub framed either side of the gallery opening. Chet took one side and Tobe the other, each crouched low and watchful. Tobe whistled like a mocking bird — the prearranged signal.

Chet held his breath. Would Ann be able to hear the whistle? Then suddenly he heard the roar of Tobe's pickup engine. The sound quickly approached the front gate. The horn started to blow and the lights flashed on and off. The engine raced and the spotlight on the left side flashed back and forth across the front of the building. Chet grimaced.

"Don't overdo it, Ann," he murmured nervously.

A light sprang to life in the entranceway and quick footsteps sounded in their ears. Someone was coming to investigate! A thick-bodied man peered from the sheltered entrance and then slid out the opening, hugging the wall on Chet's side. His beefy left hand clutched a gun, finger on the trigger, while his shaggy head swung warily from side to side.

Chet struck the man on the wrist with the edge of his left hand while his right struck the gunman a hard blow in the neck. The gun clattered on the path, and he slumped slightly. Chet's right arm circled his neck and he applied the old Indian sleeper hold. In just a few seconds the man was fast asleep. Tobe moved over and picked up the gun Chudo had dropped and slipped it into his waistband.

They silently hauled the man behind the bushes and Tobe swiftly trussed up the hulking bracero with a length of rope, like a Christmas turkey. Chet stuffed a none too clean handkerchief in his mouth as a gag. It was then that he got a good look at the man — Chudo. That left at least Harold and Julio, formidable adversaries and probably heavily armed. They dragged him further back into the shrubbery and left him.

The commotion at the gate had ceased. The pickup lights still blazed and Chet could see Ann fumbling with the gate. His heart thudded in fear. Slipping silently to the gate, he whispered, "Get back in the truck, Ann, and lock the door! It's not safe out here. Tobe and I'll take care of things from here on out."

Relieved when Ann obeyed, Chet wondered uneasily if she would stay there, as he glided back toward Tobe. In the glare of

Tobe's truck lights, Chet saw Harold's powerful diesel truck parked in the driveway. So Harold must be here — and Jessie! "Dear God, don't let anything happen to Ann and help us to find Jessie and get her out of here without any of us getting hurt," he murmured.

Tobe motioned toward the portico and they moved quickly through the entrance and into a hallway which led back to an arched opening some twenty-five feet away. Although the hall was only dimly lighted by small recessed lamps, Chet's darting eyes saw no one. They covered that distance in a rush, then peered around the archway into a long, wide hall. It was empty and silent, and Chet felt unease slide over him like an icy fog. Julio was here somewhere and he must have heard Ann's noisy entrance with Tobe's truck. And where was Harold — and Jessie? The place was eerily quiet.

A hallway veered off to the left and Tobe loped off down it. Chet glimpsed a winding stairway winding upward, in the dim light straight ahead but decided to investigate the right hallway first. Swinging into a trot, he soon came to a long, wide room, floored in polished hardwood. Perhaps it was used for dancing or some other form of entertainment. Chet sprinted across it and started through the door. A gallery with many windows opened before him and ran both directions.

The room was only lighted by the faint moonlight that filtered in, and shadows formed by a few pieces of furniture here and there along the length could hold any number of skulking men — or even another of those silent guard dogs. Fear prickled at the nape of his neck and sweat popped out on his forehead. The unknown is always more fearful than the known, he reminded himself. For a moment, he stood silently, listening. He heard no sound and a cold shiver ran down his back. The quiet was absolute and it disturbed him. Where was Julio? Where was Harold?

Straining to see down the long gallery, Chet decided to try the right wing and treading as silently as he could, and hugging the inside wall, he slipped along quickly. Moving warily, with eyes probing into the corners and shadows, Chet was soon at the end of the wide salon.

He glided toward the door and suddenly the room burst into light, almost blinding him. Shielding his startled eyes with his hand so he could see, he felt shock rock him to his toes. Julio stood in front of him, to the right of the door, with a sneer on his brutal face. Held in front of him with a muscular arm about her throat and a swarthy hand over her mouth, was Ann!

"Hola! Look what I found," Julio chortled.

Cold fear gripped Chet. He knew that Julio was completely void of mercy, indeed gloried in cruelty.

"Let her go!" Chet commanded.

"Listen at how the little gringo worm orders around his betters," Julio said with a chuckle. His voice hardened and became an almost animal-like snarl, "I beat you up once and would have killed you if El Jefe had not interfered. This time he won't be so charitable with meddlers, I'm sure. So I'm going to break you in little pieces and then peg you to the ground like my Indian ancestors used to do to their enemies. You'll die of thirst, ants or buzzards — whatever gets you first!"

He shoved Ann away from him and she tottered across the floor and fell against the wall not far from Chet. Pulling out a gun from his waist-band, Julio pointed it first at Chet and then swung it a little to cover both of them.

Chet spoke softly, "Get behind me, Ann."

Julio let out a howl of laughter as she complied. "That's a mucho shaky tree to be hiding behind, Chiquita."

Chet charged straight at him. As an obviously startled Julio tried to line up the gun on him, Chet went into a slide like a baseball player, feet first towards Julio, and plowed hard into Julio's legs. The gun went flying across the room. Chet's momentum carried them both nearly to the wall and under a straight-backed chair, which shattered.

Julio landed in a tangled heap on top of Chet's legs. Chet managed to hit him twice before both scrambled to their feet. They faced each other for a moment, Julio with a sneer and Chet with hard determination. Chet had already decided that if he got this chance he could show no mercy. This man was totally vicious, willing to stomp him to death with his boots.

They moved forward almost in unison, trading hard blows to anyplace they could land one. Chet, after a few exchanges, began to work on Julio's body. He had fought men like Julio before, men who were incredibly strong but weak in the midsection. Julio hurt him every time he landed a blow but Chet refused to go down. Every chance he got he slugged

Julio in the solar plexus with his powerful right hand. Chet saw Julio begin to weaken and he kicked out, striking Julio behind his left knee.

Panting hard, Julio fell to his side, immediately covering up, apparently expecting Chet to kick him while he was down. Chet backed off, and allowed Julio to stand before stepping in to slug him in the abdomen again, then kicked him behind the same knee. Julio fell again. This time he rose much more slowly, his breath coming in great rasping gasps. Chet waded in to finish him off. He knocked him against the wall and followed up, hitting him repeatedly in the face, neck and mid section. Julio finally crumpled, not to rise again. Chet's arms felt like lead. Moving to the wall, he leaned on it for a moment gasping for breath.

"Are you all right?" Ann asked solicitously. When he nodded, too winded to speak, Ann said with a grin, "You're quite a fighter, City-Boy."

Wincing against the pain of a split lip, Chet tried to grin. "Believe me, I got some help from upstairs! That is one muy malo hombre!" He stood away from the wall and, using some of Tobe's rope, he bound Julio's hands behind his back and tied his feet tightly together. Then he lugged Julio over to a closet, dumped him in and closed the door. "We don't want him to be found too quick and released."

"I've got Julio's gun," Ann said. "I had planned to shoot him if he took you out!"

Chet looked up in amazement. "Could you have done that?"

"You bet I could have! It would have been him or us and I didn't plan for it to be us! But you can have it now. I'm not real wild about guns," she finished, handing Chet the weapon.

Tucking the gun under his belt, Chet wiped the blood from his lip and the sweat from his bruised face. "Let's go see if Tobe has found Jessie," he said.

"I haven't found her," Tobe said grimly, as he walked down the gallery toward them. "But I see you found Julio. Good thinking, to put him out of sight for now."

He sighed, "I must have wandered around like a lost person and came back to where we started. And I haven't seen a soul. Surely Jessie and Harold are here somewhere."

Chet saw that Tobe's face was drawn and pale with worry. "We'll find her," Chet tried to speak comfortingly, but his thoughts were ranging out to other frightening possibilities. Could Harold have left his men to do his fighting for him while he took Jessie and fled? If Harold took her away — perhaps out of the country — and hid her, it might be very difficult to find her! Perhaps they never would!

Chapter 20

Jessie was standing at the window of the bedroom, straining to see out. Hoping to appease Harold in every way she could, she had changed into a handsome Levi pantsuit, with long sleeves and large patch pockets. She had chosen it for its modestly fashioned wide legs and loose, embroidered top.

She could see nothing outside, it was pitch black. Were the two fierce dogs still roaming around out there? Could that be why the back yard was unlighted, so the dogs could attack any intruders without being seen themselves? Her heart quaked for Tobe; she was confident in her heart that the vehicle she had heard was Tobe's. But why had he sounded the alarm that he was out there?

Maybe it wasn't Tobe! Perhaps the vehicle carried drug dealers — Harold's customers or suppliers. Yes, that was more likely. Harold had certainly been gone a long time. Although she dreaded his return, the waiting was getting on her nerves. At that moment, Jessie's sharp ears caught a slight noise and she turned quickly, her heart hammering.

Although she had not heard the door open, Harold stood just inside the door with a faint smile on his handsome face. "I'm sorry to be so long but I had some checking to do. Julio and Chudo seem to have vanished — at least I can't raise them on their phones. And intruders are inside the house."

The smug look on Harold's face caused Jessie's heart to lurch with fear. "Tobe's here?"

"Yep," Harold said with satisfaction. "Apparently the boys weren't able to stop them, but that just leaves me to do the job and I look forward to the pleasure." Eagerness glittered in his agate hard eyes.

"Wha— what are you going to do?" Jessie found herself stammering, her insides quivering with terror. What was it about this new Harold that made her knees trembly and her mouth dry? *Snap out of it, Jessie,* she ordered herself sternly, *this is the time to have some backbone — for Tobe's sake, if not for your own.*

Harold had not answered for a moment and then he said sharply, "What am I going to do? I'm going to get rid of those meddlers, that's what — for good!"

"Are you sure Tobe is out there?"

"I'm sure," Harold said harshly, "with two other meddlers, Ann and that reporter, Chet Upshaw!"

"You saw them?"

"Yes, I saw them. They're searching the house — my house! The gall of them storming in here like they own the place! I'll stamp them out like cockroaches!"

"Harold," Jessie said, aghast, "Tobe and Ann are your cousins — your own blood kin. You wouldn't harm them? They're only searching for me. Just let me go, and I'm sure they'll walk out of here without a word of what has happened."

Harold looked at her like she had lost her mind. Marching over to her, he grabbed both shoulders, a crazed light in his eyes. "I'll never let you go! You are mine now! And I would kill you before I let you go back to that loser of a cousin of mine!" He shook her savagely, "Don't make me hurt you!"

Too terrified to form a reply, Jessie suddenly saw the maddened glitter fade from Harold's eyes. He stepped back and said pleadingly, "Don't make me hurt you, Jessica. I love you."

Jessie dropped her eyes, shaken to her toes. *He is absolutely insane,* she thought.

He jumps from one extreme to the other in the flick of an eye and he could very well kill me — and all the others. *Heavenly Father, please help us!*

"Lie down on the bed," Harold ordered.

"What are you going to do to me?"

"Don't worry, I'm not going to hurt you," Harold said gently, "I'm just going to give you a shot to put you to sleep for a bit. I don't want you awake when our "visitors" arrive at the door."

"No, please, don't do that!"

Harold's voice took on a stern note, "Do as I say! You won't feel but a prick." Taking hold of her shoulders, he pushed her toward the bed. "Now, lie down and relax."

Jessie complied and watched Harold walk to the desk, remove the drawer, take out the box and fill a syringe. As he advanced to the bed, she closed her eyes tightly and clinched her fists. "Relax and it won't hurt at all," Harold said soothingly. "See, that wasn't bad, was it?" And amazingly, she had scarcely felt the prick.

"How long will it be before it takes affect?" Jessie murmured.

"I inserted it in a vein, so you should begin to feel it immediately. That wouldn't even be a bad way to die, would it?"

"D-die?"

Harold chuckled, "Don't worry, you aren't going to die, you'll just have a nice, relaxing snooze."

"Yes — a nice. . . ." Jessie's body went limp, her head dropped sideways and her breathing slowed to an even rhythm.

"Sleep well, my love," Harold said softly. "I'll be right here beside you when those meddlers get here." His laugh held an ugly edge.

Chapter 21

"Have you been upstairs, yet?" Ann asked.

"No, as I told you I seemed to get myself lost and didn't even see the stairs again."

"I know the way," Chet said.

"Ann, maybe you should go back to the pick-up and wait," Tobe said worriedly. "Harold is, without a doubt, armed to the teeth. And he's not going to give Jessie up without a fight."

"No, I want to see this to the finish," Ann said, with a tilt to her stubborn jaw.

"At least stay back behind us, Ann," Chet said.

"Okay, lead the way, City Boy."

As swiftly and cautiously as possible, the three moved through rooms and halls until they came to the main entrance. Chet led the way through the dim hall to the curving stairway. All of them stared upward, searching the stairs for movement, before starting to climb. Tobe now moved to take the lead, as they hugged the left hand banister, treading softly on the deeply carpeted rungs. Small recessed lamps illuminated the steps.

Reaching the top, Chet saw that a gallery, covered with thick wine-colored carpet, stretched both ways. A waist-high balustrade ran the length of the open side. On the other side of the hall, at various intervals, he could see doors. Shaded lamps shed a soft illumination.

"He's probably in one of those rooms," Tobe said softly, "but which one?"

"Why don't we stick together from here on out," Chet suggested. "Do you still have the gun you took from that first thug? I have Julio's."

"It's right here," Tobe said, tapping his belt. "Let's try each door and charge right in, so we don't warn him. Ann, keep to the side of the doors, in case. . . ." He broke off as the door right across from them opened and Harold stood there.

For a long moment no one moved or spoke.

Then Tobe took a step toward Harold and demanded, "Where's my wife?"

"What are you doing here, Tobe? There's no reason for you to be here, Jessie doesn't want to go back. She prefers to stay with me." Harold's tone was mild and friendly.

"You dirty scoundrel," Tobe said, taking

another couple of steps toward his cousin. "I want to see Jessie, and I want to see her now! If you've hurt her, I'll. . . ."

"As I said, she doesn't want to see you," Harold interrupted. His voice now held an edge.

"I will see her, right now!"

A gun appeared in Harold's hand so swiftly that Chet blinked. "You don't give the orders around here, Buddy Boy," Harold said harshly. "You're on my turf now — and in my house." His blue eyes glittered dangerously and a chill finger traced its way down Chet's back.

Then, even in the faint light of the gallery, Chet saw the grin that slid onto Harold's face, while his tone changed to a purr. "However, I suppose you have a right to see Jessica. She's taking a little nap and can't be waked up right now, but you can see her if you like. In fact," he waved his arm expansively, "you can all come in and see her. Come on in."

He stepped back, pressed a switch and the room burst into dazzling light.

Half blinded by the brilliant light, they moved hesitantly into the spacious, sumptuously furnished suite. Chet's eyes flashed about the room and came to rest upon the king-sized bed. Jessie lay on her side upon the bed, facing them, fully clothed except for shoes, her head and shoulders resting upon a fat, silky pillow. Her right arm lay relaxed at her side and her left hand was curled-up near her face. Chet quickly took in her slow, even breathing and closed eyes, and breathed a little easier. Jessie was still alive!

"What have you done to her," Tobe asked angrily.

Harold had instantly moved to stand next to the side of the bed, his left hand placed possessively upon the quilted coverlet near Jessie, while his right held the gun steadily upon the three of them.

Harold's eyes held an amused glint, "You drove your wife away, into a snow storm, no less, and I rescued her. If I hadn't, she would probably have frozen to death. So, I'm surprised you're so concerned about her now."

Tobe almost choked with fury and his eyes flashed fire, as he shouted, "I didn't drive her away. She chose to go, and I didn't know the storm was so bad. She always ran up to Ann's cabin when we had a spat, so she should have been safe. Awww, I don't have to explain my actions to you! You kidnapped my wife! Now get out of my way and let me see if Jessie is okay!"

Harold laughed. "Of course she's okay. She's just asleep!"

"Then why doesn't she wake up?" Tobe took a step toward Jessie and when Harold didn't say or make a move, he advanced to the foot of the bed, stretched out a long arm and touched her foot, and said gently, "Jessie, Honey, wake up!"

When she didn't even stir, Chet felt a cold, empty feeling start somewhere in the vicinity of his stomach.

Tobe patted her foot and spoke loudly — and a little desperately this time, Chet felt. "Jessie, wake up. I've come to take you home!"

Harold chuckled, "See, didn't I tell you she didn't want to talk to you. She'd rather sleep."

Tobe glared at Harold and then charged around the bed toward Harold. Instantly Harold lifted the gun and pointed it menacingly at Tobe. When Tobe halted briefly but seemed on the verge of coming on, he spoke softly but his eyes were two coals of glowing blue fire. "I wouldn't do that, Tobe. You don't feel like committing suicide, do you?"

Tobe backed away a step, breathing hard. "You've knocked her out with something, haven't you!"

"Let's get down to brass tacks now, Tobe. And the rest of you listen too, and listen good! Yes, I have given her something — a poison that will kill her unless she gets an antidote within thirty minutes. I'm the only one who knows what I gave her, and I'm the only one who can save her."

Chet heard Ann's quick gasp. Tobe's face had gone bone-white.

Harold stopped his tirade, and stared coldly at each one in turn and then continued, "I'm giving you a break, why I don't know, unless it's because blood is thicker than water. But thirty minutes will give you plenty of time to clear out of here and get off my property. If you want to save Jessie, you'll get out, now!"

He paused and said coldly, "Remember, I have her now and I'll never give her up. If anyone tries this again, I'll kill her, and you! If I can't have her, neither can you, Tobe. Now, what's it going to be?"

He paused and raked them again with burning eyes, "I'll give you ten minutes to find your way out of my house and get in your rig and go."

"And if we don't go?" Chet asked softly.

Harold chuckled, low and savage, "If you don't go, I'll shoot you all down like dogs!"

The room was suddenly as quiet as a tomb. Chet knew that Death hovered over their heads with a drawn sword. Suddenly, he detected a slight movement on the bed.

Like the strike of a snake, Jessie's left arm swept out and down behind Harold and he let out a startled yelp. Harold whirled around and lashed out at Jessie with his left hand, but she had rolled out of his reach to the far side of the bed. As swift as a panther Harold spun back, his gun sweeping up, but Tobe was on him before he could get it lined up. Harold struggled to bring the gun up, but Tobe held his gun hand in an iron grip. Chet moved in and swung a clip to the back of Harold's head, stunning him, but only for a second or two.

Harold fought like a tiger to free his gun, which Tobe had forced up, pointing at the ceiling. Chet put his arm around Harold's neck in the old sleeper hold and slowly Harold began to wilt, and the weapon fell from his hand. Chet released his hold and Harold caught his breath and began to strike savagely at Tobe with both fists and it was all Tobe could do to ward off the raining blows. Chet had stepped back but now decided it was time to put an end to the fight.

But suddenly before he could move, a

strange thing happened. Harold dropped his arms, began to shake his head and mutter incoherently. His eyes took on a glazed look, then he abruptly went limp and would have fallen if Tobe hadn't grabbed him and lowered him to the floor.

"What the . . . !" Tobe exclaimed in astonishment. And Chet stood speechless.

Then, to everyone's complete astonishment, Jessie began to laugh hysterically. Tobe plunged around the bed and pulled her into his arms, saying her name over and over. Jessie continued to laugh — until Tobe drew away from her and asked anxiously, "Are you all right, Honey?"

Hiccuping, she wrapped her arms about his neck, gulped a time or two and said softly, "Now I am."

"Honey, can you ever forgive me?" Tobe said, stroking her hair, "I've been such a fool. I've been nearly crazy — not knowing what happened to you and knowing it was my fault."

Jessie, moved away from him and placed her hands on each side of his face, "I-I thought I would never see your face again, Tobe." Her voice broke, "And it was not your fault! It was mine! I should never have been a bossy old nag, like that. I've asked God to forgive me over and over.

Will you forgive me?"

"There's nothing to forgive, Jessie. But if it will make you feel better, yes, I forgive you a hundred times over, if you will forgive me."

For an answer, Jessie snuggled her head into his chest. "Just hold me, Tobe; hold me tight, and don't ever let me go."

While this was going on, Chet had discreetly turned his back and was examining Harold. Ann came to his side and whispered, "Wasn't that the strangest thing. Harold just collapsed."

Chet spoke in a puzzled voice, "Yes, it is odd. He pressed a vein in Harold's neck with two fingers. "He has a strong, steady pulse."

"I know what's wrong with him," Jessie said from Tobe's arms. "I drugged him!"

"You what!" Tobe exclaimed.

Jessie brushed the hair back from her face and said calmly, "Harold's been keeping me drugged whenever he wanted to. And I knew when he told me you were here, that he would put me out before you found me. So I searched and found two bottles of valium, and syringes. I dumped the drugs into a bottle from the cabinet and refilled the bottles with water. After I filled two syringes with valium, I hid one in my big patch pocket and one under my pillow. I stabbed him with the one under my pillow."

"You're a marvel," Tobe said, his eyes glowing admiringly. "Do you know that?"

"I agree," Chet said. "I'm not sure she needed anyone to rescue her."

Suddenly Jessie's lips began to tremble, as she looked into Tobe's face. "I have never been so terrified in my life, Tobe. I always thought Harold was a little strange but he's insane! He scares me to death. And he makes his money with drugs! Did you know that?"

"Not until today."

"Are the kids okay, Tobe," Jessie asked.

"Just missing their mother. But Ann has been doing a bang-up job of caring for them."

"Thank you, Ann," Jessie, going to her quickly and hugging her. "I can hardly wait to hold Beth and T.J. But I'm so sorry I have been such a worry to everyone." She crossed to Chet and held out her hand. "Thanks awfully, Chet, for your help. Harold said Mother had called you in to help find me."

"My pleasure," Chet said. "We all made a good team. Thank the Lord you are okay."

Jessie turned back to Tobe, "Harold said Mother is in Deming, too."

Tobe grinned, "Yeah, she's going to be terribly upset when she finds out I didn't do away with you."

"Tobe!"

Tobe chuckled, "Just kidding. I couldn't even be mad at your mother today. In fact, I love everything and everybody right now."

He pulled Jessie back into his arms for a moment, and then spoke softly, "Jessie, there's one good thing that's come out of this ordeal, I've given my life to the Lord Jesus."

"Oh, Tobe, how wonderful! I've also gotten closer to the Lord through this."

Suddenly Chet broke in, "Say, I think I hear the cops coming! I'll stay here and guard Harold, if someone will go down and let them in."

Chapter 22

Harold awoke with a violent start. Had he been dreaming? Opening his eyes, he blinked and then struggled violently. Was he in the midst of a terrible nightmare? Shaking his head, he found that was about all the movement he could make. His hands were in tight handcuffs and his feet encased in shackles. Stark unbelief — and fear — gripped him when he tried to raise his feet and found they were not only in chains but locked to a chair.

He tried to clear his foggy brain and make some sense of what was going on. Turning his head slowly, he saw he was seated in a chair against the wall in his own front hall. A deputy sheriff — a burly hairy male he had never seen before, sat in a chair a few yards away, flipping through the pages of one of Harold's latest magazines.

The house was a beehive of activity. His House! They were searching his house! He could hear loud noises and snatches of conversation in the background, both up and down stairs.

Closing his eyes, he strove to remember what had happened to him. Yes, it was coming back in disjointed pictures now. His gun had been on Tobe, Chet and Ann. He had given Jessica a shot and she lay silent and lovely on the bed — his at last! Everything had been under control — his control, even though Julio and Chudo had failed, he had captured his cousins and Chet.

He shook his head in bewilderment . . . then what had happened? Vaguely it was seeping back into his brain . . . A sharp object had stabbed him in the back, he had fought when both Chet and Tobe had pounced on him. Then he recalled falling into blackness. That was all he could remember.

Someone had given him a knock-out shot. Jessie? Surely not, she had been asleep — out from a shot of valium he had given her before the others got to her room. Disbelief left him almost numb. But it could have been no one else. Jessie had tricked him! After all he had done for her! Buying her this beautiful mansion, lovely expensive clothes! He would have given her anything and everything she wanted! He had bestowed his love on her and she had rewarded him by tricking him!

Rage boiled up into his throat, threatening to choke him. "I'll kill her," he muttered. "I'll kill them all!"

"I don't think you're about to kill anyone," a rough voice said sarcastically. The hulking deputy stood a couple of feet away, glaring down at him.

"Don't be too sure of that," Harold said defiantly. "I want my lawyer."

"Now that you're awake, I'm going to read your rights to you," the deputy said, and he proceeded to do so, ending with, "Do you understand these rights?"

"Of course I do," Harold said. "I'm not stupid."

"I'm not so sure of that," the deputy said with a smirk. He moved back to his chair, sat down and picked up the magazine again.

Harold's mind was churning and hate sizzled in his breast. He wasn't beaten! Struggling to bring his thoughts under control, he closed his eyes and tried to blot out all emotion, all thoughts, and after a while he partially succeeded.

After a few minutes, he began to plan. He would get that lawyer one of his suppliers had told him about — expensive and crooked, but very good. He would know how to get him out of this!

Then the sounds around him began to intrude into his thoughts. Deputies, detectives, photographers and technical experts were hurrying about, up and down stairs, staring at him as they went by — as if he were a strange creature in a cage.

I don't know if I can stand them going through my things, all the things I have collected for Jessica and everything else that I had planned to show her, he thought. Now all my plans for Jessica will never come to pass. Tobe will win! A tight band, like a steel cast, seemed to stretch about his upper body. His breath became labored and sweat broke out all over his body, dribbling down his forehead into his eyes.

I've got to get control of myself, Harold thought desperately. Gasping in great draughts of air, he soon could breath more easily.

Then a new thought exploded in his brain: They'll find the drug shipment that was to go out today! And my collection of precious stones!

Then, to his horror, Rachel's face rose up before him. His hard-working mother would be devastated when she found out he was a drug dealer — and had kidnapped

Jessica. How could he ever face her agonized face!

Trying to blot out his tormenting thoughts, Harold struggled against his bonds. If he could only get free, he wouldn't have to face Rachel's face — or his father's disapproval. For years he had tried in vain to gain Buster's approval, now all he had earned was his certain censure.

Pushing those bleak thoughts from his mind, he wondered suddenly if he would go to prison. No! Never! I would never make it in prison! Never to be able to saddle a horse and ride across the flats again. Never to break and train a young colt again.

They will confiscate my beautiful home and all my other possessions . . . and I have lost Jessica forever!

Despair tried to latch its chilly tentacles about his heart. What defense could I use, he thought, a temporary insanity plea?

No, there was nothing temporary about his drug business — or his abduction of Jessica. Everything pointed to deliberate, premeditated planning. So that would never work.

Nothing will get me out of this, he thought despondently. What could I have been thinking of? Maybe I am crazy! But the drug business had seemed like such a perfect opportunity to make lots of money — and to get Jessica for himself.

He heard the rustle of the paper as the deputy turned yet another page.

Despair washed over him in sickening waves. His life was in shambles — ruined. What could he do? Suddenly he knew what he could do — the only option he had left. His heart leaped up and something akin to elation filled him. Wheels began to spin in his fertile brain, plans to put it into effect.

"Hey, Deputy," he called, "I've got to go the bathroom."

Looking up, the officer spoke lazily, "Is that so! What do you want me to do about it."

"Take me to the bathroom, of course," Harold said, with irritation edging his voice.

"No can do," the deputy said decisively.

Harold's voice raised a notch, "I have my rights! Get me to the bathroom. My bladder is about to erupt."

The deputy grinned and said derisively, "I'm not taking you any place. My orders are to see that you don't move from this spot and that's what I plan to do."

Harold's face suffused with blood until it was almost purple. "I want my lawyer and

I want him now!"

The officer grinned wickedly and turned his eyes back to the magazine on his knees.

Looking around him wildly, Harold saw Chet down the hall talking with Deputy Alredd and called loudly, "Chet! Chet Upshaw! I need some help down here."

Chet turned Harold's way, spoke a few more words to the officer and then strode down the hall to Harold. Before Chet could say a word, Harold said angrily, "This numbskull of a pig won't let me go to the john."

Chet turned to the deputy and spoke casually, "What's your name, Deputy?"

"Who wants to know?" the officer said insolently.

"Chet Upshaw's the name, and I'm with the Las Cruces Herald." Chet's voice softened until it sounded almost threatening. "I would hate to have to report that the prisoner was not allowed to use the bathroom facilities in his own home."

"This here is a drug dealer and a kidnapper," the officer sneered. "Let him soil his clothes. Would serve him right!"

Chet took a step toward the deputy and the officer quickly placed a hand on his holstered gun. Chet raised his hand in an appeasing gesture, "Innocent until proven guilty, I believe the law reads. Now, are you going to let this man use the toilet or do I have to see Sheriff Brady?"

"Deputy Joe Hendricks!" The harsh voice spoke from behind Chet and he turned quickly. Sheriff Brady glared at the burly deputy. "We do things by the books around here. Is that understood?"

Deputy Hendricks had jumped to his feet and was now standing stiffly at attention. "Y-yes Sir!"

Sheriff Brady turned to Harold, "Where's the nearest bathroom, Mr. Helm?"

"Just down the hall," Harold said sulkily.

"Fine!" He turned to the deputy, "Deputy Hendricks, check out that bathroom and see there are no concealed weapons, then escort the prisoner there. I'll stand guard until you return."

In minutes Hendricks was back, "No weapons," he declared.

"Leave on the leg shackles and handcuffs, just unlock him from the chair," the sheriff ordered.

"B-but how can a man take care of his needs all trussed up like a turkey," Harold sputtered.

"You'll manage," the sheriff said grimly. "We don't plan to take any chances of you escaping." He pulled his gun and motioned Harold to lead the way. Harold's eyes smoldered with rage and humiliation as he hobbled along ahead of the sheriff and the deputy, chains clinking, and people peering at him from every angle, it seemed.

At the door of the bathroom, the sheriff motioned him in. "All right, go ahead and do your business and be quick about it."

"Don't I get any privacy?" Harold asked sullenly.

"I'll push the door nearly closed but that's all. If you made a suspicious move, we'll both be all over you like a swarm of bees. Now get on with it."

Swearing in an audible voice, Harold hobbled to the lavatory. The room was not large and the wash basin stood to the left of the commode. After emptying his bladder, he shuffled over to the wash basin and turned on the water.

"Gotta wash my hands," he called to the waiting officers. Then swiftly, Harold reached out and swung the toothbrush holder out to reveal a small hidden compartment. Quickly he lifted out the syringe it contained.

He had secreted these syringes in several places throughout the house, as protection against unscrupulous drug smugglers or other enemies. He grimaced. Certainly he had never intended to use them against himself.

The syringe was fully loaded with a colorless liquid. There was a protective cap over the needle, which Harold lost no time in removing. With sure movements he positioned the needle against his thigh. For just one second he hesitated, his hand shaking, then he plunged the needle in and depressed the plunger. As the pure uncut heroine flowed into his veins his thoughts were of his mother.

"You're taking too long in there," Sheriff Brady thundered from outside the door. "Come on out."

Chet had followed the two officers and Harold, even though Hendricks gave him a dirty look. When he saw the sheriff charge into the bathroom after ordering Harold out, Chet moved quickly to the door and peered into the room where the sheriff and the deputy stood. Sheriff Brady was swearing and the deputy was standing stock still with his mouth gaped open.

Chet could see Harold slumped on the floor with his head resting against the tub and an empty syringe in one manacled hand. The sheriff knelt in the close space and placed two fingers under Harold's jaw.

"He's alive but just barely," he said.

There was silence in the little room where the sounds of Harold's gasping breaths were clearly audible. Finally the sounds ceased completely and the silence somehow was louder than the gasps.

He won't have to face the music now, Chet thought. Everything now is in the hands of the law and there is nothing more I can do.

Chapter 23

Two weeks had passed since Harold's death. Jessie lay back in a lawn chair at Rachel's old ranch house, under the shade of a canopy of huge old cottonwood trees. How peaceful it all is, she thought. The faint rustling sounds of the cottonwood leaves and the murmur of the women's voices in the kitchen as they cleaned up after the sumptuous barbecue, reflected the contentment in her heart.

"You are the guest of honor — this is your welcome home party, and you're not allowed to lift a finger to help," Aunt Rachel had stated in her brusque way. And Jessie had been content to rest.

Jessie could still scarcely believe how well Rachel had taken her son's death. But although Rachel was not very vocal about her faith in God, it had sustained her throughout her life of hardship. And strangely, Buster had been there often, with a compassionate shoulder for her to lean on. He seemed to know when to tell a funny story, and when to lend some silent sympathy with an arm laid gently about his ex-wife's shoulders. Jessie wondered idly if he and Rachel would get back together. It certainly seemed to be leaning that way.

Jessie's lips curved into a gentle happy smile as she savored the past two weeks back home with Tobe and the children. Just the way a marriage should be, she thought dreamily. She relived every moment and every word spoken on the drive home with Tobe, after her nerve-racking experiences at Harold's mansion.

As Tobe and Jessie were driving away from Harold's ranch, Jessie had slipped over next to Tobe and he slid his arm around her. She sighed and put her head on his shoulder. "You know going home together is the most wonderful thing I can ever imagine. There were times during this ordeal when I was doubtful I would ever do this again."

"Me, too," Tobe said, "and I have died a hundred deaths over driving you out into that storm. Why you don't hate me is more than I can fathom."

"It wasn't any more your fault than mine," she said earnestly.

"You know, after seeing all the magnificence of Harold's home, and even seeing you in those beautiful trappings you have on, it grieves me that I can't give you more — lovely clothes, a finer home, help around the house and garden — so you don't have to work so hard."

"Clothes and a fine home don't mean anything to me after what I've been through. You work hard but you do honest work, Tobe, and I'm totally proud of you. I wouldn't trade you — and my two kids — for all the pretty clothes in the world, or servants or a mansion like Harold's."

"I've been thinking," Tobe said after a moment. "You said they had some counseling classes at the church. Maybe it would be good if I went. This temper of mine is more than I can handle sometimes. Do you think I could get some real help there?"

"Yes," Jessie said thoughtfully, "I think you could get some help, and I need some help too. Why don't we go together. We want to make our family life the best we can. And with God's help it can be better and better."

"I've also been thinking that I've never treated Beth right, never given her much attention. Perhaps she and I could do some things together and get to know each other. Do you think Beth would like that?"

"She'd love it, Tobe, she never thought you liked her."

"Be patient with me, Jessie," he said humbly. "I've got a long way to go, but I think with the Lord's help I'll get there."

"I'm sure you will," Jessie said, leaning over to kiss his cheek, "and so will I, with lots of help from our Lord."

Jessie roused herself from her reminiscing. She could hear Beth's and T.J.'s excited voices from down near the barn. A short while before — after the delicious food had been consumed and the women had cleared away the remnants and the dishes, Tobe had extended a hand to each of the children. "Come on Kids, let's go see that new colt that was born yesterday."

Tears rose in Jessie's eyes as she recalled how Bethann's eyes had lit up when her father had invited her to accompany them. True to his commitment, Tobe was carefully and lovingly cultivating a relationship with Bethann, and her eyes were filled with adoration when she looked at her dad these past few days.

The women were coming from the house now, Clara, Jessie's mother; Carolyn, Clara's sister; Ann and Rachel. As they drifted out of the ranch house toward her, Jessie thought, *I have something else to be thankful for.* Her mother had apologized for her enmity and distrust toward Tobe and had asked Tobe's forgiveness. Tobe had accepted the apology and humbly asked for her forgiveness for his rudeness in times passed. Jessie doubted that they would ever be close friends but seemingly a healthy respect had sprung up between them, so all was well on that front.

Rachel came to Jessie's side and said softly, "Come in the house with me, I have something for you." To the others, she called, "Jessie and I have a little private matter to attend to. We'll be back soon."

Mystified, Jessie followed her through the kitchen, into the hall and back to the back bedroom — Harold's bedroom. Opening a drawer, Rachel took out a long white envelope and handed it to her. Her voice wobbled just a bit as she explained, "Harold always loved secret compartments and made one for himself when he was a kid. After his funeral, I got to thinking about his secret cubbyhole and went to see what was in it. He had left you and me a letter. I'll let you read mine after you have read yours."

With butterflies fluttering in her stomach region, Jessie took the letter and slit open the envelope. It contained a hand written letter and a legal document, she quickly realized. The letter read:

Dearest Jessie,

If you get this letter it will mean I am dead. In my business, danger is a constant companion. If I am ever arrested, I don't plan on going to prison, so that is the reason for this letter. I'm fully aware that all my possessions will be stripped from me if I'm convicted of drug dealing. So if we are together, my love, and I feel we will be, you would be in poverty and I could never bear that.

I have always loved you, so even if I should die, I have made arrangements for your future security, as far as I am able.

Enclosed are trusts, made out to you. You may have scruples about using money earned from drugs. So I assure you this money is the profits I have made from cattle sales and other legitimate ranch income over the years. I have no scruples about living on drug money, so I've saved the legitimate money for you and lived on my other revenues.

Be happy, my love, and be assured that there has never been anyone else for me.

Your ever loving admirer,
Harold

Silently Jessie handed the letter to Rachel, many emotions struggling in her heart: pity, confusion, and anguish for the way Harold's obsession had dominated and ruined his life. She accepted Rachel's letter. In Harold's letter to his mother, he had praised Rachel for being a loving and supportive parent. He was appreciative of the sacrifices she had made to clothe and feed him, and educate him. He made a plea for her understanding of his involvement with drugs, and if not understanding, at least for her forgiveness.

I would have been content to be a simple rancher, he stated, but I needed to make lots of money so I could win Jessica's love. I'm sorry if I have caused you great grief, but my first obligation had to be to try to win Jessica. You loved my father once, so you surely know how I feel.

I love you,
Your son, Harold

A sob rose into Jessie's throat as she

handed the letter back to Rachel. "Aunt Rachel," she said in a tremulous voice, "I never, ever, gave Harold any reason to think I loved him — except as Tobe's cousin. I swear that is the truth! Tobe is the only man I have ever loved."

Tears glistened in Rachel's eyes and she reached out to pat Jessie's shoulder. "I know, dear, I know."

"Did you know about this-this obsession of Harold's?" Jessie asked.

"I suspected it," Rachel admitted, "and I tried to reason with Harold about how futile it was to desire someone else's wife — but he would always cut me off and stalk off. But I never dreamed the obsession was so strong that he would resort to drug trafficking, with the thought that he could buy your love, or that he would kidnap you. I had been feeling for a long time that he was becoming unbalanced, but I didn't know how to help him. I tried several times to get him to talk to me, but he would not! He was really furious with me once when I suggested psychiatric help."

"You know, of course, that I cannot accept this money," Jessie said. She scanned the legal documents and her face went pale, "There is one hundred thousand dollars here!"

Rachel said softly, "Yes, you must take the money. You and your family deserve this money, after all Harold put you through."

But Jessie was shaking her head violently, "No, I don't want any of Harold's money. You are his mother, and as his heir, the money should be yours."

"No. Dear, I have all I need on my ranch," She paused and then laughed softly, "I am even considering marrying Buster again and doing some traveling with him. Both of us have saved some money and we will do fine."

Jessie again protested but Rachel put her finger on Jessie's lips, "You kids have had such a struggle and this money was given to you with no strings attached. It will clear out your debts and set you up for some carefree years as you raise those precious children of yours."

"But . . ."

"No 'buts', come on, we are going to find Tobe and convince him to accept this provision of the Lord!"

Early that morning Chet had driven over from Las Cruces and picked up Ann to accompany her to the barbecue at Rachel's house. Besides the tender spicy barbecue with all the trimmings that they had partaken of, the day had included horse back riding, games, music and congenial conversation. A wonderful, carefree day!

Late that evening, Chet and Ann were on their way back to her little cabin. The headlights shining on the dark road put he and Ann in a world of their very own. He felt, what? Relief, exultation, he really couldn't explain his feelings. He only knew that right at this moment he would rather be going down this road with this woman than to be anywhere else in the world.

Chet glanced at her. He couldn't see her clearly in the dash lights but he imagined just how she looked. Why did he ever think she was too short? Now, thinking back on it, she seemed just right. He remembered the calm way she conducted herself when Tobe was arrested, and she was unbelievably courageous and helpful when they had gone after Jessie in Harold's mansion. Quite a woman!

"Ann," he said, "I have been thinking of starting out on my own. I believe there is a place for a private detective, specializing in missing persons."

He saw he had her full attention. "I've been asked to help on a number of other cases in the past. You have been your own boss for a number of years now and you are a success. I'll go back to Las Cruces now that this is over, and you will probably wind up back in El Paso after you finish your new book.

"Aww . . . shucks, this is coming out all wrong. What I'm really trying to say is, I'm beginning to care for you — a lot. I would like to see more of you. Are you interested?"

"Actually, since we are being so frank, yes."

"Well, okay, then. How can we accomplish it? I can't court you if I have to drive all the way to El Paso every night."

"I can work out of any town and if you launch your business, you can too, can't you?"

They were nearing the cabin now. Chet thought, *I might never have a better chance to broach this subject.* He swallowed hard. "Would you consider moving to Las Cruces to help me start it?"

"Let me think about it," she murmured. "I might, I just might."

They had pulled up in front of Ann's cabin. Her voice was soft, "In fact, why don't you come in for a while and we'll talk about it."

Chet's heart bounded up and seemed to have trouble staying inside his body. He had started out a few weeks ago to find a lost girl and found one far more intriguing. This case had turned out better than he could ever have imagined!

They got out of the car and went up the path together.